Still with you.
A Contemporary Romance

Zaara Ali

Ukiyoto Publishing

All global publishing rights are held by

Ukiyoto Publishing

Published in 2024

Content Copyright © Zaara Ali

Cover Illustration by Naysha Satyarthi

ISBN 9789362696519

All rights reserved.

No part of this publication may be reproduced, transmitted, or stored in a retrieval system, in any form by any means, electronic, mechanical, photocopying, recording or otherwise, without the prior permission of the publisher.

The moral rights of the author have been asserted.

This is a work of fiction. Names, characters, businesses, places, events, locales, and incidents are either the products of the author's imagination or used in a fictitious manner. Any resemblance to actual persons, living or dead, or actual events is purely coincidental.

This book is sold subject to the condition that it shall not by way of trade or otherwise, be lent, resold, hired out or otherwise circulated, without the publisher's prior consent, in any form of binding or cover other than that in which it is published.

www.ukiyoto.com

"To my first love. I can forget myself, But I can never forget you."

Acknowledgement

I was in 6th standard when I started writing. It was poetries at first, then songs, and ultimately stories. My friends were the first cheerleaders I had in my life. Though I hadn't thought, it could be possible to get published. But then I got to know about anthologies, so I participated. Not knowing where I was headed. Again, my friends cheered me up and It made me want to create more. Publish more. I started working on this story back in 2021, and my friends were my only confidant. I didn't tell my parents, because, again. I didn't think it was possible. Then I published a pocket size book from Ukiyoto without giving it much thought and realized that maybe It WAS possible after all.
So I told my parents, and everyone supported me. Till this date, they have been supporting me, emotionally, financially and in ways I can't fathom.
I am grateful to all my friends (Ayesha, Shafaque and Zaki) who heard me, gave me their honest opinions and guided me throughout. My biggest supporters have to be my brothers - Raquib and Faraaz. (I annoyed the hell out of them all the while I worked on this book, which was almost 3 years, I was inconsistent.)
I am thankful to my online friend Astha too, at first I was just a spectator in her life. But then we started talking, and omg did I learn from her? Yes, I did. I started working on marketing, after she told me what I needed to do and what not.
My mom and my grandmother, of course. How can I forget them? They have been a wall of support all my life and not just while writing this so they deserve the praise.

Lastly, Naysha, my cover designer. She brainstormed the cover idea and delivered the best. I don't know if I could have done such great work without her. Her patience throughout the time we discussed the design was remarkable. Thanks for your fabulous work, love.

CONTENTS

PROLOGUE	1
THE LETTER	4
FAR AWAY	8
LOST AND FOUND	11
MEMORIES	15
21ST MAY	18
THE CAKE	22
DISAGREEMENT	26
MEDIA	31
MOTHERHOOD	34
TRANSPARENT	38
CHANEL	43
MISTRESS?	46
SKY NEVER DISAPPOINTS	50
NEW FRIEND?	55
NEED COMES BEFORE WANT	62
FLING…	68
NEW P.A. WHO?	75
SLEEP OVER	82
BITCH	88
RELIEF	93
HEARTBREAK	98
THINGS WE CAN'T EXPLAIN	105
MY LIFE, MY FRIENDS, MY RULES!	112
DINNER AT KHAN'S	120
CONSEQUENCES	129
FRIENDS FOR LIFE	136
GROUP WORK	143

FEELINGS	152
PERKS OF BEING WEALTHY	156
MORE STRONGER THAN EVER	161
THE WEDDING	165
FAILURES	173
IGNORANCE	180
LAST SHOWERS	188
THE LAST LETTER	196
PROMISES	203
A NEW BEGINNING	209
EPILOGUE	212
PLAYLIST	215
About the Author	216

PROLOGUE

Aqeel

I have been effing and blinding myself since the day I realised my feelings towards her. That day I learned two things, the ability to live and to consciously drink the poison. I could confess and lose her, or I could stay silent and earn her. I chose the latter. I was a coward, and I knew it. I knew this much, that I would be able to survive if she would be by my side but I would shatter the moment she would leave. And it was inevitable, her leaving me. Only If I knew it, I would have opened my mouth a bit earlier or zipped it tight for the rest of my life. Though I wasn't just a coward, I was stupid. Stupid enough to jump, when the boat had already left the harbour.

"Aqeel... who would you choose? Me or Luna?" She asked me. "you." I said in a single breath. If it was someone else asking me the exact question, I would have said my pet's name.

"And who would you choose between Me and your other friends?" She asked.

"You are my one and only friend. So you." I confirmed.

"And who would you choose between Me and your family?" She asked.

"You *are* my family." I said, getting frustrated with her questions. She made it hard for me to stay silent about my feelings.

"That's not fair. you have to choose one, stop being a diplomatic brat." She whined.

"Alaia...the only people i have in my life are you and dida so stop making me choose." With utmost patience and calmness, I told her.

"Then why did you choose Dida over your family?" She asked. I imagined smacking her head hard against the table. I do love her, but she doesn't get to question my decisions about my family.

" I didn't . *They* left me. Besides, I don't care about them as long as you and Dida are here with me. So please don't make me choose between you two." I dropped my pen forcefully on the table,a fountain pen to be exact.

"Okay. Calm down. Another question. Who would you choose between this world and...me?" She asked me, a mischievous smile lingering on her mouth and a playful look in those beautiful brown eyes. The eyes that held me captive every time I dared to look at them. To avoid staring at her, I started cleaning the table where the ink had spilled. The pen tip broke and so did the wall of patience.

"Alaia...you are my world. I would choose you. Always. So stop asking me meaningless questions. I have homework to do." I said while focusing on my notebook that lay upon the dining table of her house. My heart beat raced and my cheeks flushed when I heard the words uttered by my own damned mouth. The words which held so much impact against me, were just mere words, words to be taken for granted by Alaia.

"Alaia!!! Stop disturbing Aqeel and do your work. And if you are not interested in it then go back to your room and let him study peacefully." Her mother yelled from the kitchen. Then a while later she brought me coffee and patted my head. Alaia got a head smack from her mother for being the cause of my 18/20 in the previous maths test. I couldn't help but giggle at that, though when she complained about being in pain. I apologised to her and she instantly regained her composure. I didn't feel like a pushover at all. If apologising could make her smile I'd apologise a million times to the world without a single thought , for though *she* was my whole world.

"Can I ask you something too?" I asked her, my eyes didn't leave the sight of my notebook as my sweaty forehead would reveal the hidden anxiety crawling against my skin.

"Yes. Of course." She said, grinning from ear to ear as she caught sight of her dad entering home after his work ended.

"Who'd you choose? If you were to choose between this world and me?" I asked, keeping my voice low as much as possible. I knew what she would do, and yet I wanted to give it a try.

"The world! It's simple. You come in that package only, Dumbass. Don't think about my questions too much, or your brain will explode if it has not already, under the enormous number of problems you solve daily.

Give yourself a break!." She exclaimed and ran towards her father. "Abbu!! Did you find the baby pink-coloured wool, I asked you for?" She started interrogating her father about the unusual errands she made him do. She didn't care about me, the way I did for her. As she didn't have her heart beating faster around me. I was a mere friend to her, amongst many others. Indeed I was a Dumbass. I took her free and kind nature for love.

THE LETTER

Aqeel

"The last thing I want are these memories to creep inside my mind", I began to murmur as I entered my old apartment. Of course it contained journals worth of memories as I spent my childhood here with some exceptionally adorable people. An unintentional smile lingered with just the thought of those faces. A few moments later that smile vanished into the dusty air as I got into a coughing fit. The air inside was suffocating enough with the moulds growing in the rotten wood furniture we have had for years. So I went closer to the window for some fresh air. The view from my room, used to be the best, and it still was. I loved stargazing hence I spent much of my time sitting near the window lost in thoughts and dreams. Some of them grew as I did, and others were crushed. The soft western breeze brought a bird feather inside, it floated in the air before finally descending to the floor. When I looked down, my gaze fell upon a piece of mail. Curiosity bubbled inside me and I picked it up to examine. The letter had the return address to Boston. I wondered who it was from, as publishers who I've been working with only knew about my current address and this apartment had been closed off to everyone. Who even wrote hand written letter these days? I did want to receive a letter, though it felt strange when I actually did.

I unfolded the letter as fast as possible to see, who had the time and energy to write me something, that too in my old address. I wondered, for how long was this here? If I hadn't visited, the sender's effort would have gone in vain. Would they still be expecting me to reply? The moment my eyes caught a glimpse of the name my mind flooded with thousands of memories and countless flashbacks. For a while I remained immersed in those memories. This was the sole reason I refused to come here. I didn't expect something like this to be here though the feeling, nostalgia was not good for me.

She was something magical, my whole world revolved around her. Though the situation wasn't the same for me, it appeared she still found me in her closets. I didn't read the letter as I came here for some important work and I had to leave the moment my task was completed. My brain couldn't figure out the reason behind this letter, but my heart knew this feeling. One look at that door, across mine and my heart started beating abnormally faster. The weather wasn't humid, and yet sweat beads had formed on my forehead

Throughout the drive I kept thinking about the letter and her, I didn't have the guts to read it. I was so overpowered by the rotten feelings that I took the wrong lane despite knowing the road for ages. Ughh!! why the fuck did she decided to write out to me out of nowhere, and why the hell was I so into that letter??? I had forgotten her, she did that too....she must have moved on. I got over it too then why was my heart still racing so much?... .I despised this feeling.

After reaching home I started unpacking the things I brought with me. It had been rotting there for years as I didn't need them much. The truth is I didn't want to be around those things anymore... I had wished to move on with my life. I did what I needed to do except get married or be in a relationship, I didn't want to be held back in the same world again. I thought of escaping this world where I had to settle down for matters like this, and move to a world of my own that I had been longing for since my childhood. No matter how much I polished my world, it remained rough in some parts, because it had the same scars I got around 6 years ago.

Should I read it? Or should i destroy it? What must have she written in those dead pages, she didn't even like the concept of writing letters. Still she wrote me one, so it must be important. My indecisive ass couldn't decide what was to be done. If someone saw me, they'd think I had probably gone mad. I must be crazy to love her.

I couldn't concentrate on anything. So I decided to make myself a cappuccino... I only take Black coffee these days because I had to keep my sugar in check. A slight change in my sugar level might trigger my diabetes. And anyways, having black coffee, sitting near the window of my staffroom that was built years ago while marking papers was what I had wanted all my childhood. And I am not being sarcastic about it, I did want those things. People said that I was boring or that I was born with a young body but an old soul. I wanted to be a maths professor. Not because I was highly intellectual or intelligent, but because maths was the only subject that helped me escape the real world. Trust me, when you have 100 maths problems to solve, you won't have enough time to think about your life problems. And to avoid my problems even more, I had a fixed routine for everyday. If you plan your days ahead or have a schedule this would hardly give you time to make mistakes or think about them. I wasn't always like this but with the passing time and lack of people in my life I had grown into this schedule thing.

After I finished my coffee, I was going to take a shower when someone rang the doorbell. "Oh sana, I forgot that you were due today. Come inside and have a seat."

"Tea or coffee?" I asked her while putting down a glass of water

"Wait.. you won't offer me herbal tea? Last time when I visited, you insisted upon herbal tea as it was supposed to be good for our health." She teased me

"Sorry to disappoint you but today you'll have to do without herbal tea as I am out of it. And I just had cappuccino myself, could definitely whisk some for you." I suggested.

"Oh…so you do enjoy your life? I thought you were an old lady with multiple health complications and only had HEALTHY food." She laughed. "I'll take a cappuccino."

I quickly made her a cappuccino, and put together some chocolate chip cookies.

"I need your signatures in these papers. The client loves the apartment, it just needs some renovation and cleaning to do. *That* they'll manage so If you could just sign these papers, My work will be finished."

"yeah sure", I replied.

I started to read the terms and conditions mentioned on the paper. I had to make sure everything was fine. Though it seemed like the sugar had finally caught upto me as my head felt lighter and there were two sets of paper rather than just one. I realised that I hadn't took my insulin shot. So I asked Sana if she could pick up the papers later. Although she agreed to do that, I would have delivered it myself if she hadn't.

After she left I came back to sit, it was difficult for me to walk without toppling certain things. Though somehow I reached my sofa and I passed out.

"Did you read my letter?" Asked Alaia.

I was utterly confused, as I thought she was in front of me. Though it was just a weird dream. I woke up as if I had seen a nightmare. For a moment I was scared, of her, of that letter and of myself. She made me crazy. Her presence was as haunting as her absence. I took a deep breathe and reached in my pocket for the letter.

To Aqeel,

Hello, sorry if I'm bothering you with this but I really wanted to talk. I hope you have been doing just fine all this while. It's been 4 years and we haven't met each other since then, neither did we talk. I am writing this to let you know that I have realised that our situation could have been much better if only I reacted less dramatically. You already know how I am and how I handle things... pretty badly huh? Hope you still remember me... well i can't say 'love me' cause i already ruined everything years ago and don't really deserve your attention. But just for my clarification, I would say that I didn't expect this from you. I really thought we were just friends. I quiet remember the time when i was here in Boston doing my degree before completely settling in US, you use to sing " Dorothea" by Taylor Swift.....i used to think that you were just missing me as we have spent our whole childhood together and i was your only friend back then but i guess it wasn't true at all. You were always in deep thought, you liked reading, writing and being my nerd friend. On the other hand, I, being the outgoing friend always wondered how to react to your profound words. You know nuh that i am not good with words so i'll keep it short, i just want us to get back together as we were years before our fight. You might get confused as to why am I writing to you all of a sudden but to let you know I haven't really gotten over our fight and why it happened, it was my fault of course but you too were being mean. You only saw your view of this situation, not mine, but I am not blaming you for this as I know it was merely your emotional rush and nothing else. You didn't mean all the things you said to me.

Truth is I wrote this a few months ago, but I didn't have enough courage to send this to you. I would have contacted you some other way. But since we cut every ties between us, I have no idea what your contact options were. I don't expect you to reply... you can forget about this letter if it does reach you. Yet if you change your mind, here is my contact ; **********.

Sending love. Your dusky, Alaia :)

FAR AWAY

AQEEL

My sweaty palms soaked the letter making it transparent. I should hate her. She makes me anxious, just like my old self. Even after all the years, she has the same effect on me as she used to do back then. It's just that I am not in love anymore, at least that's what I want to believe. This letter will definitely become the reason for my downfall. All my progress in moving on from her, would be wiped out.

I know her very well and as this letter states, she just wants us to be good friends. Nothing more, so it shouldn't be awkward, and yet my gut says that this will make my life go 180 degrees. Do I have balls to look at her and resist falling for her again? But if she is willing to give our friendship a second chance, why should I stay back? I could just ring her up and hope it goes well. Can't people go back to normal like they never ruined someone's engagement? Is it possible for two people to be friends again, knowing that one of them loved the other at some point of time and the other didn't? Is it possible for her to forget the humiliation I cost her? Can I do 'just friends' again? All these questions ate the fuck out of my mind and the everlasting lightheadedness didn't help either. Before I could pass out again from the high blood sugar levels in my system and the growing fear of Alaia, I took my insulin shot.

I was better. And it was high time I acted like an adult rather than a scared little ugly teenager who had no idea of what he was supposed to do. I could do this. She was just a woman. A woman I loved above others. And someone, I shouldn't be afraid of, my friend. So I called her number. It rang three times before she answered.

"Umm..hello!? I-"

"Aqeel? Is that you?"

"Uh. Yeah." I was speechless, exactly how I used to get whenever she opened her pretty little mouth. I am doomed.

"OMG!!??! Am I dreaming? You son of a BITCH!!!! You called? That must mean, you received my letter."

"Get a grip! It's just me." I tried to tell her, well, more to myself.

"No. Let me tear people's eardrums. Because you CALLED. I thought the letter didn't get to you as it took you months but it was you. So it could also mean that you hid it somewhere so you could avoid contacting me." She kept on going as if she had only 60 seconds before death would consume her.

"Let me speak, would you?" I politely asked her.

"Yes of course, you idiot." I swear, I could imagine her rolling her eyes at me. And it made me chuckle.

"What are you laughing at? huh?" She accused me.

"Nothing. I just missed you." I didn't believe my words. Didn't I spend years forgetting about her? Writing sad poetries because I was heartbroken? And she was the reason behind the shattered pieces of it.

"Did you? really?" She doubted.

"Kind of. I mean its not humanly possible to forget someone like you. Because you would bully the shit out of people, if they did." I heard her laughing over the phone and smiled. What was I doing? "Well, kudos to you. You wrote a letter. I received it today, when I went back to my old place for work."

"I am glad Aqeel, that you called. I feel lighter, now that I know you missed me as I missed you a ton."

"But it's never too late

To come back to my side

The stars in your eyes

Shined brighter in Tupelo

And if you're ever tired of being known

For who you know

You know you'll always know me

Dorothea (ah-ah)

Dorothea (ah-ah)"

" Mmm, I think this was supposed to be my line. It has been years since I last heard you singing, and you still suck at it." I chuckled

"Yeah yeah whatever, go ahead and make fun of my voice. At least I have the confidence to sing. What's the point of having a really good voice and guitar skills, when you can't even gather enough confidence to sing in front of anyone." She complained. I remained silent as to who would tell her. I only sang for her, as she was all that I cared about.

"What? Why are you silent now? It's as if I said something I shouldn't have. Don't make me feel like that. I wanted you to sing for others too as you did for me." She grumbled. Thats the difference between us. She never saved herself for anyone in particular. She was everyone's and nobody's at the same time. While I, I stayed the way I was, for her.

I could hear someone calling for her through the call. "Be grateful that I have some work today, so I can't talk to you much. But I will catch up to you later....bye! We'll continue this topic later!! And thanks for replying to my letter." She hung up the call. And That was her. She did as she pleased. And that made her ten times more attractive. I guess we all love a bit of toxicity. I kept thinking about her all night, till the sun came up. And I had to start my daily grind again.

LOST AND FOUND

ALAIA

"Which one looks better?" I asked.

"Wear whatever you want...you're gonna look stunning either way!!"

"Yeah, but I still need to know which is a better choice. See, this pink dress is too dinner date type and this pair of shirt and trousers are too formal. I want to look casual, as if this was a normal friendly get together as it actually is. But anyways, I need your help today. My fashion knowledge isn't working for me today."

"I know it's a normal get together but you are panicking as if it was a date. Don't worry, it's just your stupid childhood friend and not someone you are supposed to impress." Daisy blurted out.

Wow I was shocked. she wasn't just a slut but a bitch too. I gave her a death stare.

"What?" She asked as if she was innocent. I chuckled. "Listen babe… you wouldn't be able to walk down the streets if I leaked any of your videos. If you can't keep your hands away from my male models then you should at least respect my people."

"Did you film me?" She asked, horrified. "No, but someone else did. When you were busy making out in my latest collection in your vanity." I fixed my lipstick and took a last look at my makeup.

"Oh my god! What are you gonna do with that footage?" She asked me with a worried look. I liked that look.

"Well, it'll rot in my storage for some time. And if you continued with your behaviour, it might make its appearance on social media. I just need to make an anonymous tip to the media and your career would be as dead as your hair. Don't forget about the outfits you stole from my wardrobe." I gave her a sweet but bitter smile.

"Wait, you know about the outfits?" Her eyes widened. "Absolutely yes. I keep track." I squeezed her cheeks and went to change my clothes. I chose to wear the pink dress, If not for Aqeel then for the media who were waiting for me to walk out of my hotel room. I made a comeback, here in Kolkata after working from Boston all this while. This was a sudden decision though I missed being here. And people would accept me anywhere. I made sure that my brand does better and captures the attention of people. The initial reason was Papa, as he didn't want to settle in Boston so I had to come down here. And I will be close to Aqeel too now, when we are trying to patch up. He and I agreed to meet today in a cafe as I was back in India. He doesn't know that I am back for good and won't go back to Boston.

It wasn't easy to come back here, when my brand was established elsewhere. But the idea originated in Kolkata, and I must do it from here. I had been working on this for a while now, even before I wrote that letter to Aqeel. I only hope for this to work, I know the journey is going to be rocky. But I'll still have my office in Boston which will be remotely managed by me. The only way up is to satisfy my customers and expand what I started.

I dismissed Daisy as I didn't need her anymore. And went out, as expected the media was there to capture my first few hours back in Kolkata. I posed for them and answered a few questions related to my brand and avoided the personal ones. Then drove to the cafe with the help of google maps, as I have forgotten half the streets already. The city was the same, nothing much changed but my memory betrayed me. I reached there before the time we agreed on, I guess I was a little too excited. While waiting for him I ordered myself a soft drink.

He came just in time, and I waved at him from my seat. He waved back and came forward to take the seat across from me. "Sorry, did you have to wait longer?" He asked while panting a little. " No, No actually I was early. But did you come here running? Why are you panting so much, here, have some water." I said while passing him the water bottle. He gulped half of the bottle in one go, I guess he was really thirsty. "I ran out of gas, and uber kept cancelling my ride. So I took a bus, unfortunately it took a different turn and I had to get down and run here." He nervously chuckled.

"Is this how you manage your students as a teacher?" I laughed

"You mean Professor?" He corrected me.

"Yeah whatever, but you should be aware of your car and its condition. The least you could do was check up on it a day before." I advised. "You should consider thinking about your own teenage self. You were so carefree and irresponsible that I had to clear up your mess every time." He said. "That was our past. A lot of things have changed since then and so have I. I am mature now. In fact I manage a luxury brand myself. Do you understand the term Luxury? It takes years for a brand to get recognised as a luxury one. If I was any less sincere in my work I wouldn't have been here now." I told him, and did a small hair flip to brag. "I can see that." He teased me. " What? I am telling the truth, plus you have changed too, it's like you have been melted and poured in a different mould. Something about you is very different. I don't know exactly what, but I can feel it.

"Anyways, who are these people who made you so mature? And did you by chance marry?" He asked. "I will say that being lonely in a different city with no love, no loyalty, you become mature on your own. And no, I didn't marry. It isn't in my priorities right now."

"I can agree to that, without any friend or family member by your side. You become your first priority, you have to take care of yourself and focus on your career, be kind to others and just like that you forget about your carefree personality. Everyone joins the boring, intellectual life filled with meetings, work, classes, expectations, and some more work." He said

"You know what? keeping things in the past I like this version of you. You were always the serious type but I can see that life has been tough on you as it has been for every one of us. But it only made you stronger, and better. Sorry for being one of those people who caused you difficulties." I mumbled. "Hey! It's not your fault. Don't blame yourself for something you didn't do. I was immature, and I made some mistakes. I assumed some things on my own and ruined both of our lives. If someone *should* feel guilty, it's me." He squeezed my hand which was lying on the table. And I smiled. "I also had something to ask. When exactly did we last meet?" He asked. " It was four years ago. At Dida's funeral." I replied. "You visited?" He asked in return. " Yeah, I did and we met too. You hugged me and cried because you missed dida. I don't think you remember. I left immediately after that day and then we never talked again."

"Dida's passing away wasn't easy for me. She was someone I loved, and after her there was nothing that could make me happy. Working on my career, the academic-validation if you call it really helped me get through the grief. I worked really hard and went from a middle school teacher to a University Professor. It was life changing, I went from a semi-dependent person to a fully grown independent man." He said. "I feel sorry for our loss, Dida was the root of our family and relations. She held everyone together, after her demise everything fell apart. I am glad that your job saved you." I said. After chatting for a while, Aqeel ordered his salad. And damn, I was Shook. "Aqeel!! You are eating salad!!?. ohhh god where is my old friend? Did you kidnap him and take his place?" I laughed. "Hehe, not funny...yeah I am on a diet. It isn't like me to be on one, but my dietitian made me do this. My health wasn't in a good shape after all the pressure I took over myself. So my body stopped functioning properly. And I was diabetic to start with."

"I need to thank your dietitian for sure, whoever it is. You never really cared about your health, and constantly took huge amounts of sugar intake every day despite having diabetes. By the way, how is your family? And your mom? She used to be so worried about you....you and her never really had an understanding relationship though. She always asked me...if you were fine. I hope she is okay." I asked. "Mom is fine, maybe…" He replied half sure of his own answer. "Maybe?? Don't tell me you still don't talk to her." "I don't." He casually admitted. "Dude really?!!"

"Will you stop lecturing me please...can you? I agreed to come here so that we can hang out. I don't wanna talk about her. You tell me how your mom is?" "Fine! Wherever she is." I replied.

"What do you mean?" He asked. "Um....A year ago, she had a road accident and she died on the spot."

"What!? Oh my god, I am so sorry...Are you doing alright after her? It must be lonely, I can understand the impact of losing someone. She was the only person, whom you loved and the only family you had along with your dad. It's so sad...I don't have words right now. How is your dad doing?" I knew this must have hurt him, as Ammi loved her as her own son and he reciprocated it with love and respect. "Things happen...This is gonna happen one day. Though I wasn't ready yet. Anyways, Abbu is fine. It was hard for both of us but he seems fine now." Is he though?

MEMORIES

AQEEL

We talked so much that my jaw started hurting. It was pleasurable to meet her after so long, I bet I would have never tried to contact her myself. There have been so many changes in our life, that it seemed like we were meeting for the first time. So many unshared topics, stories and sorrows. But the connection was still there between us. We might have been apart for years and yet a phone call away that was preceded with a letter. As if we both were waiting for the opportunity to come and hang out just like old times. For which I am grateful that she made an effort to reach out to me. There were some stories left to hear and share but our meeting had to end. I came back, but my mind was still there. It's ironic how much power she has over me after all this time. I couldn't think about anything else but her. What she wore, how she laughed, and the way she looked at me. Though the way I see her now, has changed. I am so glad that my fears didn't catch up to me and I didn't fall for her this time. She only appeared as a friend might do and not like a butterfly I would chase.

After talking to her I realised that she was lonely, just like me. No friends. I couldn't believe it when she said that. As I only knew her younger version who used to be a popular kid. Everyone knew her in school, our apartment, and basically the whole town. Competitions? She won them all. Grades? always on top. However she never forgot me, wherever she went, I went along not willingly but dragged by her. And yet I did *that*, I don't completely regret it till now. The few moments of delusion I knitted were beautiful.

I took my medicine and grabbed my laptop. I was so full that I couldn't even think about food at that moment. I ate pizza even though I had ordered myself a salad. But I couldn't resist having a slice, then it became two. And in the end I had to finish everything, as Alaia ordered more than she could possibly eat. I was tired and wanted to sleep. But maybe my mind was too awake. Too busy thinking about that same person who was responsible for my sleepless nights back then. I changed my position multiple times yet it felt uncomfortable on my bed. So I went to the kitchen and drank some warm water to help digest all the food a little better. And then moved towards the balcony....a cool breeze touched my face and sent shivers down my body. Monsoon was near. I sat down on my balcony swing and gazed at the sky. I wonder how the world would look if I saw it with a different person's perception.

What was I? What did I like? Questions like these arose from the graveyard of my thoughts. It wouldn't help if I decided to stop now. So I began thinking more precisely. Under the dark sky, it was just me and my inner self. At this moment even my silhouettes were judging me. No matter how much I tried, I couldn't forget anything. I had built some walls and now I was just rotting in there. Never really tried to connect to the people outside. The only string between me and this world was my work. And everything seemed darker when I was not able to do it. All the rays coming from the sun were being absorbed by the darkness these walls held inside them. It consumed all the happiness. And just like that I fell asleep outside on the balcony.

Even the sun didn't bother me...I was fast asleep when I heard someone banging on my door. There were loud noises of people screaming and chattering. I sluggishly walked towards the door and opened it while scratching my bed head.

"Roop? What are you doing here? Do you need something?" I asked Roop who was the one on the door.

"Aqeel....wake up!!! We don't have time, you need to grab your things. We are supposed to leave." He said in a hurry.

"Huh? Things? Leave?What are you saying dude?" I rubbed my sleepy eyes as everything was blurry.

"Aqeel!!! The building is on fire. We really need to leave. Half of the people have already evacuated. Firemen are on their way." He explained

"Wait! Wait! Ok I get it. We are on fire. Sorry, I mean the building is on fire and we need to leave." I checked my phone and there were like 10 missed calls - from Sana and Roop. Sana? OH! The documents. I hurriedly went inside and wore my clothes, grabbed my bag, keys and then I left with him. Roop's family had already left. Though he stayed behind to help others like me. We separated our path near the coffee shop where I had my breakfast and contacted sana about the documents. I freshened up in the coffee shop's restroom and went to the University. Thankfully I had taken a shower yesterday.

After my classes, I went to that coffee shop again to meet sana. I apologised to her for not picking up the calls. I had slept till late, and given that all my classes are in the late afternoon or evening, shows that I was no longer the morning person I used to be. There we discussed the papers and I signed it. I gave her the keys even though she already had the spare keys. But since I had no use for those, the people who bought the place might need it. For the rest of the evening I spend it on the coffee place itself. I had to think of a place where I could go and crash for the night but before that I called the security guard of my apartment and enquired about the condition of our apartment, thankfully the fire got off but the building was still filled with smoke. No one told me or maybe no one knew how the fire started but we'll get to know that once we get back there.

So I booked a room in a hotel nearby cause I didn't have any other option apart from my parent's home, but that would be the last place I'd go. After checking-in, I spotted Alaia. I didn't remember her telling me which hotel she was staying at, but it looked like destiny had everything planned. It worked as a driving force as she wrote to me and now it was bringing us back under the same roof, technically building.

I couldn't sleep as I had overslept this morning and the recent events had a depressing effect on me. So I decided to watch a movie. It felt disgusting while I threw away my desert. The next morning when I woke up and checked my phone. There was an invitation sitting on my text and it was Alaia inviting me to her Birthday Party. BIRTHDAY??? I checked the date and it was indeed the 21st of may.

21ST MAY

ALAIA

I wore a maroon slim dress from my own collection, and to accessories I wore a pandora's heart shaped rose gold pendant and a Micheal Kors mini parker rose gold watch. I'll be forever grateful to myself for cutting my hair short in high school. It flows with my vibe so well, that I wouldn't even need to accessorise. But today, I wanted that extra kick. I was wearing my black toe pumps when I got a text from my assistant telling me I was late. To my own party. I was going to host a party for the first time after returning to Kolkata. It had to be a blast. Sadly, Abbu bailed on me saying he won't be able to make it as he was not feeling well. Was he really sick? Or just angry because I wasn't staying with him? I would have gladly stayed with him but he wouldn't stop telling me to get married. And marriage was not in my list of priorities right now. I went to the venue before everyone else, as I was the hostess and was supposed to welcome everyone. I had high hopes for this party, as this was not just a birthday party, It was networking. People from different fields were going to attend, as I didn't leave anyone out, nor would people lose this chance to meet me or talk about me. Being a little self-obsessed is fun, besides I knew my worth. There would be friends and foes, and everyone would enjoy it, I'd make sure of that.

"Where is the guy you were talking about? Is he gonna come or not?" Asked Dhruv.

"If it was any other party, he'd never come but this is *my* birthday party you are talking about, he would never miss this." I bragged. I looked around, the venue was full and yet people kept showing up. One after another they came and wished me a happy birthday. There was a pile of gifts on the gift counter. At first I arranged them to make them look good, but after a hundred of them I gave up on aesthetics. We took so many pictures and videos that I got tired of posing for them. I was to introduce Aqeel to so many people I knew, and they were waiting for him to show up. These people knew him by name, but no one had ever known him personally or met him. He'd kept his real identity a secret, which was going to be shared among these people. I was shocked when he revealed it to me that he was behind all those romance books. I had always known that he had a thing for writing, but in my mind I had this idea that he would at least use his real name to publish his work. I was becoming restless, as Dhruv told me to stop waiting for him as he wouldn't appear. But he did, and made my anxious mind calm down. Aqeel came in looking like a complete groom material, wearing a Black Tuxedo with a tie and a silver toned embellished lapel pin pairing with black shoes. I wonder when I last saw him looking like a piece of snack. My jaw almost fell to the floor, watching him walk towards me. Did he always look this fine? His thick and black curly hair, eyes alert, probably looking for *me*, jawline sharp enough to slice my fingers if I dared to run my fingers on it. I shook my head to throw away the thoughts that just came to me. That's just my friend, my childhood friend who was once obsessed with me. Dhruv tapped on my shoulder and said- "Stop, you are drooling." "What?!!" I freaked out. "Chill! I am just kidding. Will you care to tell me who you were looking at like that?" He asked. I pointed towards Aqeel, exactly when he saw me so I waved at him and asked him to come where I was standing. "It's the person I was talking about, my ridiculously talented friend." I bragged once again. "Are you sure he is just a friend?" He teased me. "I was." That was all I told him when Aqeel tripped because of an invisible obstacle while he was coming towards me. Someone helped him get balanced on his own two feets. I stopped the laughter that almost came out after seeing him trip but I controlled myself. "Doesn't look like how you described him to be." Dhruv said. "I know right! He has become more handsome, stress seems to work great on him." I said.

"Hey!" He greeted me. "Hey! Are you okay? Did you hurt yourself?" I asked out of courtesy as I couldn't just laugh at my fallen friend like old times. "No, I am alright! Don't worry. And a very very Happy Birthday to you!! I am really sorry but I had forgotten about your birthday. Blame my forgetful mind." He said. "It's okay, as long as you come and join me to celebrate my happiness. I was afraid you'd ditch me. Now, will you please let me introduce you to my colleague. This is Dhruv-casting director of CxStudios and Dhruv, this is my friend Aqeel." I let them greet each other and chat. Thankfully Dhruv initiated the conversation or Aqeel would just stare here and there awkwardly as he barely knew anyone here. But surprisingly he carried the whole conversation without any awkwardness. I forgot that he was now used to giving lectures in front of hundreds of people. His confidence was much better than it was back then when we were students ourselves.

I had met Aqeel earlier in the hotel I was living in. I didn't know the reason why he was staying there but since we were living in the same place I asked him to ride with me. Once we were out of the venue and headed to our hotel. Aqeel spoke up. "I don't know if you'll like it or not and looking at all the presents you got today. My gift looked smaller which is why I'd feel more comfortable giving it to you in private. Here, this is for you." He said "Oh, please. I'd love whatever you have for me, I'd be happy if you just came and didn't bring a gift at all. Your presence mattered the most." I opened the package...It was a small heart shaped platinum pendant."Oh dumbo...you know that I adore platinum and pendants both. It's very pretty and precious. I haven't seen any other gifts till now, still I already know that *this* is the most thoughtful gift ever." I said. And I meant it. "You know, this was the first thing I saw and I immediately knew that this was the one I wanted for you." He said. "Thank you very much, though upon everything else I am glad that you came. Dhruv was so excited to meet you." "Dhruv?" Asked Aqeel. "ohh!! I didn't tell you right?? See dhruv and I are colleagues. He is a casting director who helps me with my models for photo shoots related to my work." I asked. "And?" He asked. "You write novels and stories nah...and Dhruv works with many directors and producers too. So when I had just basically told him about you...he told me that he was actually looking for you for days so that he could talk about some work related to your novels." "Really??" he asked, clearly not taking it in. "It seems like I am pretty famous everywhere." He continued.

"Yes, that's the point. You are famous! And people want to work with you. I know many people who love your work. It would have been really good if only I knew it was you all along. May I know why you are using a pseudonym instead of your own name?" I asked

"Because I wanted a change, to start fresh you know and also to avoid unnecessary attention and publicity." I couldn't help but laugh. "People would do anything to become famous and known, and here you are trying to hide behind names." My laugh came out with ugly snorts. I would have never laughed in such an ugly way as people might judge me, or click weird pictures of me. But with him, I could be anything, I could be me. "Think whatever you want to think about me, I don't even attend my own book promotions." He joined me in my monstrous laugh.

"Sorry to ask but you'll have to do me a favour and meet some people." I said. "What do you mean by that? I already met so many tonight."He asked. "Oh, that was just networking. Now the real work will begin." I said and reassured him by telling how good he was at his work as I very well knew that he had imposter syndrome. Though he kept saying that he wouldn't fit in with the people or how he hasn't worked with people like them before.

THE CAKE

AQEEL

I didn't take much interest in what she had to say about collaborating with Producers on a movie adaptation. As I would like to stay away from these people, as much as I hate being publicised, I also hate what they do with my favourite books. None of the recent book adaptations were good, and I would like to save my books from this disaster. Besides, my audience could be satisfied with just the ink on paper, they don't need horrible casting and role play. Don't even start on how they would change the setting and dialogues to make it more appealing, as if the book wasn't selling thousands of copies without them. Anyways, I wasn't going to let our tradition slide that easily. So I asked Alaia to go inside as I had some errands to run before I could rest.

Since our 12th birthday, we have been making Oreo cakes for each other. Of course, we hadn't done it since the last 6 years but this was a perfect opportunity to celebrate this new chance we had given to our friendship. I wasn't home, which made it difficult and even more exciting when I went to the nearest grocery store and bought the stuff I needed. An oven safe tiffin-box thingy, oreos, some whipped cream spray and candles. I came back to my room without informing Alaia and quickly changed into t shirts and trousers. It was the most problematic but fun part of the process. I smashed the oreo packet multiple times with a flower vase, spray bottle, water bottle, and other stuff to make a fine powder of the biscuits. Note, that I had separated the cream beforehand. There were crumbs everywhere around my room, but what does it matter? Alaia loved oreos and so I liked to pretend. I made the cake in another ten minutes, decorated it with the whipped cream, it wasn't exactly pretty to look at. But I was glad that we were doing this after being on hiatus for so many years. And I hoped that it would make her feel good, if not special. I covered the cake with nothing but an invisible cloak. I wasn't sure how she would react to this, as this is not something she would expect right now. Would she see it as an attempt to bring back the joy we had, back then when all we cared about was us? I knocked on her door, while balancing the cake on one hand. She opened the door but didn't exactly look at me, she was on her phone trying to write a better caption. Never mind, I might have peeked. I coughed to grab her attention, though she was a little too immersed in her post caption than one should be. So I called her name, and she instantly looked up at me, then at the cake.

"No!! You didn't!!" Her face instantly filled with surprise and joy. "Yes, I did. How is it?" I said.

"It looks horrible!! How did you even make it here?" She asked before taking the cake from my hands, her hands definitely didn't brush past mine. This time though it didn't send tingles down my spine, or awakened any butterflies in my stomach. "It's an oreo cake, what do you even need for it? Oreos??" I chuckled. "Still..You remembered. I shouldn't be surprised as it's *you*, and you would do anything for *me*." she said. I raised my brow in confusion. "What?" "I didn't mean that you should, but that you always went lengths to make me satisfied or happy. And I am always grateful for that." She smiled.

Once again she busied herself in her mobile, trying to click pictures of the cake from different angles. I needed to change the mood, I felt too nostalgic and not joyful at all. We were back as friends right? We were making change, we forgave each other, or did we not? Things had to change or it would start feeling nauseating. We were adults, but the child in us didn't have to die so soon. Which was why I had bought a foam can too. Alaia was too absorbed in taking pictures that she didn't notice me taking out the can from my back pocket. And before she could detect any of my movements, I sprayed foam on her face, and instantly took a picture of her. It didn't matter if it was hazy as long as people could make out that It was *her*.

"Oh my god! Dumbo!!! What the fuck?? I just took a shower." She yelled, almost making my ears go deaf. I couldn't stop my laughter which overpowered her voice. "You should have known that I was going to pull a stunt like that." I continued laughing. It was amusing to see her face covered with foam, which she tried to wipe with her hands but only ended up spreading it on her clothes. "Come here! I won't let this slide easily." she warned me. And I knew immediately to run away but it was a closed place and not our apartment's garden, so we both ran in circles around the room, over the sofa and bed, toppling whatever came in front of us, and spoiling the fresh sheets. I ran with whatever stamina I had, but got tired after our tenth round around the house. "Ahhhh!!! Wait a second! Man, you have a lot of energy for being in your late twenties, show some mercy!" I kept running but with less intensity now. "I am tired too, babe... So just stop running and give up." She said while panting. I knew very well that she wouldn't stop unless she took her revenge so I stopped and let her have it. It was her day to win. So I stopped abruptly on the sofa, but I had no idea that she was right behind me. Before she could process that I had stopped, we both collided and fell on the floor together. I fell on my stomach first, and she fell on top of me. She didn't even think for a second before taking the spray can from my back pocket that I had safely kept and sprayed all over my neck, and then face. It was only then that she took her weight off from my back, I kept my mouth shut as I didn't wanna get beat up, but she got a little heavier. My back felt as if someone had dropped a big rock on it. I stayed like that for a few minutes before rising on my feet, and I found that she had cleaned her face already. I guess it was my turn to do that. So I went and washed my face with her facewash. And came back to the room's light turned off and candles being lit for the cake.

She cut the cake, and we both tasted it. And the rest of the cake rested on the tea table while we continued chatting for another hour. When we realised that it was very late and we needed some rest so that we can get back to our work tomorrow with a fresh mind. I went back to my room, changed my clothes again as it still had some foam on it, and slept. The next morning I woke up late, so I had no time for breakfast. Just took a cold shower and went out for Uni. I had a lot of classes to take this day, so I couldn't pick Alaia's call. When I got off work in the evening, I made sure that I called her back. But she asked me to call back later as she was getting ready. I was gonna go to the hotel anyway so I thought of having that conversation there with her, whatever she called me for. I called Roop and asked him if he got any news about our apartment, and he said that the cleaning and inspection of the apartment was completed this morning and it's safe to go back now. Which meant that I won't have to live in this hotel room any longer, there was some of my stuff there and if I picked it up, I could just go back to my own house and rest. I went to the hotel, took my things and then went to Alaia's room. But it was empty. The receptionist told me that she checked out this evening. Maybe this was why she called me, to tell me that she was checking out. But the question stands, where did she go? She seemed busy when I last called her, so this time I sent her a text asking where she was and what she wanted to tell me, if there was anything to tell. I bought some take-out, as I had no energy to cook at all after last night and the number of classes I had to take this day.

After an hour, I was back home, relaxed on my living room sofa with food on my plate while watching netflix when I got her reply to my text. She told me that she was on a work trip, and gave me Dhruv's number. I wasn't supposed to call, as he would call me himself as told by Alaia. The number was for recognition. I tried to ignore the call which followed right after, too fast. But it would be rude if I didn' pickup. " Hi! It's me Dhruv, I hope I am not disturbing you." He said. "No, not at all. I was warned by Alaia, that you'd call. So what did you wanted to talk about?" I asked

"She didn't tell you right? Basically the producers I work with, were trying to reach out to you for a book adaptation. But since you have strictly told your publishers and your agent to not accept any of these requests, they couldn't approach you. Though when Alaia told me about you, and I in turn told the producers about you, they were willing to have a meeting with you, privately. And Alaia fixed the date and timing on your behalf, saying that you would certainly do this. I was a little suspicious that she didn't tell you about the plan, and now I am being proved correct." He said. "I am very sorry but I'd have to politely decline, as there were reasons I didn't take interest in this before and don't plan to do it anytime soon. Can you please talk to them and say that I cancelled the meeting? I'll talk to Alaia about this and make sure she doesn't do this again. I had no idea that she would fix the meeting without even consulting me." I said. "I know, she told me everything about why you were not interested in a book adaptation, but can't you meet these people once? I mean it as a request, these people have been trying to catch up to you for so long, and are willing to hear you out. They have promised Alaia and me that they won't change anything about the characters or the story. It will be as it is now, so I am requesting you to give it a chance. If you don't like their ideas, you won't have to do anything. But just this time, help us all out by meeting these people." He said. "Uhh…Okay. I guess. Only this time though, if it goes well then we can think about it but If I didn't like what they have to say, I won't meet anyone else." I said.

"Alright, then I'll text you the address and the timing for the meeting." He said.

Very good, Alaia. You are the only person who can make me do things I don't wanna do.

DISAGREEMENT

AQEEL

On normal days, I'd like myself a slow morning. Sipping on my coffee, reading a book or listening to songs. But today was different, I had to mentally prepare myself for what I was going to go through. I thought of all the possible ways by which I could cancel this thing. I was only going to the meeting for Alaia, once I do what she wants me to do, she'd be happy. I went to the designated place, It was a hotel room. I wondered if these people always had their meetings in hotels, instead of in their offices. When I entered the place, I only hoped for it to go the way I had imagined. They would suggest some changes, and I'd decline politely. I had to cancel my classes for today. But I was sure, my students were going to love their day off.

It was a suite, bigger than any other rooms in the hotel and much more luxurious. The butler helped me in, and asked me to sit in the living area. There was something off about this whole meeting, something I hadn't thought about. And the fact that I had no knowledge about who I was meeting with, made me even more anxious. I waited there for ten minutes, when the butler came twice to ask me for coffee or tea. Then finally a woman emerged from her bedroom, she was probably in her 40s. And I noticed something more suspicious, she was still in her *nightgown*. Wasn't it supposed to be a meeting? Don't they care about themselves, if not for others?

"Hey! I knew you were talented, but I didn't think you'd be so hot to look at." She came right towards me with a cheeky smile plastered on her face. I chuckled, trying to hide the nervousness. "Did I wake you up? I thought I came at the correct time, but it doesn't feel like that anymore." I said. "Oh, don't mind my attire. I love my comfortable nightgown a little too much, you'll get used to it." She laughed. I was sure, there would be no next time so I didn't have to get used to it. She asked the butler for some whiskey for the both of us. "Sorry, but I don't drink." I said. "Whiskey? Then we'll get you something else, how does wine sounds to you.". She asked. "Oh no, I meant I don't drink alcohol. And thanks but I won't take anything, so please don't bother." I said. She just nodded, and sipped on the whiskey the butler brought for her. And I couldn't help judging her for day drinking, but may be thats who they were, these people, they didn't follow the rules common people did. While she drank her whiskey, she looked me up and down, as If she was checking me out. I couldn't do anything but turn a blind eye, I felt extremely insecure and self concious. Why was she checking me out, what did she want? It was all that I was thinking at that time, and her remark as soon as she saw me. These weren't good signs, but I was waiting for the worst ones. "So, I have read some of your work, and it seems like you only write young adult and romance genres. But frankly saying, I wanted something more spicy, you know like dark romance, and ...smut. There is a high demand for those kind of books and movies. If you could write me something new, It would have been a pleasure to work with you." She said while still checking me out. I fixed my coat. "So you are asking me to write something new? Outside the genres I work on?" I asked. "Exactly." She said, and walked towards me with the whiskey glass on her hand. Then she sat beside me and touched my hair. I flinched. I shifted on the couch a little, away from her. She crossed her legs, and looked towards me with lust in her eyes. I wasn't mistaken, I very well knew what it looked like. I was praying, internally, to be saved. I didn't want to stay in the same room with her, let alone on the same couch. She opened her mouth to say something but I interrupted her. "Listen, I am not gonna agree on anything new. I wasn't even interested in doing an adaptation, I just came here because my friend asked me to. But since you don't want anything with romance or young adult fiction, I'd have to politely decline this offer. I am not interested in writing adult fiction or smut. Okay?" I explained. "Maybe I can change your mind. You know, writing and making dark romance is very fun and I bet you won't regret it." She shifted a little on the couch towards me. And I couldn't bear her anymore, so I stood up. "Sorry, but no!" I said and walked towards the exit. "Are you really gonna reject this offer so easily? Do you even know how much you'd be paid?" She asked. "I know, and I am rejecting it all, gladly." After that I walked out of the room, without even taking a look back. I texted Dhruv that the meeting was over, I didn't bother telling Alaia as she would throw too many questions at me and right now I wasn't in the mood to talk to anyone else. I mean, I never wanted to work with them. But I hadn't expected the offer to be this. Write a dark romance with a lot of smut, get paid in lakhs and probably a night with the producer herself. A complete package of what I didn't want.

Dhruv asked me to meet him , and texted me an address. "Why are we meeting in a club?" I asked him on the phone. "Would you rather want to meet me in a Fancy ass 7 star michelin restaurant? or maybe in a children's park? You should have fun, when it comes to you." He advised me and I wondered if he was still talking about the club or the meeting I just had. "Okay I'll come only". I arrived at the location 20 minutes later, and saw Dhruv wandering around the parking lot. He must be waiting for me then. "Hey! Man you are late, it's only a ten minute ride from the hotel." He said. "Sorry! Took a short washroom break, on my way here."

"Fine!" he said. "And yeah, enjoy yourself while you can. My friend is throwing a party here, so take full benefit of the free drinks." "I don't -" the words were still half inside my throat when he spoke again. "There are non-alcoholic drinks too. Don't worry." I smiled. We entered the club and in the next few seconds, Dhruv vanished amidst the crowd. There were too many people, loud music and girls. On the bar, in people's arms, laps and basically everywhere. I took my seat, on the corner stool at the bar. "Hello sir! What would you like to have?" The bartender asked, and I tried to avoid looking at her exposed breast. I want to have fun too, but not the physical fun everyone talks about. "Anything which is non-alcoholic." I said. "Will a Diabolo grenadine work?" She asked again. "Does it have sugar in it? Sorry, I am diabetic." I asked. "He'll just take water, thanks." Affirmed Alaia. She emerged from where, I had no idea. I had thought she was still on her work trip. "I see you are back then. Weren't you on a work trip?" I asked her. "Yup, I was. And I am coming here directly from the airport. Couldn't miss this party." She squealed. "So tell me, how did the meeting go?" She asked the question, I wasn't ready for. "I rejected the offer." I admitted. "Huh? you rejected what? Why on earth would you do that? Ughhh." She gulped her drink on one go. I eyed her drink a little too much, which didn't go unnoticed by her. "Its not alcohol." She clarified. So I continued with my story, as I'd have to tell her one day. "They weren't interested in my story." I said "So?what did they call you for?" She asked me, confusion blurring her mind. "The producer wants me to write a new story. Something in dark romance." After hearing my words, she broke into laughter, her confused face now making funny sounds. "I can't imagine you writing in that genre. But still you could try, It'd be fun." She said by taking a short break from her laughter. "Thats not it. There is more. I mean I would never write that, even though I enjoy reading it. But that's just not what I'd do, It's out of my comfort zone." I said "You are saying that you read that genre?" She laughed again. I wonder what was that funny. Everybody enjoys dark romance, that doesn't mean they would go around having sex with anyone they come across or talk about it out loud. "And what's the other thing?" She asked, still not over her laugh. "The producer tried to hit on me. And If I had stayed a little more, she'd have made me strip." I might have exaggerated it, but it felt like that only. When she kept checking me out, and god knows what she was imagining in her mind. Surprisingly Alaia became silent. She stopped laughing and looked at me with shock. "What?" She asked, as if she didn't hear it properly the first time. "I said what I said, I am not going to repeat it. I feel filthy by only imagining how she looked at me" And for once I thought she was serious, but she started laughing again. And I reconsidered the person who I should be mad at. "You are saying that a woman, who is extremely picky about who she walks with, sexually approached you?" I felt like she was amazed by the act that woman had pulled on me. "Yeah, that is what happened. But I am not really enjoying this Alaia, so I think you should keep it down." I muttered. Annoyed by her reaction, I already made up my mind to leave this party and go back to my world where people don't normalise Sex in exchange for work. "Okay, but do you realise what you did? I mean she would have paid you in lakhs, if you only pretended to enjoy it. You wouldn't actually have to sleep with her, just play along for a while until your work was done." She said, "I don't want money, Alaia. If it means that I'd have to stand a person like her. You don't understand that I am not okay with this." I said, angrily

"So, you'd just reject all that money?" She asked."Yeah. What would you do if you were in my position? Sleep with a guy, because he says he can help you up the ladder?" I didn't hear what I was saying to her. "What? NO! Of course not, but I would at least try to pretend. And not reject money, when it is what matters in this world."

"It might matter, in your world. But not in mine."I blurted out.

"Okay! Then go to your world, which includes your desk at your home and the one at your university. Because your world doesn't include living people in it right?" She barked. And it was impossible for me to react to that so I left. Surprisingly she followed me to the parking lot, a few steps behind me. She kept following me without saying a word until we were in the parking lot, alone, away from the crowd. I halted, she followed suit and stopped right behind me. "Am sorry, I didn't mean to hurt your sentiments." She pleaded. "I am sorry too, I shouldn't have said those things to you. But you have to understand that I am not like you. I like my comfort zone a little too much, and would never trade it for money." I said. "I know, I know. It's just I didn't want you to lose this opportunity, but since you don't want to be involved in such things I won't pester you anymore. But you have to understand that since we are friends, sometimes my world will leak into yours, and yours into mine. You have to be clear about your thoughts regarding my lifestyle, it's not like I go around sleeping with people for work. In fact I have never slept with anyone except one." She said, And my attention went to the words she said, *except one*. And maybe my expressions were too transparent for her to find out the curiosity taking birth inside me as she admitted. "It was Uzair." I slowly nodded to her. I excused myself by saying that I was tired and needed rest. The fact that Alaia lost her virginity to Uzair, clouded my mind. It wasn't that I cared anymore. And yet, I couldn't help but think about it. All that time, she knew that I had feelings for her, but she chose to ignore it, and kept living her life with as much fun as one could think of. I mean, I wasn't upfront about my feelings back then, but my behaviour towards her was evident.

MEDIA

ALAIA

After Aqeel left, I didn't go back to the party. I felt guilty for pressuring Aqeel on something he wasn't fond of. So I texted Dhruv that I had a headache, and I wasn't lying. I checked-in in my hotel room and went to bed after having several glasses of water. The next morning I woke up to the alarm which went off for the fifth time. I was taken aback as soon as I unlocked my mobile phone. Not so good after a katzenjammer. There were more than 500 notifications from Instagram, Facebook and approx 17 missed calls from Dhruv and Marina, my assistant. I couldn't wrap my mind around what exactly happened? As there wasn't any Pr marketing program scheduled for today. Also these Unwanted publicities were scary to entertain.

The headache should have been gone after the sleep I got, but it looked like I would have to bear it for another day. I opened Dhruv's text and it contained a link which showed Aqeel's name in big bold letters. Something struck and sobered me upon seeing his name on it. What? UMM.. why was Aqeel in today's headlines? After I saw what was written there, every colour from my face that I imagined being present there faded away. I could already feel Aqeel drifting away from me, and being hurt from what happened. The headline showed - Author of " Pretty Littles Secrets " Aqeel Baig involved in Casting Couch? Easy road to Showbiz?

The media is a snake, it can sense the hidden secrets of people from far away and destroy their reputation by spilling their venom all over the place. At that moment all I wanted was the walls to crumble on to myself so that I could be buried alive. How did the word come out? Was the first question that came into being, though it seemed like I answered myself. I am DEAD! SHIT, SHIT ! I should call Marina back. No Aqeel...ugh who should I call first? Aqeel, I should definitely check up on Aqeel. But to my great disappointment His phone was switched off. So I called Marina but her line was busy. Then I turned to Dhruv. And thankfully he received my call. "Hello, Dhruv?" I asked. "Hello, Alaia. WHERE WERE YOU?

I called you SO many times.?" He asked, sounding very concerned. "I am so sorry, I overslept. But How did the word got out?"

"My guess is, the producer leaked this news as she didn't get what she wanted. Besides we were at a party yesterday, and the whole drama between you and Aqeel was a mere spark to this flame. Someone recorded the whole argument that went on between you and Aqeel and posted it online. It became a sensation last night only. We were so hungover and busy in our own world that we couldn't stop this. And this morning the printing media took it on themselves to make it a worldwide news." He said. "Have you talked to Aqeel?" He continued. "No, I tried but his phone is switched off. He might not know it yet, but I am sure he'll be horrified and angry after seeing this." I panicked, bile rising upto my throat. "Hey, are you there?" Dhruv from the other side, asked for me. "Yes, I am. And I might need your help to come up with something that can solve this mess. I am not able to reach out to my Assistant, otherwise I would have asked her only. Please, Dhruv. Help me out. I don't want Aqeel to hate me, *again*."

"Listen up Alaia, I don't know why he would be mad at you as this is not your doing, you were just trying to help. But still, I would suggest you to set up an interview for Aqeel. His identity is already out now, so there is no point in hiding behind names anymore. He needs to share his experience with that producer to everyone else. So that people would know that it was her and not Aqeel who demanded for sex in return for work. I know my relationship with her will be ruined, but what needs to be done should be done immediately. Besides, I am not interested in working with her anymore."

After that call I felt all sorts of emotions. I felt miserable and lonely, not because I was alone. But because I made Aqeel's life even more difficult just by showing up. I already presented myself for ignoring his feelings when he had loved me with all his might, because I didn't want it for me. I didn't want my friend to become anything else, and now I was close to losing that friend I wanted to save. Why couldn't I just love him back? Why can't I stop pushing him further away from me? Whenever I tried to help him for his benefit, I always ended up hurting him. Why can't I understand that he is a grown up and doesn't need me to walk him. He can walk himself, he can run. But as soon as he is in front of me, I lose control over myself. He seems like a lost child, and all I want to do is run towards him and help him. Sometimes it's hard for me to understand that he might not want my help, or worse, doesn't need *my* help. But he is my friend. He is *mine*. And I will continue to help him, even if I have to go against his will.

I immediately rang some numbers and talked to a radio channel, and set up an interview. Aqeel was hot news, and everybody was looking for him, and a chance to talk to him. They needed more juicy stuff, honest replies and gossip. Which they were going to get *soon*. I would provide it to them.

MOTHERHOOD

Alaia

My days here in Kolkata were getting busier and nerve wracking and this was making my heart heavy. It used to be a lot easier back in Boston. I had planned the day earlier this morning, fixed the interview and informed Aqeel. It wasn't easy for me to convince him for this interview, after what took place with the previous thing I had planned for him. He was worried, as this would be his first public appearance. He even told me to cancel it by saying that it wasn't necessary. And he would be just as fine as always. But he didn't know what would happen if people kept believing in this news. They needed the true version of this story, or else it would ruin his reputation. He didn't know the power the media holds against us, and what they would do if we didn't clarify things. At last he agreed to do it, asking me to not plan on things before asking his permission. I had to agree to this condition, I had to chain myself up.

It was time for me to relax and not in the way where I pampered myself. I needed to talk to someone, someone who would give me strength, courage and believe in me. Someone who would trust me, so I went to meet *Abbu*. I wish Ammi was here. I hadn't paid him a visit after I came back from Boston.

I had this idea that my father was lonely because he lived alone and missed his only daughter, me. Instead, I was warmly greeted by five other grey-haired handsome men, probably Abbu's friends. And he emerged from behind those men, a tall black-dyed haired equally handsome man, my Abbu.

He greeted me with much affection and surprise. "Look, who decided to finally come and see this old man!" He was beaming with joy, the kind of joy I was looking for in other people's eyes. He came forward and hugged me tight, nearly leaving me breathless. "Meet, my friends. They were keeping me coming, while you were gone."

"And I was gone for a long time, sorry Abbu." I said, hugging him back. I greeted everyone in the room, even though I didn't know them but I was glad that Abbu had company. Everyone left, giving me and Abbu some private time to catch up. "So, how are you?" Abbu asked. "I am fine." I said with a dry sigh, a big fat lie. All the work from shifting my base was catching up to me. At this rate I would either get migraine or a weak heart. "Just because I am old, doesn't mean I can't differentiate between a lie and a truth. I know what has happened and how upset you must be." He said.

"Really? And how do you know what exactly happened?" I asked him. "Well I saw the news. And I know, whenever something happens with Aqeel you get really upset. And you always went to your mother for suggestions after that. But since she is no more, I might come handy. This old guy right here isn't that useless you know? Though I am glad you came, for whatever reason. I missed you a lot. So sit tight, I am coming with some refreshments for you." He said and kissed my forehead.

I felt like a weight was already off of my shoulder, and felt like crying. It was so nice to be back *home*. I always felt like it was Abbu's taunt to get me married but, it was the bitter sweet memories of Ammi which kept me from coming back to this place. While tackling all the reasons to cry I managed to put on a fake smile just for the sake of Abbu. Guess I made the right choice to settle back here, after all. As I wouldn't wanna experience the same thing again with Abbu. I wanted to be by his side for however long he would live.

I waited for ten minutes, when Abbu came outside with ginger tea and hair oil. "Abbu, no! Please do not use hair oil!" I complained. I don't quite remember the last time I put hair oil. "Shut up! Nothing bad will happen to your hair if you put some oil on it. Look at my hair, it still shines. Besides, I know your mom used to do your champi twice a week."

"Yeah, your hair is definitely shining because you *dyed* them. Besides, Ammi used to force me to do that." I chuckled and resettled on the floor, took the tea cup from him and our chit-chat began.

"Abbu...thank you so much. For not getting mad and understanding me."

"Isn't that what every parent is supposed to do?" Asked Abbu. I hummed in response and delight which I got from the head massage. "When did you even become this good at massaging?" I asked, with my eyes closed.

Abbu said "It was your mother who taught me, I was a miserable one earlier. She didn't like to disturb you whenever her head hurt so instead she told me." After a brief pause I said "Abbu, I miss Ammi." while the tears rolled down my cheeks.

"You should have come earlier, what took you so long? It would have been your mother's words…" said Abbu. " I know what happened and I know there is an explanation for that. The Question is Why is this affecting you so much? You always said that this kind of things happened in your industry. So what is the real reason behind your worry?" He continued

"Go on and tell me. I will be a good listener, Promise." He assured.

"I…I just feel, *empty*. I didn't think I had someone beside me before I came here. After Ammi's death I was so paranoid of losing yet another person. Which is why I wrote to Aqeel. I wanted him back. Yet somehow I don't believe that I deserve him, Abbu. I feel like I will ruin his life, If I stayed. It doesn't feel like it used to be between us. Something is off and I don't know what? He was very nice and warmly welcomed me back in his life. And yet.."

"Can you tell me in detail.. Like why do you think it's different?" He asked

"You know what? I think it's just my guilt. I shouldn't have left him. He didn't do anything wrong. He just *loved* me, unconditionally. And what did I do? I ignored him, and his feelings. I knew it, but I didn't appreciate what he had to offer. And now I am regretting it." I admitted.

" I know that you were wrong. I was completely against it, how you broke your lifelong friendship with him." Complained Abbu.

"I hate myself too, Abbu, it's just that, I liked him too much as a friend. Also, I was too serious with my relationship with Uzair back then."

"Uzair was fine. But Aqeel *is* fabulous. His love was genuine. If it wasn't you who got involved in relationships and insisted on love marriage. I would have paired you two." He said. "What??" I asked, completely shocked.

"You have no idea, but you two would have made a really good pair. Now, finish your tea before it gets cold. And tell me what you'd like to have for lunch? I'll make it for you."

"Sorry, but no." I said " Arey, just trust me, I am a good cook now." Abbu said proudly.

"Sure you are, I can totally unsee the food packages that you have piled in your kitchen." I laughed. "Aqeel has an interview this evening, and I am supposed to go with him. I can't be late."

"That is why you shouldn't leave on an empty stomach, dear. I'll just take 20 minutes to make our lunch and to assure you, I have your mother's old cook book."

"Perhaps, I'll stay for another 30 minutes, so off you go, make me a good old Ammi kinda lunch." I demanded with a smile.

TRANSPARENT

AQEEL

It is evident that everybody needs to have a coping mechanism. They get their choice of things that might help with depression or on a day to day level of stress so they don't fall apart. I usually take a break from work and spend time reading or cooking my favourite comfort food. Though as of today, none of them worked. I kept thinking about Alaia, that producer, and the interview I was supposed to give today. This was going to be my first interview, and definitely not an easy one.

So to clear up my mind and stop thinking about it all, I decided to go for a run near Rabindra Sarobar Lake. I tried really hard to persuade Alaia into cancelling this interview as I didn't think I could do it. But she made me believe in myself, I personally had no idea If I'd be able to talk about it at all. Or that people would believe in my words, I was just a newbie, would they listen to me or the producer herself?

I remembered coming here, during my college days. On days when there was too much to do, too many thoughts clouding my mind that I was left procrastinating most of them. I used to come here and just sit near the lake and people watch. There was peace in watching people meditate, read books, and walk their dogs. It soothed my heart and cleansed my soul. The sweet spring mornings filled with warm sun and cool breeze.

Alaia was right, I had made my desk my life. Even my hobbies were indoor ones and didn't encourage me to go outside. I wondered If I was a full time writer, I'd be confined to my room. And wouldn't even know, if something went wrong in the outside world. So I took a long breath and thanked Allah for letting me live a life in such a beautiful world. I decided to run for 30 minutes. At first the idea seemed great and not tiresome. 30 minutes wasn't that much, right? The first ten minutes felt like I was trying to climb a steep hill rather than running, but I kept running, thinking it would get better. Another 10 minutes in and my chest started heaving, I was struggling to even run in a straight line. I knew I was out of shape but this much? I needed to get my priorities straight. Medication alone won't help me, I need to take care of my body.

At last I couldn't finish my goal of 30 minutes. So I went back home, took a shower and then went to the University. I covered as many classes as I could, had my lunch in the college cafeteria to save some time and went to the location Alaia sent me. When I reached, Alaia was already there, talking to the show director. Looking at the set-up, it finally dawned upon me what had happened with me this past week. It felt like someone dragged me out of my room and threw me out in the streets, naked. I stood at the entrance, People scanned me from top to bottom as if I was an alien or worse a victim. It felt exactly how one would feel if they were stripped off in front of everyone. All of me was visible, they knew me, knew what happened to me, knew why I was here. I had loved playing the smart, introverted, mysterious guy all this long. But people would see me differently now. They would judge me, because of the characters I write, because of some scene that went wrong or someone I killed. Not literally, but in books. They would judge me because of who I am with, and although I would like to say that I don't care. I actually do. These opinions, judgements drive me crazy, and all this while I thought I could be saved, because *I* was able to hide my real identity, I was wrong. One way or another, they would have come to know who the person behind those books was, who I was. And maybe today was that day. So I braced myself for whatever was coming for me, and stepped inside.

While they fixed my hair and makeup before shooting. Alaia bickered with people, about how it was getting late and we shouldn't have bothered with makeup as I was looking impeccable without it. I chuckled but noticed how she cared about me and knew that I didn't like all this stuff. I remembered what had happened in our past. Me confessing to Alaia on her engagement day. Uzair cancelling their engagement and cutting ties with Alaia. End of lifelong friendship. Being the reason for their parent's broken hearts. As I sat beside her, I couldn't push these thoughts away. They fed on my mind, until my shot was ready.

Sometimes I think about what it means to be happy and at peace. Whenever I read something or watch a movie about lives, personality, choices and topics like that I figure so many things and nothing at all. It takes me some time to rethink and relearn what I already know. Seeing things from a different perspective every time I write something down makes me phase out. On most days when I am sitting in front of my half filled manuscript, I look at something beyond and just think. Think what it feels like to be in a different body living a different life and looking at things in an obviously different way with many kinds of opinions. Some people complain about overthinking and I do it myself too, but this is one of the major reason I was able to create something. Something of my own. Thoughts. And when I was writing them down, I was also giving them colour and a world to live in. And very few judged it, but mostly they related to it. Because it's written and we tend to believe what's written. Just as people believe in published newspapers and not circulating messages on whatsapp. We believe that if someone has written it then it probably has a meaning and purpose. Though people hardly believe what we say verbally. That is the reason paper and ink has more weight than any other form of knowledge. Umm.. that's not a hundred percent as I like learning visually more but yeah this is it.

This is what I imagined myself saying at an interview, earlier when I knew I was never gonna give one. But look at me now, I was going to give an interview, which was less about my *books* and more about me. I was too deep in my mind, when a girl came and snapped her fingers on me to get my attention. I figured she was calling my name for a while now, but I had zoned out.

"Got you! Sorry for the long wait, but we'll start in just a few minutes. Coffee?" She asked, her eyes shone brightly as if she was a child who finally got the thing they wanted for so long. Before I could say about how I'd want my coffee to be black and sugar free, she said it herself. "You know what? I'll get you a black coffee with no sugar." She vanished and came back in a few minutes with two mugs in her hand. She offered me the one with 'Wait! I am refuelling my soul.'written on it. I couldn't help but smile at that. Alaia was now sitting with the team on the other side of the glass wall, in the control room. And I was here with the Rj, inside the broadcasting room. "I am Haniya." The Rj introduced herself, forwarding her hand for a handshake. I followed suit and shook her hands. "Even though I wanted to keep it down. I can't. I am your BIGGEST fan. I love your books, and always wondered about the person behind it and see where I am now. I must say I don't hate this job anymore." I couldn't help but chuckle at her reaction, and she started blushing after my reaction. Soon the team announced the beginning of the shoot and Alaia wished me good luck from the other side of the glass wall. I know, I was in this situation because of her but I hadn't thought that she would make time for me and wait here while I got anxious upon each and every question. My anxiety was through the roof, but the Rj, Haniya was nervous herself, So I felt less lonely. Being in the same room with a person who was as nervous as you, made an invisible connection. I wasn't alone, and Alaia was on the other side, looking at me and encouraging me. Whenever we took a short break in between, both Haniya and I gulped down half a litre of water. The Makeup artist came and helped us wipe off some of the sweat that accumulated on our forehead, in spite of the ac inside the room.

"Actually, I suffered from obesity since my childhood and it took me years to get in shape. So I know now that my health should be my top most priority." Haniya said. For a second I wasn't sure if she was talking to me. Her suddenly jumping on a sensitive topic like that shocked me. "I knew that you were diabetic, which is why I offered you black coffee. It's not like I was being weird, sorry if I made you uncomfortable." She apologised. "No, it's okay. Why would that make me uncomfortable?" I asked, unsure if I missed something. "I don't know, what if you think that I was forcing my own choice on you?" She said,

"No, no, not at all." I said. I didn't realise what was wrong with her words as I was used to people deciding for me, especially Alaia. Though I realise now that not everyone is as controlling as her, I get it. Her behaviour comes from a protective nature. Haniya had a sweet smile and whenever I glanced at her I couldn't help but smile back. We continued to talk about how she loved my books and asked me for a signed copy. I couldn't say no to those bright eyes that hinted of nothing but pure innocence. And then we were shooting again. It went for another hour as I had to take a few extra takes, didn't expect any better from me. When I glanced towards Alaia, I found her dozed off in her seat. She must have been tired.

Something about Haniya struck me, she wasn't just a fan. It looked as if she knew me, knew the real me behind the characters I made and didn't judge me for it. Despite being nervous about the whole interview, I was at ease. As there were not just one but two people inside this studio who saw me for who I was. It's not common for me to make a friend this fast, but with Haniya, time didn't mean anything as she knew everything there was to know about me and I was getting curious to know about her too. On her request, I signed a copy of my book for her and in exchange I asked for her number. She was surprised at first but beamed with joy when I said that I would like to be in touch with her. And as for me, I was happy to find an honest, innocent, and pure person inside Haniya.

They had to sprinkle water on Alaia's face as she was fast asleep and wouldn't even budge.

"Sorry buddy but you missed the fun part." Said Haniya to Alaia.

"Yeah, I have never been this transparent to my thoughts and words before. I am thankful that Haniya was there to cheer me up and of course *you* who stayed here this late just for me." I said to both of them and indeed I was grateful for them.

Alaia was glad that the interview had finally ended and we both could head out now. They needed to edit the clips and put it together before it would be broadcasted on their channel the next day. But just a few seconds later, Alaia's bright face changed into something grim. I wondered what was the matter behind that sudden mood shift, so I followed her gaze towards my arm which was entwined with Haniya's. I hadn't even noticed that myself but when I looked at her, I realised that it made her upset, so I quickly but politely slid my hands out. Haniya didn't notice anything, and even if she did, she must have thought it to be my shyness.

On our way back home, I told her whatever happened while she was fast asleep. But it felt like she wasn't listening to me at all. She kept looking outside the window and didn't even nod when I asked something. I gave up after some time. I had no idea what made her so upset, or it might just be her tiredness. But I didn't think about it too much. As my mind was occupied by someone else's thoughts. Fresh and new thoughts. Alaia dropped me a few streets before my apartment, as she was supposed to take a different turn. I didn't mind it at all and took an auto from there to my apartment. My car was still outside the studio, they said that they'd send me back my car at my address, as we had decided to carpool instead of going separately.

CHANEL

ALAIA

It was around 2 am when I came back. I didn't have the energy to even change my clothes. So I just laid down on my bed and tried to sleep. The images kept haunting me, The flashbacks from last night. I had no reason to be upset, no reason to be jealous of a girl who barely knew him. But was I jealous? Yes. Why? I don't know. It didn't matter how much I tried to forget about how happy and chill Aqeel looked when they both had their arms entwined together, or how much I tried to force a smile in front of Aqeel. I felt utterly upset after ignoring Aqeel the full time we were on our way back. I even left him mid-way, as it was impossible for me to see him without imagining him with Haniya. I cried my eyes out until darkness swallowed me in a deep sleep.

The next morning, I woke up to the sound of my doorbell. I rose up from my bed and saw myself on the dressing table mirror, I looked miserable and dirty. But I couldn't just leave the person waiting outside so I went to answer the door, looking like a mess. "Who is it?" I asked.

"Good morning ma'am, I am your new intern, Shruti. Marina ma'am asked me to meet you here and also to take you to our New office." I now remembered her from the interview I took several days back. She was as nervous as she was the first day she saw me, but I knew her well enough. Her CV wasn't that impressive but I had seen the glint in her eyes, the passion I wanted in my employees and interns.

"Yeah, I know. Wait for me, while I take a shower."

"Ma'am, the meeting starts in 10 mins." Stuttered Shruti.

"Then why the hell are you late?" I asked her, disgusted at my own condition. It's not her fault that I had to accompany my friend for his interview and came back really late.

"Actually I was waiting for you to open the door for half an hour, but it's okay, take your time, I'll just remind you that we have a shoot too and if we go late for the meeting we'll be automatically late for the shoot. Also

Marina ma'am asked me to pick up the jewellery too. May I know where it is?" She asked me, sweat dripping from her forehead and shins.

"Hey! Slow down, one thing at a time, okay? The necklace should be somewhere near my bed. I am off to shower, please find it for me." I said. I had very little time, but I couldn't just pull up to a meeting without showering first. So I quickly took a shower, while I did that, the thought of Aqeel with some other girl still lingered around, even in my bathroom. Shruti called my name from outside and asked me if she could check inside my luggage for the necklace. I asked her to do whatever she needed to, while I quickly slipped inside my clothes. When I went outside, she was still searching for them and even after I finished getting ready. "Did you find them?" I asked. "I am afraid not." She looked at me, terrified. "What? It must be inside, check properly." I started feeling anxious, what if we didn't have it? "Ma'am, I checked everywhere, it isn't here. What should we do now?" She said, almost crying. "You must have missed somewhere, where would a necklace go on its own? I haven't even seen it since I came back." And the realisation hit me, I *hadn't* seen it. The last time I saw it was when I picked it up from Chanel's office in Mumbai. "Oh shit!" I blurted out. "What happened ma'am?" Shruti asked me. "I think I left it somewhere. Maybe at the airport." I slammed my palm flat on my forehead, the necklace was worth THIRTY lakhs, and it was a *sponsored* piece, for my fashion show. "Oh my god!" Shruti exclaimed.

We both were panicking at this point and paced around the room. I called Marina, and asked for her advice. She, being the experienced one she is, calmed me down and told me that she'll contact the Airport facility and ask them about the necklace.

I took a breath of relief, we both did. "What is happening to me? Why can't I function properly?" I complained. "Don't worry ma'am, it's only natural to forget things." She assured me. "Is it normal to be jealous of a girl who took a slight interest in my friend?" I asked, to someone who I shouldn't have asked. "Might be possible, if you like your friend." She shrugged. "Really?" I found it rather funny, could I like him? "I think we should leave, or else we'll be super late." She requested. "Yeah, yeah sure." And we both left for my office. Thankfully we weren't much late, and the meeting went just as fine. The investors were already impressed by my work, they just needed a tour of my new office here in Kolkata, to make sure I had settled properly and the work was going on as it was supposed to. Then after the meeting, we went straight to the shoot location. Marina, my assistant, was very competent and experienced. She took care of the models and the clothes. I just had to be present there, to look upon things and the photos before it went out for further editing.

Finally after the shoot I went back to my office, to check up on some more things before I could take some rest. Of course shifting here from Boston wasn't easy, even though we had been planning this for months, and had everything prepared before I made my come back. Things were a little rocky, though it'll all get back to normal soon.

I plopped my head on my office desk. It was a long and tough week.

MISTRESS?

ALAIA

"Why are you behaving as if your world has turned upside down? Let me remind you that I have got your back, don't stress on a piece of necklace." Said Marina.

"Sometimes you act like my mom. If she was alive, this is exactly what she would have told me. But it's not only about that necklace." I whined. "Then what is it about, my child?" She asked.

"Nothing. Can you get me some coffee please, I think I have a headache." I pleaded. "I am not getting you coffee, you have had at least three cups already. Give yourself some rest okay? Maybe take a holiday if you are not feeling well." She advised me.

"A holiday? That seems like a good idea to me." I yawned, my words half understandable.

"Who is taking a holiday? Sorry if I am interrupting something." I looked up from my desk and saw Shruti peeking inside my cabin. "Can I come in?" She asked. Marina and I nodded. "I am suggesting that your boss take a holiday, as she seems really tired and stressed these days." Marina said to Shruti. "But where should I go?" I whined again. "I think a short trip to a beach will be therapeutic, as you can't take a longer leave since we have that fashion show coming up." Marina said to me. "But I don't want to go to a beach, what am I even gonna do there all alone?" I complained. "Side effects of not finding a boyfriend and rejecting the ones who approach you. How long are you planning to stay single?" Marina asked. "I don't think I am in the mood to discuss it, Marina."

"Can I suggest something?" Shruti asked us. And we both nodded again. What else could we have done? It's not like I had a list of places I wanted to visit. "Will you be open to going to a college camp?"

"College camp?" I looked up with surprise. "Yeah, I mean. My college is organising one in a few days. And I have my pass too, which I am not going to use as you know I just joined this internship and it's not appropriate to take a leave day just yet." Shruti said. Marina and I both looked at each other, because of how absurd the advice was.

"And you think that *I* will go to a college camp?" I asked her, tilting my head a little.

"I know, it would be weird, you going to my place. But I can talk to the teacher in charge and they'll understand. I just thought that maybe you'd find a common ground with all the students as they are all in designing. And the campsite is near a lake, so you'd be able to relax too." She said, weighing her words. "I don't think it's that bad of an idea. You just need a vacation from your work, and what more good can it be from spending a day with people who share your interest." Marina suggested.

"Okay, I'll see." I said.

I drove back home, my hotel room. And slept without bothering about dinner. The next day was as busy as any other day. I didn't get much time to relax or to have any thoughts about anything except work. I had to work on my collection which was to be displayed at that fashion show. Everything was getting together piece by piece, I had to make sure that the arrangements were perfectly done before I could go on a vacation. I could have planned something else, could have booked tickets somewhere else. Though as if something kept pulling me, kept attracting me towards that camp, Shruti talked about. Even Marina was pleased by the idea, after some time. I was still thinking about how it would feel to be amongst students, amateurs. It's not like I know everything or think very highly about myself that I can't join them. If I was a guest, It would have felt different, though I was taking a student's pass for free to spend a day with teenagers. Was it a wise decision? No. Was I in a desperate need of a vacation? Yes. Did I plan on something else? No.

"Am I really doing it?" I spoke to myself. Apparently, the camp sounded too tempting once Shruti said that they were going to do activities like dance parties and stuff. But with one condition, No devices. I found myself driving towards the location anyways, I had the pass with me. It's not like they were gonna throw me away. "Straighten up Alaia! You have gotta enjoy today." I cheered myself up. I departed at around 7 in the morning, and reached there by 9. I promised myself that I wouldn't check or use my mobile phone until the camp was over as a *holiday* should feel like *one*.

It was not a popular campsite but as shruti had mentioned, it was found by the students. Near the city, in front of a lake there was a place with nothing around it. No lodge, no restaurants, no people, kind of like an abandoned place. No one ever visited the lake, so it was quite a place students would use for a picnic. I wondered how the college would have agreed for this location?

Best location for someone to die, get kidnapped, or possessed by a lake side ghost. Or most interestingly a place for hookups, if you went in the woods for a while no one would even bat an eye. Still, the place looked very calm and contained, cool breeze, tall trees, huge wild flowers and INSECTS.

At first I couldn't find the exact location and blindly trusted the map. But as I approached the lake, I could see the students unloading from their bus. I took a breath of relief, as I wasn't lost yet. So I looked for a parking spot, idle for my car. A guy with a buzz cut appeared in front of my car. I honked, but he didn't budge. He kept walking at his own slow pace while I kept screaming at him to choose a side. Then I realised that he probably had his headphones on. So I got out of my car and caught up with him. "Hey buzz-cut!" I tapped on his shoulder and he looked back. His square face, with defined jawline was even more handsome with the hazel eyes which were now facing me. He took off his headphones and asked me if I needed anything. "Can't you walk on the sides? I was trying to park my car here." I said

He looked around for my mustang, and nodded to himself in approval. "Yeah sure." He said with a smile, his brown complexion shining against the morning sun.

"Also could you please call your teacher, I need to talk to him." I asked him while getting back inside my car. He simply showed me a thumb and yelled his teacher's name to where he was. I looked outside from my window and saw that someone was driving that bus towards us. Towards the place, where I had decided to park my car. So I started my car to park before someone else did. But my car wouldn't budge, I tried accelerating but it only sunk deeper in the mud. As I continued trying, the buzz-cut guy stood still and saw me struggling. His teacher was just behind me, but there wasn't much space for it to move past me. So it stood, and I continued trying to free my car from the mud. But it didn't, only sank deeper. At last, the guy came and asked me to come out. I protested but he was just trying to help. So I let him, he then began to try to unstuck my car. The teacher gave me a greeting bow and helped push the car. After a while, I don't know how, but they were able to unstuck my car. I thanked both of them, the teacher introduced himself as John, and his student as Kabir. I opened my mouth to introduce myself but Kabir interrupted me. "And you are? You look a bit old to be a student, and yet too young to be Sir's wife. Are you his *mistress?*" He asked, with a cheeky grin. "What the actual F- " I blurted. "Shut up! Kabir." Mr John yelled at him. "Sorry, he is just trying to be funny. All my students are like that, a little too frank than they should be." Mr John said to me. "This is Alaia Mirza, the CEO, Founder and Designer of NXDE. If you don't know her then at least don't assume her relations with anyone." He said to Kabir, who was looking at me with amusement plastered all over his face. I rolled my eyes on him, annoying but handsome. "It doesn't seem like a nice parking location to me." Mr John said and I agreed with him. "It's okay, we'll manage something. Let's go and introduce you to my other students, hopefully they won't embarrass me like him."

Mr John hurriedly gathered everyone together, beside the lake and made them sit on the grass. Everyone was curious as to what was going to happen.

"So, we have a surprise guest with us." He announced. I was thanking him internally for introducing me as a guest and not someone who snatched a student's pass. "As you might know the

CEO/Founder/MAIN DESIGNER, of the luxury brand NXDE, miss Alaia Mirza. She has taken an interest in our camp and have blessed us with her presence." I was hiding behind Mr John's enormous back while he announced my presence there, I only came out once he took my name. And with my appearance, half of the crowd who knew me by my face roared with excitement and the other half who had only ever heard about me were astonished.

SKY NEVER DISAPPOINTS

ALAIA

After the announcement, everyone rushed towards me, except Kabir, which I didn't mind as he barely knew me. But the others, who knew what I was, welcomed me with great fondness and pleasure. It was easy for me to adjust between them, as everyone belonged to the same world as me. They were all design students like Shruti, and I didn't think her advice was wrong now, that I was having fun with these people. We started our camp day by playing some games like volleyball, badminton and tag. Funny how most of us were adults and still didn't mind playing games meant for childrens. As I was the outsider, I automatically became the chaser, it wasn't as if they were trying to separate me from the crowd, at least that's what I would like to think. I had taken this day to detox, to clear my mind and have a day just for fun, because I had overworked myself these past few months while shifting here from Boston, and there was more work waiting for me as soon as I would go back. So I decided to spend my day on a positive note. I took immense joy in chasing after people, one by one I caught everyone except Kabir. I couldn't run fast enough, he was always ahead of me running as if I was a monster. After we got tired from all that running and falling down multiple times because of the slippery mud, we ate an early lunch. And then some more games, until the sky turned into a pinkish-blue colour, I loved it. We all adored the sunset and took pictures, and then the real camp began. Fire was lit, music started playing over a speaker, and we made some barbeque. They didn't let me do any work as I was their guest, even though I would have loved to help, my cooking skills were of no use to them. So I helped them fill their glasses with soft drinks. We ate, sang and danced, even Mr John couldn't keep himself calm when his favourite song was played. I then realised the reason his students were so frank with him, he didn't care about manners, etiquettes or whatever that would keep the fun away from him. He was equally frank to his students, and danced with them as if he was just another student. I wondered what Aqeel's relationship was like with his students. He wasn't the outgoing guy, neither was he the boring one if felt comfortable.

I was tired, not the kind of tired I usually get after work where the only thing I would like was to take a shower and sleep, but I was tired after having fun, the carefree fun that didn't include people who would judge you if you happened to fall down or break a leg. They were students, who wanted fun, rather than a source of gossip.

We all sat in a circle around the fire we had created. Tired but not ready to leave the place just yet, everyone was silent including me. Watching the fire, savouring the beauty of heat and cold together. The weather was chilly, as we were outside and near a lake. Clouds formed above our heads, the moon glowing from behind the grey clouds. I remembered the days when we, Aqeel and I used to play like this, all day. And then, we would get tired and sleep beside each other under the moon in our building terrace. Those were some beautiful days, which won't come back anymore, though it would keep us together, keeping aside the problems we create as an adult.

I was looking at everyone, who were either sleepy but won't let go of the ongoing conversation or behaving like a drunk person and throwing random dad jokes once in a while. Though one person was missing, Kabir. I went out to look for him, out of curiosity. He wasn't gloomy or arrogant, and yet he didn't strike up a conversation with me like others, I wondered why? Did he find me rather uninteresting or unimportant? I walked out of that circle and towards the bus. I saw a flash of light coming out of the bus, so I peeked inside and found him rummaging through a bag which had Mr John's name on it. There was only some light, which came out of his mobile flashlight, that I could read the name on. I couldn't make out what he was doing with the bag. I didn't ask him anything or made my presence noticeable. But I felt a little suspicious about him so I went to ask Mr John to check up on him.

"Oh! He asked me if I had a power bank, so I told him to take it from my bag. Don't worry, I trust him, he isn't the type of guy to steal. Lest you think badly about him, He is actually a nice guy, don't let the words he said to you this morning get to your mind." Mr John said. I nodded at him with a smile. "I got it, thanks." Kabir said to Mr John, catching upto us. Mr John went away to talk to others, and left me with him. "I heard everything. Are you trying to get back at me for what I said this morning?" He asked, facing me now. "No, It was a mistake, I misunderstood you. That's all. Besides what you said this morning, was absurd and yet I took it as a compliment." I said to him, crossing my arms in front of me. "It was a compliment." He said with a sly smile. "What do you mean?" I asked. " If you took that as a compliment, I am sure you would know the reason." He winked at me. "Well, now I am curious about why you planned to call me a mistress."

"A woman in her late 20s, beautiful, talented, smart and sexy like you, can easily attract a married man like Mr John. Even though he is too loyal to his wife." He said. "That's a really weird way of complimenting a woman, you should choose your words wisely." I advised him and walked away.

I was disappointed in myself after doubting someone for no particular reason. I was only a few steps ahead when he caught up with me again. "People tend to have so many opinions about others and disappoint them with their words so easily but look at this sky, It never disappoints... right?" And here he was trying to start a conversation. "What are you implying?" I asked. "Nothing, just another weird way of complimenting the sky." He looked at me and grinned. It felt more like a taunt than a compliment. I had enough of him, he confused me, annoyed me, and brought out the curiosity in me no one had done in a while. But I chose to ignore all of this and didn't say anything further. When Mr John waved at us, I went up to him. "Hey! I am really sorry but I forgot to mention that we were staying the night here. And we only took the calculated amount of sleeping bags. If you are okay with it, you can take mine and I'll sleep inside the bus." He suggested. "No,No, that won't be necessary. I can sleep in my car, It would only be better seeing how many insects there are. I have used almost half of the mosquito repellent on me today." I suggested. Other students protested and offered me their sleeping bags, but I disagreed and decided to sleep in my car instead.

"But we parked your car somewhere else, it's a 10 minutes walk from here. Apparently that was the only safe location for your car, in front of a police station." Kabir stated.

"Kabir, you should escort her to her car." Mr John demanded. "Why *me*?" Kabir protested. "Because *you* parked the car there, who told you to park so far away?" Mr John complained. "I mean I did it for her car's safety. What if someone stole it?" He said. "What if the police towed the car away?." I asked with my brows furrowed in annoyance. "Do you think *I* am that much of an idiot, who would use the Police's parking spot without asking for their permission?" He debated. "And they gave it to you?" Mr John asked with wide eyes. "Yes?" Kabir shrugged and I watched the exchange silently. "Anyways, take me to my car, lest you want to risk my life by sending me there alone." I demanded. "And why should I care?" He asked. "Because I am a woman in my late 20s, beautiful, talented and sexy, who can be easily abducted and misused." I tried not to smile while I reused some of his words. "Smart." He added. "Yeah, that too. Thanks for reminding me." I winked at him. Mr John, unaware of our little conversation, was confused and uninterested. He waved us off and wished me a good night.

We both went together, I walked ahead and Kabir followed me from behind like a bodyguard. The lane was narrow and scabrous which went in a single direction. There were small slanting trees with elongated heart shaped leaves, which I suppose were false white teak as I remember reading about it somewhere. There were huge tall trees with orangish pea-like flowers that I couldn't name. It was so dark that I couldn't see any of the flowers properly or it was just my lack of knowledge about the flora of my very own city. If only Ammi was here, she would have named every single plant well. The place was lonely and it reminded me of Aqeel and how he would have loved this place, and with that I remembered that he didn't even know about me being there. But then I thought that he wouldn't even care if I disappeared. I am not exaggerating it but yeah I think it would take him some time to give me that same place again. Even though he behaves the same way he used to do earlier, I think he needs time to forgive and welcome me with the same affection.

All the while I was thinking about Aqeel, Kabir was silently walking behind me watching the trees and what I observed was probably a bird that was chirping even in the darkness like that. I looked over my shoulder at him, right when he was watching me. I tore away my eyes from him. But he came forward and walked at my pace. "Don't think that I have a fascination for you just because I complimented you."He said.

"Aren't you a little too forward? Thinking too highly of yourself?" I asked. "NO." He said. After a few moments he asked me-" why did you come here in your mustang, don't you think it's a bad place to flaunt your car."

I was a little annoyed by this question as why would someone ask such an unnecessary question at a weird moment like this. "I only have this one…how was I supposed to come otherwise?"

To which he responded with - "Oh I thought you would have a whole collection of cars with your annual income, but it's ok you know being minimalist and all. Anyways you could have taken a cab or just come with us, but looking at your situation right now it's best that you have your own car with you."

"I know, right? I mean why did yall plan to stay the whole night here in this lost place of zero inhabitants? Shruti never told me about this stuff or else I wouldn't be here."

"May I ask you, what was your reason to come here? As I know it very well our Uni didn't invite you, I was in the management crew and it wasn't planned at all." Asked Kabir.

"I didn't plan to come here, I was suggested. Don't ask me why? but it was Shruti, who asked me to. I don't completely regret coming here, if you are curious."

"Well it's a great place, the fewer people there are, the more peaceful and beautiful it will be, that's why we chose this, given it is free of cost." Said Kabir.

We reached the place after some time. I got very tired after walking, though thankfully it was time to sleep. I felt bad for Kabir as he had to come drop me here. But he did park my car here in a stranded place, so he deserved it. "You can go now, I'll rest in my car." I said while fishing for my car keys in my pocket but it was hopeless to do so as I didn't have it. It was with Kabir all along since the time he parked it there. Before I could ask him for the keys, he handed it to me and started walking away. I turned towards my car and unlocked it, and sat inside in the warmth of my car.

NEW FRIEND?

AQEEL

I didn't hear anything from Alaia after that shoot, nor was I able to call her. I did text her a few times but she didn't respond, so I waited for her. Though a new person was there, taking my full attention towards her. It surprised me how we started chatting over ridiculous topics, as we didn't know each other much. The awkwardness that keeps me silent, everytime I meet someone new, has vanished under her influence. She told me that she was a fan of my books, though something about her made her stand out from other readers. I felt very secure talking to her, and didn't even have to hide anything. Because she seemed to know me so well. As if the characters didn't matter, their story didn't matter, instead she had studied the person behind them. She studied me. My identity was anonymous to her as to everyone else, and still she managed to understand the feelings hidden behind the words.

Haniya brought out the curiosity in me, no one had done in a while. I thought that If I asked for her social media id, I would come out as a desperate person. But I was curious to know more about her so I searched her name on social apps. I couldn't find her, I don't get how people stalk others online, I couldn't even figure out her social handle. Though being young is like a blessing, you don't think twice before following someone online, or accepting their request unless you are a freak like me. It's not bad, thinking, though sometimes it is worthless, what are you thinking this much for? Are you going to figure out the space after thinking about it 24/7? Absolutely not, you need logic, maths, calculation, reasoning, relatability etc to get close to what space is. Still, who is there to stop me? I'll think about my lunch menu for 4 hours and then end up eating the regular.

At last I gave up, and settled with the information I had of her till now. Though I grinned with pleasure and excitement when she casually texted me her Instagram Id and asked for mine. We immediately followed each other, and I browsed her page for a while before going to sleep. The other day we decided to meet outside. I thought about it for a while as it's hard for me to go outside these days, as somehow people found out about my place and now there were media outside my apartment every morning. At first it was about the talk show and the chaos, then it switched to different topics. Haniya told me that this will be a forever thing now, and I can't escape this. I'll have to deal with certain rumours, a few mean tweets, and many fans who will try to pull here up just to have a glance. I knew it, which was the foremost reason I didn't want people to know about me. Though I'll have to deal with the consequences alone. I panicked the first day I went outside after the show, as there were like 50 people with cameras ready to take my shot. Roop came to my rescue and helped me get past all the people as I was getting late for my classes. Since then the number of reporters have lessened so I don't panic much and do as they want me to. Sometimes they just go away after a few clicks and on other times they ask me questions, which I choose if I wish to answer or not.

I wanted to meet Haniya, I wanted to be in touch with her and no one would be able to stop me from doing it.

Today was the fifth day, I looked out from my balcony and there was no one, I took this as an opportunity and left as soon as possible. It's an hour prior to the time we decided we'd meet. So I went to the cafe, ordered a black coffee and sat while I worked on my laptop. Ten minutes after that, I noticed some people outside who were trying to come in and were refused by the cafeteria staff. The staff member was a teenage part-timer with minimal knowledge on how to manage a crowd, so he came and asked me politely to go and talk to those people. They were here for me, apparently they followed me down here just in case they get some spicy pictures of my date. But it was just me alone, working, so they were kind of disappointed. I went outside and did as they said as long as it was okay with me. I am not used to these things, in fact I did everything in my possibilities to avoid coming into the media. But ever since I met Alaia, things have gone out of my hands. I don't blame her for that, yet one can't deny the fact that a storm follows everywhere she goes and she is the only person who can calm it down. Apparently the industry was now boycotting the Producer who approached me, Haniya told me it was Bollywood's cancel culture. At first no one dared to say anything against her and silently kept working with her, and when a newbie like me opened my mouth to admit what happened to me, they started trolling her and boycotting her. And in return I was getting all this attention.

After several awkward poses and weird questions which I brushed away, they were done. And I was finally able to get back to my work and coffee which went cold. Time passed by very quickly, and I wasn't even able to do any work. As I got busy stalking Haniya online, I mean how do you not? I feel like a hypocrite now. She is the same, online and offline if I had to go by looks. I kept scrolling through her feed, trying to find out what kind of a person she was. And I found out nothing new, she was just as sweet, goofy, and pretty as one can see her in real life. I didn't realise that I was so engrossed in her feed, until she caught me off guard.

"Hi!" She greeted me from behind, peeking at my phone. And I smiled like a fool. I may have been a little too absorbed to not notice her coming inside.

"Hiii, um…" I tried to explain to her about what I was doing.

"Hey it's cool, I gave you my profile so that you can take a look, there's nothing bad about it. If you had searched about me and stalked me behind my back that would have been a little creepy, though." She said, settling in the seat across from me.

I giggled at her words, which she noticed and giggled back.

"So what did you find?" She asked me, folding her hands in front of her, as if it was an assignment.

"Well, I found out that you are quite a book yourself, an open one." I said.

"Hmm..and do you know what I found out about you?" She questioned me. "What did you find?" I asked, getting curious. "I found, that you are a *Liar*." She exclaimed. "What?" I was confused.

"Yeah, didn't you know? You are a perfect liar. I thought that you didn't know many people, but after looking at your posts I realised that you have a ton of friends."

"They are not exactly friends, they are my students."

"Who posts photos with their students? I bet you are one of the teachers, who are immensely loved and respected by their students."

"You can say that. They are all very sweet, it was hard not to post their pictures."

"I know that's what I am saying, I thought you were a loner and I was absolutely wrong about that."

"I'll say I am fortunate to have found sweet people like you, who tag along with me on my worst times. So it becomes impossible for me to neglect you all." I said these words without giving it much thought and it never occurred to me that it could mean something to her.

And it definitely did, because she blushed under her honey glazed mouth, which made her face glow up as the sunrays shifted and pour all the light over her demeanour. She had light brown eyes, and a warm tone to her face which glistened may be because of her moisturiser cause otherwise she didn't look like she had makeup on. She lowered her face out of embarrassment, and some of her hair fell upon her eyes, which she tried brushing away but couldn't do. I wanted to help her so badly, but my indecisive ass couldn't decide sooner what to do and what not. I think it annoyed her, or maybe it was me who didn't do what she wanted, cause she took her hair and tied it with a little rubber band which magically appeared in her hands.

She stopped smiling and motioned towards the waiter. I remembered that I had completely forgotten to order something for her. She did it for herself and asked me, What would I like. I ordered the same drink as earlier as I couldn't have it at that time.

"Sorry" I said, not knowing why. But she heard me and blushed, again. And this time I didn't zone out, instead I took it as a blade in my heart just like a warrior would do in a war zone. This isn't war though, I don't know what this was. Some weird high school stuff was happening. To break the awkward silence I asked her why she wanted to meet me here. She was better than me, as she straightforwardly told me "To see you."

"Huh?" I clearly heard her but I felt a little confused and blushed, she saw that I did.

"Don't get all worked up, I am not asking you out, though I would have loved it if you did." She gave me a playful snicker, I couldn't really tell what she meant by that though out of pure instinct I took her hand in mine and Squeezed it. I could feel my heart thumping, and hers too while I was holding her wrist in my hands. As if our hearts could talk, it told me I could trust her. And that she wouldn't break my heart if I ever opened it upto her. We weren't kids who would play shy and delay things, though I took immense pleasure in slow burn and I was unsure of Haniya's intentions. Did she really mean what she said? Would she accept my proposal if I asked her out? Was it too early to do that? We just met a few days back and this was our second meeting. Would I come off too desperate if I asked her out now? Can I even do that? It took years to confess to Alaia, when I was so sure about my feelings towards her. But regarding Haniya, I have no idea what I feel, how *I* feel? Do I like her? Or is it just a crush? Was she casually flirting with me or did she really want me to ask her out? Though there was no time to delude about things or assume anything on my own. I didn't want to have feelings for her unless it was mutual, I didn't want to love again just to watch them leave from my life. So I loosened my grip on her hand. Her expressions changed a little bit, and then went back to normal when the waiter brought our orders. For a while we both remained silent and sipped our drinks. Then she suggested "You know there is a book fair going on?"

"Really? Where?" I asked, relieved that we had shifted from the previous conversation. "Ice skating Rink, Book Chor is holding the fair in Kolkata for 2 days." She said, "Interesting! I have stopped going to fairs as I order my books online and get some newly released books in my mail. That's why I had no idea." I continued sipping my coffee. "Would you come with me, if I asked you to?"She asked. "Only if it's a date." I risked my chances of talking to her at all by saying this. But it was worth the risk. I had wasted enough of my time after Alaia, thinking about confessing to her every hour but stepping down the moment I got an opportunity. I don't think that it would be wise to do the same thing in the case of Haniya. What if she takes my indecisive ass as an uninterested one? "Glad to know that you are interested in dating me. It's a date!" She beamed with joy. And there was this feeling inside me, the euphoria of achievement. I internally thanked Allah a hundred times that she was interested in me the way I was interested in her. I smiled and took her hands in mine, again. I was speechless, but she wasn't in need of words. She had plenty of them, mine. "Shall we go?" I asked. "Yup." She replied. And we both gulped the last bit of our drinks and left the cafe after paying the tab.

She took me to the book fair as if I was going there for the first time. She held my hands as if I was her child, but she was the cheerful, kind hearted, curious, innocent being who was close to being a child. I was nowhere near being one, the child in me was dying. As the world wasn't in need of a man in his late 20s behaving like a child. As I grew up, all the people I loved either died or were snatched away from me. I had to become mature, not just because I was old or because I was alone. But because I had to learn how to love oneself. I had to embrace my own self by holding my hands, by hugging my own warmth to calm down. I had to walk alone, I had to raise myself from the ground when everyone left. I could have easily depended on someone. I could have gone to my mother, but the mere feeling of being uninvited made me change my mind.

We both strolled inside the place and looked for our new reads. My Tbr was already very long, and I added a few more to it when Haniya suggested it to me. We both discussed the books we had read till now and the adaptations we were looking forward to. People had to interrupt us because we were talking very loudly, as if we had met after a really long time and had too much to catch up on. It really felt like that, I was meeting her after a long time, the familiarity was there. Although we had never known each other, this was probably the first time we met. The other time was for work and we hadn't opened up to each other like this. I saw a person inside her, someone I used to know. Maybe I had known her, just not in this world. And now all I wanted was to get to know her in this world. But how?

"Can you sign this for me?" Haniya found one of my books and asked me to sign it for her. "How many author-signed copies do you want to possess?" I teased her and took the book from her to sign. "Many" She admitted with a childish grin and I couldn't help but chuckle. I was signing her copy, when other people noticed me and asked if I was in fact Aqeel Baig. "Yes, I am." I said with a soft smile. "Oh my god! I'll faint. Why are you so handsome? I didn't think Authors could be so handsome too." One of the girls from the crowd asked me and I was taken aback. No one had complimented me like that, let alone a stranger. I looked back at Haniya and she was gone. I smiled at the girl and she pretended to faint and I went wide eyed. When the girl laughed at her own silliness, I was relieved and scratched my head in embarrassment. I signed their copies too and clicked a few pictures. Then I went to find Haniya, and found her behind a bookshelf trying to reach for the book at the top. So I took it out for her, and for the first time I was glad of being taller. "So, how was it?" She asked, looking up at me. "Why did you leave me alone, I was searching for you?" I asked, leaning against the bookshelf with my hands crossed in front of me. "I wanted you to interact with your fans without any distractions. They were so happy to meet you, you should really do book signing events more." She said while picking up another book of interest. "So that you can get my signature again?" I asked, again trying to tease her. "Yes. I would get my books signed by you, whenever I can. Or I can ask you to sign my T-shirt too." She pointed towards the back of her dress. I laughed. That's when her phone rang. She picked it up as it was from her mother. She looked terrified after whatever her mom said to her, the brightness from her kind eyes disappeared completely as if she saw a ghost. I got concerned, did something wrong happen? Were her parents alright? Too many questions bubbled inside me. "I have to go. I'll talk to you later." She said, shock engulfing her light in its darkness. I tried to ask her about what happened, but she didn't even hear me and left. I would have dropped her, if she gave me a chance though she left without a goodbye. Something happened, something wrong. But what?

NEED COMES BEFORE WANT

ALAIA

I took a breath of relief, I could finally rest, after having a blast of a day. It really helped my mind to relax and forget about work for a while. I put my phone on charge, and stretched my arms and legs. I body was aching, but in a good way.

I heard a knock on my car window. I couldn't see who was outside as it was dark, so I rolled down my window, hoping it wasn't someone creepy. For my safety purposes, I had pepper spray and a sharp *nail filter*. Gladly, it was just Kabir. "Did you forget something?" I asked. "Unlock the car." He said with a note of urgency in his voice. "Why?" I asked. "It's raining! I'll get drenched. Just open the damn CAR." He commanded. I unlocked the car and he pulled a shotgun. I looked outside my side of the window and it was indeed *drizzling*. Though he could have easily walked down or ran to the place. "Do you have water?" He looked exhausted, as if the day filled with running and playing around was finally catching up to him. I passed him the only water bottle I could find.

"The water tastes awful!" He complained, making a face. "Yeah I know, it's been sitting here for a week now. I forgot to change the water." I admitted. "You could have warned me." He frowned

"Oh. Yeah. Sorry." I said. He snickered, but it didn't last long. He was more exhausted than I had thought. I had no idea what to do, it's not like I asked him to park my car here. Though I was grateful, I didn't know these people and still they welcomed me and hosted me with pure joy. I had fun, and the memories we made will surely remain with me.

I looked at Kabir who was more or less fine now. But there was an awkward silence between us, which was getting more awkward by every passing second. I had nothing to say to him so I kept my silence but he might have had something he was curious about, as he broke the silence which had clouded our minds. "What is your top priority, Business or Fashion?"

I won't lie, the question puzzled me a little bit. "Both?"

"No, I mean. Would you compromise your profits or your designs? If you had to?" He asked. And I couldn't wrap my mind around what he was trying to ask me. "I wouldn't compromise at all. I mean I can handle a little loss but not more than that. And compromising on my designs? *That* is out of the question." I said. "But may I know the reason behind your curiosity?"

"It's just that I didn't know who you were at first but seeing how *famous* you are among everyone I got curious and googled you. I came to know more about what you do and don't. And I am not exaggerating but I *was* shocked to see the achievements you have made in a short period of time. Which fueled my curiosity a bit more and that's why I just wanted to know more about your ideas related to business and stuff." He said. I nodded. "If you were from any other field, I would have understood. But being a fashion major, how did you not know *me*? I am not implying that everyone should know me, but at least you could have had an idea just like everybody else. Instead, you misunderstood me as Mr John's Mistress." I asked. "Hey, it was a joke, okay? I just thought you were sexier and made that comment. I know, it wasn't appropriate. You just have to forget about it, okay? Or do you want me to apologise?" He asked. And I chuckled at it. "It's okay. As I said I took it as a compliment. But mistress? Really? If you thought I was sexy, just say that. Why put a label on it? Is every sexy girl a mistress to you?" I continued. "You said you didn't mind and here you are complaining." He said. "And about you. Yeah I don't know you or want to know you. Because I am not interested in Fashion. I am just passing my days until I get enough knowledge about business." He said. "Looking at you, I can tell that you are not interested in fashion. You are wearing clothes that belong to Fast-Fashion brands." I made a remark.

"WHAT?" He checked himself after my accusation on his fashion sense and I knew he didn't understand anything. Did he really miss all his classes? How does he not know about what Fast-Fashion was?

"Just look at yourself, you are wearing what is popular these days and not something that would actually look good on you. Where do you shop from?"

"I don't know, my mom does." Okayy, so he was a momma's boy, Interesting. "Okay, so this is not something you should be blamed for nor am I gonna blame your mother. Fast fashion is known as such due to the availability, budget friendly and trending material. But incase of my choice, I prefer fashion which lasts. Sustainable pieces which may be over the budget for some but there it's *me* who tries to make it not so costly and yet available for everyone.

That's it. That *is* my business plan. Many went against me but many stayed. It was like a revolution at first as there were a minimal number of sustainable brands. And yet, *this* was my plus point. There are many people who love my designs and support it."

"Doesn't that prove that your main focus is in Fashion rather than Business"

I pondered upon the question for a while and he was right, for some parts. "No No, You are going completely wrong. I mean… yeah, I am a fashion designer so my foremost priority is that, but I do *care* about my business. Which is in fact Fashion. So they both go hand i hands."

"Ok, whatever you say. I should go back now the rain must have stopped, bye." He opened the door and with a gush all the water and wind came inside the car, he immediately closed the door. The rain was much heavier now, and it looked like a storm was starting outside. "Ugh!! It's raining so hard. How am I gonna head back?" He said frustratingly. "You could have left at that time only, the rain has only gotten heavier. You won't be able to make it back." I said. "It was raining at that time too, how was I supposed to walk back?" He asked, his brows raised a little bit. "It was only drizzling." I replied. "Yeah so what? I hate rain. And don't think that I wanted your company. That's the last thing I wanted. I remember you accusing me of theft." He reminded me. "Oh, please! That was a misunderstanding." I said with a slightly raised voice. And he laughed. "It's okay. Would you mind If I stay here for a while? Until the rain stops?" He asked me. "Yeah, yeah you can stay. Find yourself at home, I mean car." I suggested. "I'll inform Mr John." He said. Then he made a call and talked to Mr John. "Sir said that it's a cyclonic-storm and not a regular thunderstorm. And that we should not leave the place at all." He told me. How in the world was there a cyclone? The news didn't mention one. I got as annoyed as one can be, as I myself hated rain. "Where did this uninvited cyclone come from?"

"The cyclone wasn't supposed to hit here, it changed its direction midway to Bangladesh so We just need to wait for it to get over. Mr John said all their tents are either broken or wet, so they all are inside the buses. And we must not go anywhere."

"Don't you think we are in danger too?" I asked frowning.

"What do you suggest then? Should I talk to the constable there, I am sure they would let us in?" He asked me pointing towards the small police posting. "You are suggesting that we spend a night in a police station?" I raised both my brow. "Well it's safer than *here*." He said. "No way! I am not going inside that police station." I said.

"Why not?" He asked. "Because Its a *police station*."

"We are screwed." I sighed.

"Yes we are." He said it so calmly that I wanted to punch him in the face.

"Aren't you going to rest? If you can shift in the back, it'll be best for both of us." He suggested.

"Are you planning to sleep here?" I asked, pointing towards the car seat.

"Of course, do I have any other options? Or are you planning to kick me out right now?"

"Oh, please. I am not that cruel." I couldn't help but get angry, the way he smirked after accusing me of wanting to throw him out, it made me furious. What does he think of me? and why was he being so frank with me? I was literally older than him. Shouldn't he at least have some respect for me?

I crawled to the back seat opposite to the side he was sitting on, so that I could relax and he could recline too. But he didn't do anything and sat idly. We had lost network signals, so we didn't have anything to do except sleep. But with the cyclone outside and the extreme calmness inside I was unable to sleep. So I just tried looking outside the window, which terrified me as the trees which were looking peaceful just a while ago were now on the brink of falling out. The wind was blowing with such a speed, I was afraid it would blow away the car with itself and we'd get lost somewhere. The visibility lowered than it already was as all the dust from the ground was now swirling in air like a spirit who had been angered or awakened from a deep sleep. My heart sank every time I heard the wind getting stronger.

I thought Kabir was resting and we wouldn't have to engage in another conversation anymore, but then he opened his pretty and immature mouth again. This time, he was looking around the car, checking the gears, steering and other parts of the car as if he was grocery shopping. Then he asked "Why did you choose a Mustang? You could have chosen GTR. It would perform well." I wonder if his nickname was 'question mark' cause he just happens to have some ridiculous amount of questions. I tried to be calm this time and said that I preferred the Mustang as it was a *CLASSIC*.

He looked back with a frown and said "You know that GTR has a better design, and higher speed, right?"

"I already said that I like Classics plus the Mustang has better handling, get it? Anyways I would never invest such a huge amount of money for experiencing luxury."

"That money is worth the car, Also I think the Mustang is overrated."

"Do you know what I feel? I feel that *your* opinion is overrated and I hate pricey things."

Kabir shrugged and said "Okay. Do whatever you like with your money."

"You didn't have to specify that, anyways if you don't want to sleep then let me get mine." After that argument I cozied myself in the back seat and he remained in the front. I pretended to sleep so that he would stop bothering me even though the storm outside was loud af and as the time passed, it grew even more making it unbearable. So, eventually I gave up and sat upright, finding Kabir asleep soundlessly. I wondered how he could sleep so easily beside the noise and stress this storm had brought. I reclined his seat so that he would be comfortable, in return to the efforts he made for me today being just a stranger.

The world looked like a mess, it gave me major anxiety about people who might be living in slumps and Kutcha houses. Their house must have blown away or broke, the situation they were put into after this storm and several storms which had occurred till date was the worst. I had never put myself in their shoes until this day when I was having to live inside a car while everything was crumbling outside. Being born in a middle class family I was always pampered with the best clothes, stationary, makeup, devices and anything one would ever want despite the hardships my parents had to go through. They never let me suffer, and this is how I was going to pay them back. I don't mind what people think of me when all they see is my luxury stays at hotels, my car or my wardrobe. My plan from the very start was to buy my Ammi *a Bungalow*, as she always wished to live in one but couldn't afford. She was no more, but I was going to keep that bunglow under her and my name, which I made from scratch. I had been secretly working on it, before coming here. Abbu doesn't know anything, as I wanted to surprise him once the interior was done. I hope he won't mind living in it, cause he always preferred flats and still remained happy with whatever Ammi wished.

I wasn't able to sleep so I checked my phone. But it was useless, I couldn't check my socials or make a call as there was no network. Aqeel had texted me a few times, asking if I was okay. But I wanted to know about *his* condition. I hadn't reached out to him after that interview. I had no idea how people reacted to it or what happened with the producer after her real story was leaked. And the thing I was more worried about was, Aqeel and that Rj. They seemed to have become friends, I just hope they weren't in touch with each other. I could understand if he wanted to date someone, but the thought of him dating some other girl made me nauseous. I hated what I had to witness, I hated his arms in someone else's. Why did I want to snatch his arm away from her? I felt so possessive of him at that point, that I almost cried. And I don't even know the reason behind my behaviour. Could it be guilt? Or was it love?

FLING...

AQEEL

I can't believe I went on a *date* with Haniya. I knew for sure there was a spark between us. But I was sceptical that it would be a friendly one only. But she was interested in me, and wanted me to ask her out. And what is more surprising is that I asked her on a date. A book-store date. Could it be any more beautiful? Could I really start something with her, something romantic? Was it possible? After Alaia, I never came across a girl so magnificent, so alluring and kind. It was already hours after she left. I came back home and started working on my current story. Though I couldn't focus. I kept staring at my hands, which dared to touch her today. And sent sparks down my spine, as I remembered her touch. I have no idea what the universe has planned for me, what Allah has planned for me. But I am ready to take this risk, I took one today and gained a date with her. Maybe if I push myself a little, I'd be able to gain another one.

She is free spirited, friendly, and sweet. The most beautiful thing about her is that she understands the other person really well, and then treats them just the way they would like to be treated. It comes naturally to her and she doesn't have to think about it unlike me who over analyses everything. It takes millions of years to open up or talk to someone when it's not related to work, but she is someone dogs will run to. I mean usually the ones who are overly reserved like me and only go near their master, they find a comfort spot in her lap and might just sleep there.

I am not a dog, but I would run towards her if I was.

I met Alaia after so many years, I thought she had forgotten me but then the letter came and everything changed. My thoughts about her changed, she was guilty for my mistake. For something, I ruined it. She loved Uzair and I loved her, what a love triangle, huh? I hated myself for what I did but eventually grew out of the hate. I think I would have hated myself even if I never admitted my love for her. Admitting it made me suffer less than I would have but it was the opposite for her. She had to go through a breakup, our friendship went down the hill and then her mother also died. I wonder how she handled it alone. Slight changes in my life results in a 3k word paragraph. Picking up writing whenever I overthinked led me to the career I had right now, I don't regret it even a bit. But, could it be a coincidence or was it yet another plan of Allah?

That I have found a girl, after so many years of being single right after I patched up with Alaia. Things got settled between us, We might have found closure. And I was finally able to move on, I had moved on but still there was something inside me that didn't completely let go of her idea.

During the day I only had a few refills of black coffee and a sad pastry so I was starving. I made myself a quick sprout salad and put chicken breasts in the oven to roast. I watched some netflix and ate my food while I had my eyes peeking over my phone which lied there dead. In the previous few days, people have somehow found my social media accounts and from then My dms and follow requests were sky-rocketing. It bothers me a little bit but not too much as my notifications were muted. Though they weren't the ones I cared about. I was waiting for Haniya, she never texted me or called back. I picked my phone multiple times to make a call or just text her asking if everything was okay. But I still wasn't sure about my position in her life. A date wouldn't change much, we still weren't something. We didn't have a name, a label. Were we friends? Each other's date? Or couples? It was too soon to decide. I was delusional, but not enough to delude myself as someone she would care about. Not when I was an author, and she was a fan. I never really met my fans, so I had no idea what their idea about me was, as a person. But it seemed like they liked me. Not just for my stories, but for me. What if she was just another fan? All she did was to ask for my signature. Could I really mean something to her? Or was this just my illusion?

Next few days were busy catching up on lectures, notes, some extra classes and tuition. It would be an exaggeration to say I was treated like a celebrity but that was what happened. No one knew I was an author to one of the best selling novels of the year 2025 and 2027 except a few of the teachers whom I had sent wrong drafts, accidently. They saw some of the upcoming pieces but didn't realise immediately as they were raw but after it was published and they read the final print, it was inevitable. But now when the truth was out in the open, I couldn't do anything but accept it and I did with my whole heart.

However I would have loved it if it came without the cheering of students as soon as I stepped inside my classroom. I had always had a sweet relationship with my students given the heartfelt conversations we had several times. Even so I never ever let them near the core of my heart. They were like electrons revolving in the outer orbits but my stories made up the nucleus. Now it was as if the barrier was taken down and there was no force which would hold them in the correct place. The energy I got from the black coffee I had before coming to the campus, got completely used up in calming down the students. We did not study that day. Half the time they argued with me about why I never told them the truth and half in answering their questions related to the books they had heard about till this date. Some even admitted that they had always suspected me to have some dark secrets and that they were proved correct. I couldn't help but laugh at their assumptions. And then one of them asked me a question which brought me out of my comfort zone and I hadn't thought about that question before hence, didn't realise what might be the answer. I didn't see who was the original person to ask the question and before I could pin-point them, nearly every one of them joined in and asked " Who is your muse?"

I gave it a little thought and realised I didn't want to answer that. Why would I wanna talk about something so miserable? It's stupid, my love was stupid, I was naive and didn't know if the timing was right, if the person was right. Although I could swear that the person was right, I was the foolish one.

"Asking someone what their muse is, Is pointless.

If they could admit it.

If they could confront it.

It wouldn't come out as poetry" I said these words so casually as If i was teaching them another lesson. But they knew, I knew, It was my reality. I was thankful they didn't drag that topic for as long as the bell rang and the class was over. After the not-so-hectic but confusing day I went back home and made myself fried rice with the leftover ingredients from which day? I couldn't recall. And waited for Haniya's call, checked my phone every five minutes to see if she texted and cringed over my own actions.

I wanted to know where we stood. Did I make her angry which was why she was not reverting back to me or something really serious was going on back at her house? It made me feel bad, for whatever the reason might be as in the previous few days we have had many conversations through text. And by that I could say that she was a fast texter, though there was a possibility that she was not interested in me anymore. These thoughts were eating me out, and yet I was happy to have a crush on somebody after so many days? Months?

My crushes didn't really last long, I either grew out of it, or I realised that they were out of my league and it wouldn't workout.

It was past 11 o'clock in the night, and I was getting impatient. At first I thought of texting her first but then also I didn't want to look desperate. And if I didn't do anything someone else might take her away from me. So I took my last and only option, I texted Roop.

He told me to meet him in our apartment park in 5 minutes. I went down and found him holding a cigarette. He threw it away as soon as he realised I was coming close. " I haven't had one in months, I promise. I just craved one today." He defended himself without even me questioning.

"Fine! I am not your dad! But did something happen?"

"Yeah, if you were my dad, I would have been on the ground kneeling in front of you. Why do you think something happened?"

"I have my reasons, but you seemed eager to talk so I assumed you had something to say too…besides this is the no smoking area, be careful. Now, spit it out."

"Had a fight with kriti, nothing major but nowadays it's getting regular. Same routine everyday, I go to work, Listen to my boss as if I was his slave rather than his employee, come back and listen to kriti's and then sleep without a word of affection. So I thought it might be of help if I come down and chat with you."

"You should have contacted me then, we could have caught up earlier. What are friends for? Partying together? That's it?"

"I didn't come here to complain or cry…tell me about you. Anything new? We can always discuss household problems. But you have been the talk of the town for the past few weeks." He chuckled. Roop was not just my neighbour, he had become a close friend so he knew about me being an author.

"I met a girl."

"Woah!! So you finally agreed to find a match."

"It's not like that, we just saw each other twice. She is the one who took my interview that day"

"Is she beautiful? And what's with this I saw her twice. If she is beautiful and interested, don't even think about delaying it and ask her out."

"Hey, slow down buddy. I just mentioned her name and here you are planning my wedding. Besides, I did go on a date with her." Saying it aloud made me blush.

"Well I never mentioned a wedding, I just asked that you should go out with her but if you *are* thinking that way you may even marry her. How many more days are you going to stay alone, huh? and for how long are you going to listen about my married life problems? I deserve to listen to yours too. And it's good that you are already making progress."

"Yeah, probably. She does seem interested, otherwise she wouldn't have asked to meet me. We met a few days back and since then she hasn't contacted me. Actually there was a family emergency which was why she left midway our conversation though she promised she'd call. I want to know where we stand. I have two options: first to call her and ask what's going on. Second, I could just wait."

" Well there is no harm in asking her about her situation, you never know she might need someone right now. Also, don't be a coward, you are not in school or college right now. You are a fucking adult, go and ask her out while she is around and single."

"I guess, I don't have any options left now. I have done huge damage to people's life and my own by holding on to feelings. Lets give it a shot"

I opened my phone to write a text to her and that's exactly when I got a text from her so I started typing a response when her next message showed up. It said "I am at your apartment."

I looked up at Roop but he was already peeking through my phone. I slapped the back of his head lightly and asked what I was supposed to do now.

"It's obvious, You should go and pick her up. Might as well enjoy this *fling*."

I went for another slap but unfortunately missed it. Then, without giving her a reply, I went to the entrance and talked to the guard to let her enter. Then she parked her car, and I invited her upstairs. To which she happily agreed and came with me. We sat down, and I asked her for a beverage but she refused and said " I came here to apologise."

"For what?" As if I didn't already know, she was the one who wanted to be in touch but then ghosted me. "For not clearing things up." She replied right after.

I was confused, but she continued. " I didn't have a family emergency, but it was urgent and heartbreaking. My neighbour's son died and a day after she herself died. Which is why I was disturbed these few days and couldn't reach out to you. I of course didn't expect you to call me and hence I am not sad about it. But the thing is- I was thinking about you all the time. It's not uncommon for me as I used to have a crush on you without even seeing you. I have been in love with your words ever since I started reading so I thought it was that similar feeling. But upon meeting you personally and talking to you I think I really adore you."

" As a writer or-" I questioned.

"As a person. I think I like you. For whatever you are. I am sorry for being so bold, showing up at your door steps, it was not a brilliant idea. On my way here, I thought you would want me to go away, instead you invited me here and I am thankful to you for the affection and respect you give even though you don't owe me anything" She said.

"How rude of you to assume I would make you leave. Besides I waited for you to text, when you came here I was actually thinking of texting you and ask, if you wished to talk to me or not"

"Really? But why/" She asked.

"Because I think I might like you too, I am very grateful to have you here inside my house. It would have taken me years to invite you home" I blurted out.

She chuckled and took a look around the house. "Your place is very nice, simple and yet beautiful, just like *you*." Her complimenting me so easily, made me blush.

I get these complements almost every time but I had no idea why I blushed so hard and she noticed it too. We both went silent for a while as she looked around my place, it was fairly neat so it wasn't a problem though I didn't want her to go inside my room yet, the weather was humid so I had my clothes scattered in my bedroom for drying. When she turned towards my bedroom door, I panicked and thought of striking up a conversation which might distract her, and it did. Or else you can say that she read the room and came back to sit on the couch. "What happened to your neighbour's son?" I might have stepped inside very deep, as she looked uncomfortable for a while before she started speaking again.

"He was in a coma, I guess his body gave up after being in that position for more than a decade. For his mother, she couldn't bear the pain of losing her son after all the years. She must have waited for him to come back to life."

"It must have been hard for her, I hope she and her son both find peace." I said.

"Amen" and She started sobbing. Maybe she used to be close to them. I searched for tissues but they weren't there. Handkerchiefs must have hidden themselves so I proceeded to give her my own handkerchief, though by then she had already wiped her face with her scarf.

" He used to bully me, everyone knew about it except my parents. They seemed to turn a blind eye when something was bothering me but his mother knew. She always scolded him for me. I was happy to have someone to support me until one day she hit on the back of his head with a cricket bat owned by him. He fell to the ground, while blood rushed from his head to his shoulders and then to the ground while he was kneeled down grabbing his head. Upon seeing this with my own eyes, I fainted. Later when I woke up in the hospital, I asked my parents what happened to him and they said he went into a coma. His mother was quiet for a few days, and spent each day in the hospital waiting for her son to wake up. When the hospital bills went higher than what she could afford, she had him discharged and cared for him in her house. I thought she would blame me for what happened, instead she said that he deserved it and it was his fate. Though you can't expect a mother to just abandon her child, she loved him with all she had. She worked twice the amount she used to do and became his full time nurse too. My mother and I used to help her sometimes, I was partially responsible for this situation hence I worked as much as I can to pay off what I owed to them"

She wasn't crying anymore but looking at her dark circles I would say she had definitely cried back home. I don't know what's stopping her from crying more, does she feel embarrassed or has she passed that stage. Anyways I failed to realise that it was almost 1 o'clock in the night and she was here sharing the most drastically sad story. What could I possibly do to comfort her?

NEW P.A. WHO?

ALAIA

Last night was a horrible experience. Kabir woke me up at 8 in the morning as everyone was leaving and I was supposed to do too. Initially we were going to leave by 6 in the morning but due to the storm we had to wait. I thanked everyone including Kabir before leaving, they were beyond happy to have me again even though I was 200% sure I was never coming back. I mean I didn't hate the experience, but the fact that we got stuck in a storm made the day a terrible end. It was too early to go to the office so I went straight to my hotel room which was booked for two more days as I had an event to attend . The days were rough on me so I should be as tough as I could. And by tough I meant, I need to have my hair done in an updo and wear the sexiest but formal clothing cause Why not?

It took me an hour to quickly shower and put on my clothes and makeup. I spent another 20 minutes eating a small breakfast and then headed out for the day. I went through my phone while I walked towards the parking lot and checked the news related to Aqeel. It had been like 2-3 days since his interview aired and people were going crazy after that interview. I needed to talk to him about that day. And I wanted to watch the show too, but I had work. So I only got to hear the podcast version of it while I drove towards my office.

It was a 20 minute ride but I sat inside my car to finish the show. I know it was not my place to be jealous but this girl 'Haniya' was a little annoying. She was pretending so hard to be sweet to Aqeel but I could see right through the desires she held for him. Of course one would, He was the one who wrote several best sellers and teaches in a high end university. And his *looks*? He was the brown munda of our locality, it was just that he didn't dress nicely, Or looked after him at all. But his fashion sense has improved since then, and his handsome face has gotten even more handsome. I wonder why I never looked at him the way I looked at him now. He definitely was taking care of his skin and all, and the stubble alone was killing me, that day on my birthday. But him being the unaware naive guy he has always been, would never know how crazy he could make girls like Haniya, feel. I hope he realised Haniya was flirting with him, it was my fault, I shouldn't have dozed off. I could have protected innocent Aqeel from this little witch, or it can also be that he was enjoying it. He was not the type of person to enjoy a flirtatious talk but what if he was? I had known an amateur teenager and not the adult human who wrote about love and betrayal.

Was this so called Rj stealing my friend from me? Or was she aiming for a boyfriend? Ugh! It made me want to smack someone on their face or throw my mobile phone. Anyways I'd deal with her later but first I had to ask Aqeel, how *he* was carrying himself these days with all the more attention on him now that he was upfront being the writer of all those best sellers. Were there more girls chasing after him? I bet he has guys falling for him too, otherwise he wouldn't have gotten himself in a casting-couch situation given he was the most popular writer these days. Production houses must be looking for a brunch, out with him and discuss their upcoming movies. Maybe I could talk to some of them and fix a meeting, as Aqeel must be too anxious to even pick a call.

I pulled myself together and went inside my office. It was a hodge-podge inside, everyone seemed to be so busy and there was no one incharge. I looked out for Marina but I couldn't find her. Something crazy happened behind my back as no one paid attention to me, not even one person wished me a good morning or asked me about my holiday until I came across Shruti. She was in her pyjamas and looked shocked to have me here, was she not expecting me? I asked her what happened there while I was gone, and if something unusual had happened, why didn't they bother to tell me? And where the hell was Marina? Shruti looked tensed more than she had ever looked nor that I had seen her working here much, but still I could sense it.

After a little hesitation she told me that the Chanel thing was taken care of and everything was going well. Though Marina had been hospitalised. I was taken aback, as I knew she had a heart condition. I shouldn't have put so much pressure on her. Still I asked Shruti to explain everything, to which she replied that Marina suffered from a heatstroke the morning I left for the camp. But as I was already stressed, they thought it was better if I didn't know. I mean, Who *were* they to decide such a thing for *me*? Fortunately Marina was blessed with a longer life although she was prescribed to stay indoors and rest. So work wasn't even in the picture.

One day without marina, and everyone was freaking out, this showed how much she was responsible for everybody's well being and a good work environment. I suggested Shruti to take her place for the time being but she refused, excusing herself with being under-experienced and already having been involved in other tasks. But to my surprise I was going to take her advice again. As much as I didn't want to, I'd have to look for a new personal assistant rather than just picking one from my other employees as then we'd have less number of people working on the ongoing projects. So I asked her to put up a Requirement post on different job search websites. It was a huge decision to shift my main office from our Boston to here, and in that process only, It took me three and a half months to find the employees and designers we have here. Some were loyal enough to move out with me, I would be forever grateful for such hardworking and talented people. Now I was just worried about how much time it would take for me to find a new PA. Marina was my first and only PA I have ever had. She was one of those beautiful people who willingly shifted here. I knew she did it for me and for NXDE, even though she excused herself by saying that she was moving out for the sake of her family who had been here all along.

In the late afternoon, I went to the hospital to check up on Marina, where I met her daughter, a mother of triplets. We talked about marina's health, insurance and her severance pay. I apologised for all the stress I put her through, but her daughter thanked me instead, for loving her as my own mother. She said that Marina always talked about me and at some point it even made her jealous. But it was all good now, and I only wished for her improvement. I returned to the office in the evening and was greeted by a huge crowd. They all rushed towards me at once which startled me, but thankfully the staff handled them. I went inside my room and called for Shruti. I was surprised how fast she had taken care of everything being just an intern. Maybe I should put her in an actual position. She came in a rush and told me that people had already shown up for the interview. Fast as Furious. Our whole evening went by listening and rejecting people. My head started aching by looking at the pile of Cvs we had gone through and the ones that we didn't. I had been put in a situation but that didn't mean I'd hire just anyone. I had several shows, events and parties that I needed to attend. And without the help of a capable PA, I was definitely going to go crazy.

One by one people came and went away and slowly slowly the crowd thinned down to zero. There was no one left, but it was just the first day and believe me I had seen worse.

Though Shruti came up with yet another advice for me, I was starting to think that she would suit the job of an advisor rather than whatever she was doing. But I had nothing else to do and listen because that's what a boss does, more like a leader. She suggested that I should try hiring the students from her batch, the people I met a day ago. I was not disappointed but not yet impressed by the idea. Though I could entertain this thought, so after 20 minutes of discussing the perks of having a PA in the fashion field who would be a student, crazily enthusiastic about learning and working simultaneously we concluded that it'd be a great shot.

The next morning, I was handed another pile of CVs, if Shruti wasn't working on designs with Rabia I would have hired her right there and at that time because she worked like crazy. And I *needed* that much craziness in my job. I was blessed. Though I was praying for these few candidates to be as competitive as her to match Marina's level. While I was going through the CV, I found out that Kabir also showed interest. Was he serious? I thought he didn't like this job. Anyways, I decided to ignore practically everything for a while, meetings and shows were put on hold until I found myself a decent person who could take over Marina's position. How cruel and weird was this world? A person suffered from a heart condition which made them unable to work anymore, and what did the people do? They replaced them. As much as I hated this fact, I was one of those people who did this. I had to. There was no other option. Health conditions needed care and rest. While Business needed attention and unlimited passion and hardwork. There was no place for emotions when working.

People were filling up in the waiting room as the time was right around the corner for the interview to begin. A few of them came and went away but I'd shortlist them later. Then with a rush, Kabir came inside and sat without even taking my permission. I didn't see him in the waiting room and that must be because he was late. That was not fair for the ones who were waiting for their turn.

"Where are your manners? This is not your college camp, it's *my* office. Besides this is not even your turn so go back and sit until you are called." I declared.

"I am really sorry, ma'am" He said it with a mocking tone like a school kid playing rebellious with his teacher. This kid right there made me furious. I took a few small breaths to calm down.

"It is indeed my turn as I saved myself a seat, my friend helped me as I was running a little bit late. Sorry for the inconvenience. I would like you to consider my kind apology and proceed" He said with a more formal tone now. There was something strange about this guy, he always had this sour taste in his sweet speech. It's as if he wanted me to serve him this job. "I don't hire corrupt people, and never a person who forgets to sugar coat their bitter thoughts." I said. "So does that mean you like fake people?" He asked with a teasing tone. "I like people who know how to behave when they are talking to someone older than them. Besides, you could use some manners. Go take those classes where they tame down rowdies like you and then think about working for me." I was toying with him. He wasn't *that* much of a rowdie. He just misbehaved with me a few times, and I didn't even mind it as I was busy enjoying looking at his handsome face. But I wanted to see what would happen if I acted a little bitchy with him.

So I decided something fun. I was going to give him a hard time. If he thought that I was going to treat him equally like his batchmates. He was utterly wrong. I tried to dismiss him but failed. There was enough stress in life these days, and I could use some moments of fun by acting all bitchy with him to see how he reacted to that. I didn't care about others at that time, not even about hiring a PA. I wanted a game, and an entertaining one so I faked a phone call and went outside to attend it, leaving him there. On the other side I asked Shruti to take someone else's help and talk to other candidates and then give me the shortlisted names. While he waited for me in my office, I quickly grabbed myself a sandwich and a matcha latte. I hadn't had a great lunch in a while. So I went to my favourite restaurant, but Chef Ranveer was on vacation and I didn't want anything else from that place. Anyways I loved sandwiches from the street side shop where I used to grab snacks when I was in school.

After an hour of munching on my sandwich and drinking my delicious latte I thought it was enough so I headed back inside, only to find Kabir outside my office room chit chatting with my accountant, Sameer. If he wasn't a guy I would have thought he was just flirting to pass the time, though there was a small chance Kabir might be gay. Why does every *hot* guy has to be gay? I shoved these filthy thoughts in the trash area of my brain. He was gay or not, I shouldn't care as he was a *student*. And I shouldn't be thinking about *students*. Their chat started to look serious as I got closer to them, Kabir had his back towards me so he didn't know about my presence and I asked my accountant to not make my presence known. I was shocked to hear him talking about business, profit, loss and what not with him. He sure was into business and was using every damn second of his life to get there. If he really wished to become a businessman, he should start finding ways to create a business and pen down an idea. I would suggest he use his designing degree though he barely knew anything about designs. From what I heard, he seemed very passionate about it, and yet he had no idea what he would actually do. He needed an idea, a business plan.

I stopped eavesdropping and went inside my room, the shortlisted names were yet to arrive so I called for Kabir and decided to have a question and answer round. This time he was a little polite, he asked for my permission before coming inside and sat, he even apologised for misbehaving earlier which surprised me a little. *This* much improvement in such a short time period? No, this couldn't be right. Something was fishy.

"So why do you want to work for me and why should I hire you? You have no prior experience of working except a summer internship in a library and you certainly don't have good communication skills, public speaking skills, marketing, leadership qualities etc etc."

"Thank you very much for counting all my flaws, I know I am no good. But it's about a chance, I certainly know what a personal assistant's job is and I lack many of the qualities but if you give me a chance I can prove to you how well I can work. Also, if you don't know, I adore your business strategies, which was why I came here, although I had no interest in doing this job. I want to work with you so that I can learn from the best. I don't care what you think about me but I think highly of you as an Entrepreneur. I wasn't used to it, but I changed my mind. And if I had to work my ass off for that I would gladly do it." Oh! So that was his plan. *To learn from the best.*

"Listen, I like your determination, but don't you think in order to become an entrepreneur you either need an incredible idea which would change the future or a very basic one which would earn you millions. You surely know about the competition in this industry, there are more than hundreds of companies which have been trying to replace me since the very beginning. I didn't have an incredible idea, but a mindset which I liked to put in front of others and amaze them with my achievements. I *knew* what I wanted to do when I was 15 and I made it happen. Do you have any plans for the future or are you just wandering here and there looking for it? Because Ideas are a little surprising, you never know where you'll find it, and it might even work. Here, I can't give you anything but just an idea which you can implement if you want." I was amazed by his level of concentration and curiosity, there was this hunger in his eyes for knowledge, for lessons, for ideas. And I was full of them so I looked straight in his eyes thinking he might find one there. But he broke eye contact, And I was intimidating and it was hard to maintain eye contact. But I thought he could do that, given he dared to act rebellious with me.

"I know what I wanna do, I just need your assistance. And as I can see you are in need of one too, We might be good for each other." He said. *Good for each other?* Could that be possible? He had *many* things he wanted to gain from me and it was evident he could in fact get all of them. But could I gain something from *him*? Could he give something valuable to me? Was he *trust-worthy*?

"Tell me your plan, and I shall decide." I said. I was practically gambling at this point. I knew there were options, Shruti must be shortlisting the names right now. But I was invested in this conversation.

"Something like, what you do, I have zero interest in it, but it might make my mom happy and of course I'd be able use my degree." I was impressed. It was exactly what I would have advised him.

"Nice. But I have to say, I couldn't find even one reason for which I should hire you. What you told me would help *you*, and not me. If I happen to find something worthy in you by tomorrow you'll be receiving your acceptance email or else not."

I didn't look at any other candidates' interview answers and he did get an email that evening. Yes I was *that* impressed by him. I saw a spark, the same one I had when I was his age. I was ready, but he wasn't. And I was capable of helping him, so why not? Let this be a gamble.

SLEEP OVER

Aqeel

It was around 3 am when we finished talking. I was concerned about Haniya's parents, they too must be sad and I didn't even know if she took permission from them before showing up here. Whatever the given circumstances were, I was still a stranger to her, so I was not sure if they were feeling safe for her to spend the night here. Though it would sound very wrong If I asked her now about this, so I just carried on with the conversation we were having. We shifted from her neighbour's topic a while ago and were discussing some shows. I think she was fine now, and I should have stopped worrying about it but once the cloud of sadness takes over somebody it shows the grey even after several rains. We were up for so long and got hungry so I made us some peanut butter sandwiches. I felt great as I was finally able to share my peanut butter. Earlier no one used to touch it because they didn't find it interesting. Alaia used to puke whenever she tried to take a bite of my peanut butter sandwich, it's weird how I even put it in some of the sauces and noodles. It tasted amazing, I wonder why people disliked it so much, however not everybody shares the same taste buds. We were all made a little different, and there is always that other difference which blended with us completely.

Just like an enzyme which had a receptor, we people also had other people who might have a different configuration than us but we fitted with each other very well. At first I thought about Alaia and then about Haniya, which one of them was the other half? Then again I thought if I and Alaia were meant to be, we would have been together and not with somebody else. Though currently, Alaia didn't have another half, she was alone, I might have Haniya otherwise she wouldn't have come to me at such a weird hour. I knew she didn't come to apologise, she came because she needed someone, and I might have been the better option for her at that instant. I hope she didn't regret coming here, I hope she felt less bad after talking to me, venting, sharing all the stuff which worried her and made her heart ache. I hope I was the comforter she needed, unless I made her look miserable for crying. I make sure I never do so, as I myself never cry in front of any person, thinking I'd look bad or weak or they would just make fun of me behind my back, I didn't want anyone to feel that way. I wanted to become *the* person they come to when in need, and I would help them with whatever I had inside.

We ate together on our living room couch, when I realised that she needed to sleep. So I went inside my room and fixed it to make it hospitable for her. I asked her to sleep in my bedroom and I'd either sleep in my study or in my living room.

"I can't sleep alone." She hummed with embarrassment.

"Huh?"

"I can't fall asleep alone, my maid sleeps with me in my room. Sorry that I bothered you today, but you were the first person that came to my mind and I came here immediately. I told my parents that I'd be in the studio so they have no idea I am with you, not that they care. But can I ask you to sleep with me, as in, in the same room?"

"Oh, okay. I'll keep you company. I'd have to sleep on the floor but I guess that's okay. I'll come back outside once you have fallen asleep."

"If I ask you, will you sleep beside me? We could cuddle." She fidgeted with the kurti hem. I could see a faint red marking her cheeks. She was proposing that we cuddle. Where was I? Was I in *heaven*? How was I supposed to say no?

"Will that be okay?" I asked hesitatingly, not sure if I heard right.

"Please don't overthink it or else I'll feel bad for asking. If you like me even a little bit then come with me." She said, her cheeks showing a darker shade of red now.

"A little bit?" I asked and she nodded.

"It would be my pleasure." I said, and indeed it would be. I was practically living my dream. My crush asking me to cuddle? It indeed felt like a dream though it was an unbelievable reality.

We went to our bedroom and slept together. I thought it would feel uncomfortable to cuddle a girl, as I hadn't done it in my entire lifetime, but somehow her hug was warm and comforting, which fixed something inside me that I didn't even realise was broken. I didn't know how to give a proper cuddle so I just lightly patted her head and shoulders, but she came in for a hug and it soothed me instead, I thought it was supposed to do that to her. I don't remember falling asleep but I remember waking up early in the morning, as much as I wanted to leave her there and walk outside the room as it was a lot for me to take in, I couldn't. So I slept again, holding her hand. She was now facing away from me but her hair was touching my face. I thought it would bother me, but it didn't and in spite of the interruption it did, the smell of it made me want to preserve it.

Did it feel like *this* when the feeling was mutual, when both sides were in it together? I didn't know how a mutual relationship would be, although we were not in any position to be called a couple, yet. It still felt amazing to be loved and to be able to love. Love was a much greater word for me now, as I barely knew about Haniya's intention but when I had her hand in mine, her sweet smelling hair on my face, when we had cuddled all night long, chatted over some sandwiches and slept soundly like a child in each others arms it felt as if we had been in love forever. As if I had seen her morning face daily, and we had shared enough awkward conversations that we didn't need to hide our burp from each other, anymore. Nothing had happened so immense that I could name it as love or like and yet I was content to have her for a mere night in my silly apartment. It might just be me dreaming about it with my eyes wide open, or I had really came across a person who cherished me as much as I did. She must had something within the boundaries of her heart for a stupid person like me for which she came straight to me and opened the gate, told the guards to put their weapon down and let me enter through the front corridor of her heart. Even if I was just a dervish to her empire, I would gladly take a stroll in the garden of her aching flowers and pray for them so they grow and become as beautiful as ever. I wanted her to be happy, and I also wanted to be the source of her happiness. She might be the one opening the doors, but it would be me who'd live there like no one else, and then maybe she'd close the doors to her heart and let me live there until it's time for us to die. Yes, I was being delusional, and I wouldn't stop.

I was hesitant, even though I had already had several dreams. I'd wait for her to admit her feelings and only then would I disclose mine as I could never afford to lose the love of my life, again.

It's funny how I spent years loving Alaia and how it had only been a few days loving Haniya. And here I was measuring both the loves equally. Loving Alaia was not my choice, it happened itself. I was attached to her, never saw any other girl with the same feeling inside until this day. I had shared more memories with Alaia, but none were as mature as these. We were friends bound to help each other and love each other, hers was platonic and mine was romantic. We were in love with each other but had different priorities, she was my first, I was her first too but only when she had to choose between *friends*. I didn't blame her for anything, we shouldn't blame the other person who hadn't fallen in love with us.

I fell asleep again, all these thoughts might have bored me as I had gone through them multiple times. When I woke up I didn't find Haniya by my side, rather she was in my kitchen brewing some coffee. And yet again I dreamed of having her in my kitchen, daily, working busily on her own terms and I'd just be there and watch her.

I stopped watching her as soon as she turned around, my cheeks turned a darker shade of red, making me look like a tomato. I wondered if she saw me, and how she would react if it was a daily thing? I informed her that I was going for a shower. That was when she uttered the most painful words that made me realise, I was looking at the future and neglected the present. She asked "Already washing away my scent?"

It threw me off, did she say those words to just tease me or did she really meant it? I hope what she said came from affection and not just a friendly flirt cause I didn't mean to wash away her scent, I would rather want to be engulfed by it.

"I'd wash it off, only if I could hug you again and fill myself with your smell."

"Of course you can." She said those words with the most honey sweet voice you could imagine as if it was nothing. I could cringe upon my own words later, but I would like to enjoy these moments first. I took a quick shower and then we ate an egg sandwich along with the coffee she brewed. I had forgotten to ask her about clothes, she had slept in the one she was wearing last night. We were too observant to care about clothes but now her kurti looked creased and it would look bad if she stepped out in that. Well, I might have also wanted to give her my clothes as a sign, a sign that I was claiming her and as for her, I'd ask her for something of her own. This sudden sleepover was a sad party. I wanted her to come more often, remember me more often and for that she needed a part of me and I *her's*. She changed into my Pjs which were slightly bigger for her, though she looked even more cute in baggy clothes. I would rather see her in baggy clothes all comfortable and cute rather than a sexy dress which would show her curves. Remembering about her curves, I could still feel my hands around her waist as if it was made to hold her. She had an hourglass figure, and could easily pull off a cocktail dress and yet I craved to see her in a saree, beautifully draped, wrapped in a silky dream. Not too revealing, not too sexy but enough to make her shine just the way she was. Ahh!! *me* and *my fantasies*.

I didn't ask anything else, we both were busy in our own world. I was too nervous so I just walked around and pretended to work and she used that time to chat with someone. I was pissed, why was she chatting with someone else when she was with me? Was I not entertaining her well enough which was why she was talking to somebody else? I thought of asking her if she was going to go back home or not, I had a class to take and I was running late for it which made me restless. But just the thought of asking such a bizarre question made me feel bad and rude, like how could I ask *her* to leave? Nor could I just leave her here alone, it would be more rude. So I just stayed in that situation, restless as ever. When I got a call. It was from Alaia. I picked it up and waited for her to say something first, when she said hello I replied "Hey! good morning. where were you?"

"Hi, I'm so sorry for being MIA. I had too many things on my plate so I couldn't ask about your situation. How are you?"

"I'm fine. And you don't need to apologise. Is everything okay with you though? You sound tired."

"Yeah, I am fine now, it's just that, I am having to work a bit more than I am used to as my old PA retired due to some illness and there is a new PA who needs a little practice in the field. I am mentoring him for the time being. What about you? Does it feel adventurous or is it annoying you, now that you're in the limelight? But I'd say don't worry, once they get another spicy story your topic will stop circulating."

"Oh it's fine. It was a little difficult at first but I think it'll be worth it. As long as I have friends like you, I'll be good." I eyed Haniya, while talking to Alaia and there was no doubt that if I could spend a night with her like this, everything would be alright. I kept talking to Alaia and watched Haniya while pacing around the room when I tripped and fell down with a bang.

"Hey! hey! Are you okay? Wait, let me help you up. You should watch the way while you are walking around the room. Are you hurt somewhere?"

I was delighted at how much Haniya cared for me, I smiled even though My lower back was in pain. On the other side, Alaia was asking me, if I was okay, what happened and if there was someone with me and other stuff. I said that I was completely fine and Haniya was with me so there was nothing to worry about. And that's it. She suggested that I take a rest and then ended the call.

After Haniya asked me a few times, I admitted that my butt was hurt. It was embarrassing but she was concerned so I had to tell her. She giggled and asked me to lie down on my stomach until the pain went away. She also gave me an ice pack from my freezer which I put on my butt. It healed quickly, maybe because *she* gave me the ice pack. Ugh! I was being cringey.

Before leaving, Haniya asked me for my schedule, and if I was going to take any classes. She left me her hair tie. I wore it in my hand and went to the university.

BITCH

ALAIA

What the hell was that bitch doing there? I knew she was eying Aqeel the day I saw her in the studio talking so casually to him. But what the heck was wrong with Aqeel? Why did he invite Haniya over? She had no business being there. If they really had some business to talk about, they would have met outside. But at Aqeel's apartment? Really? What happened while I was busy in my own fucking life. It was not getting any good, no self-care, no picnic, nothing could help fix my mind right now. I was his childhood friend, the friend he used to have a crush on, the friend he loved, the friend whose engagement was called off because *he* decided to confess in front of all the guests and he hasn't invited me home yet. And this new girl, she just came into his life and she became more dear to him than me that he straight up invited her home? That early in the morning or did she stay the night too? Did they sleep together? as in did they *sleep* with each other?

Why was I stressing out though, if he wished to have a one night stand with a nobody like *her* then he might as well fuck every girl around. I didn't want to think about him, he didn't care about telling me that they were in touch after that interview so why should *I* destroy my morning because of them? It shouldn't hurt me this way, I didn't even like him, all I wanted was to reconcile with him as a friend although he was just giving me a corner in his life to rot there and see him with others.

As much as I thought I would not think about it again, I did and it made me feel worse. Kabir kept throwing certain questions to me, sometimes I told him to ask someone else or when I was calm I tried to explain to him myself even though it was a hassle to have him around all the time. I regret choosing him so impulsively just because I liked his passionate self. Only one thing was stopping me from throwing him out the door, my need for someone to manage my meetings, calls, shows, events, the people I met, my visits to different places and of course to help me with my goddamn brain which forgot to cooperate sometimes. Just like now, I was not thinking straight. A new bitch scared me with just the thought of losing

Aqeel again. We might have been apart for so long because it took me so fucking long to decide if I wanted to have a friend or cry over an ex who left me as soon as he looked in his competitor's eye. That must have scared him to death, I do remember the day. It was my engagement, Aqeel was supposed to show up as the bridesman. I was so observant in the arrangements and getting ready that I totally forgot to check up on him and at the time of the event, he didn't pick anyone's call and went MIA. Though just after we exchanged our rings, he showed up as a goddamn villain would do and said *it* infront of everyone that he loved me and wished to marry me. Uzair the fucker misunderstood it for an affair and without even asking me for an explanation, threw our rings and fled away. His family accompanied him, I was bawling my eyes out on the stage while everybody stood there and watched the drama. Aqeel had left before Uzair, maybe because he was too ashamed of the confession he made.

From that day, Ammi used to say that if the circumstances were a little different she would have accepted Aqeel as her son-in-law and that Uzair was no match for him. I realised much later, maybe after Ammi's death, that she was right. If Uzair was really nice he would have waited for me to say something but instead he just let himself get carried away because of a mere confession. I very well knew it was inappropriate, though I could never, I would never blame Aqeel again. As I didn't know myself, how *he* felt, how much in love he was that he couldn't watch me get engaged to someone else. It was a bold move, and I know he wasn't the type of person who would do something like that. Although I don't know him anymore, I'm not as good as I used to be. I have said it earlier but it seems more clear now, that he has changed. I should really stop thinking. And also, it might be completely different from what I was thinking. Maybe she was just his fan and came for a signed copy. Let's believe in that, for now.

Kabir dashed inside and startled me, that's when I realised I gave more thought to the recent situation than I should have. It's regular now, him coming in with a rush and without my permission. He definitely was a rebel. He had his hands full with what looked like tiffin boxes to me. There was food, I assumed they were home-made.

"Hey, um sorry I didn't ask your permission, again. These are for you, I have also given them to others."

"What are these?"

"FOOD."

"That I know but who made these and mind you, *eating* is not allowed in my office, I myself eat outside."

"I made these, I mean I helped my mom make them. It was her birthday and she usually bakes a lot, so she gave me some for y'all. It's yours and mine, I have already distributed to others. And sorry I didn't know food was not allowed here inside, I'll eat mine outside in the dining room and you can eat wherever you would like to. Also if you don't like it, you can return it to me. I won't force you to eat it."

"Well I never said anything about *not* accepting it. You can take yours and go look over my schedule and tell me at what time I have to leave for my flight." I missed the other event I was supposed to attend as it took everyone including me a while to settle down without Marina by our side. Kabir was passionate, though he was still an amateur and needed lessons. So I was having to teach him all the while he worked for me.

"Thanks, You have a flight at 2pm which is in 2 hours so if you wish to be on time you must leave *now*."

"Okay, and from the next time you'll be accompanying me so be ready for that. And give my wishes to your mom." I looked up at him and he seemed *happy*. "Alright, I'll tell her you wished happy birthday."

I hadn't had breakfast that day as I was doing intermittent fasting before the event. It was the inauguration of a cultural centre in delhi. So I didn't pack much, just the essentials like my wallet, some makeup for touchup, documents, and a different dress which I was gonna wear that night. Everything fit inside a small bag so I took it with myself and didn't leave it for the luggage compartment. I didn't know what to do with the cake Kabir's mom sent. I didn't want to eat something so high in calories after fasting nor did I want to give it to somebody as everybody had their own share and it was made specially by a mother. Whenever I saw a child with their mother, I got a little jealous. I wanted to spend more time with her, it felt as if the time I had with her wasn't spent with as much love as I needed to. So I took the tiffin with me inside my bag. I kept it for a time when I'd actually be ready to eat it, maybe I could have it after a little lunch.

As I thought, I didn't have any time to grab lunch. The event was supposed to start at 8pm. I boarded the plane at 2 and reached there by 4. It was another two and a half hour drive to the location. If I could I would have stopped somewhere but we were getting late, I needed to change and get ready for the event. So eventually the intermittent fasting lasted till 11pm when I finally got something to eat. Appetisers. You don't get served main course these days, it's not in fashion. As if I cared, but if you gave sushi to a person who could eat three bowls of rice was a joke. On my way back to the hotel room, I was practically starving and needed to eat something. We were driving towards a restaurant to grab dinner but the Delhi traffic didn't let me do that. After being stranded on an island, a person would eat whatever comes in front of them and that was how I ate the cake. Taking bigger bites at a time, and practically just swallowing it. I became a vacuum cleaner and inhaled all of it. I was full after that, so there was no point in going to the restaurant anymore. We took a U-turn from further down the road and went back to our hotel. I was tired and when you eat after a long time being empty stomach your body refuses to move. And that's how I slept in the dress I was wearing. I had brought my Pjs with me but didn't get the time or energy to change into them.

I slept peacefully until it was interrupted by Kabir's call. It was 6 in the morning, and he informed me that my return flight was at 8 am. I boarded the flight looking like a zombie. As I got very little sleep, I had under eye bags. Which was noticed by Kabir when he came to pick me up at the airport. "Wow! You look fresh." How kind of him to remind me that I looked like a trash bag. We went straight to the office as it would take me another 2 hours of drive to reach. I sometimes think about why we had to have our home/office in a place exactly opposite and far away from the airport. It always took more time to travel within the city than to go somewhere outside it. He didn't let me grab a coffee as according to him I was tired and what I needed was rest and food rather than caffeine. *How considerate, right? Ugh!* So I took a quick nap before starting my day in the car, and when we reached our office he gave me another tiffin box. With sandwiches inside, *my favourites.* He said that his mother would like to send me home cooked food as I looked thin and weak, she was basically stalking me online. I didn't object, couldn't refuse home cooked food as I was craving it the most. Also because I loved the cake Kabir's mom baked. My mother was a fabulous cook but a terrible baker. She used to bake on special occasions, sometimes it was burned and sometimes undercooked. Though we still devoured it as if it was cooked by the chefs from heaven. Now that I don't have her around, I miss her silly baking and delicious cooking.

I ate the sandwich, it was delectable. He took both the tiffin boxes from me and said that his mother would be happy knowing that I ate it. We started working on all the pending work that we'd left because of Marina's absence. It was slowly getting back on track. I think it would work out with Kabir as my PA, he was no match to Marina in the sense that if he worked hard he was more capable of doing the work than she used to. I can't complain, she was my best choice at that time and he was trying to become better day by day. He learned fast, listened to my words, had poor manners but it'd be okay as long as it was with me but if he dared to misbehave with other staff, I'd fire him, right away. I knew what he was before hiring him, though I feel he was too compassionate to weigh him down because of his too friendly nature with me. Sometimes he behaved like we belonged to the same age group and it was alright to chat and joke around like friends, while sometimes he was just as childish as a 10 year old would be. Which was something I could deal with, I hope so as he was curious for the work I was making him do. If he ever tried to teach me how to work or behave as if he was superior I wouldn't bear him a minute longer. I had only known him for a few days though I think I understood him. He was trying to behave the way he wanted to with his mother, he wanted freedom of speech and rights to choose his own career. And he was doing exactly what he wanted all along but without making her mother worried. It was a nice way to work on one's career so I don't mind him.

Whereas there was one thing I would mind a lot, which was Haniya. I was feeling like she was bad news for my and Aqeel's friendship. Ugh!! I felt like a teenager worrying if someone would snatch away my crush from me, but she was too quick to not worry. I saw her holding on to his arms the day they met, her innocent face made it easier for her to grab someone's attention. If she really had a plan to make Aqeel fall for her fake self I was not going to just stand here and see this shit. If Aqeel was not feeling comfortable enough to invite me home, I was going to destroy that comfort by showing up at his apartment. Sure I didn't know his address but that's not something I couldn't figure out after it had been circulating around the internet.

RELIEF

Aqeel

-

I would have but I decided to not hide the hair tie she gave me. Each one of my students and teachers noticed it, but they just gossiped about it in whispers. If they had asked me about it, I would have proudly told them that it was my girlfriend's. Our interaction was enough proof that she liked me too, *if* I was not being delusional. I would think about the hows, when, and what's later but at this moment, I'd just like to be with her. Be the one she thinks about. Her hair tie kept reminding me of her, I couldn't smell her in it although she'd be able to do that in her case. I *should* ask for her perfume brand, that information might come handy if I ever need to gift her.

Haniya informed me after reaching her studio and also that she was *missing* me. I got the text during my class but I could only check it several hours later. It immediately made me cheerful knowing that she thought about me just when I was doing it. So I called her without a second thought, but to my bad luck she didn't pick up. Later, when I was back home, resting in my living room, She called. I literally jumped to grab my phone which as in charging near my Tv Set-up. If I had been anywhere else, people would have thought that I was crazy. What was fascinating was that I *was becoming crazy about her.* She told me that earlier she was taking a shower and then got caught up in chores which was why she couldn't receive my calls. I said that it was okay and she could have called me once she had relaxed. But then she said that it was all okay and she had taken some time out for *me*.

"Can I ask you one thing?" I asked

" Absolutely! Go ahead, don't be shy." She said with a mild giggle.

"Why do you talk to me?"

"What do you mean?"

"I mean...why do you stay in touch with me even after that day of our interview? No pressure, its a casual question and I was just curious if-

"I *want* to talk to you, do I need any reason to do so? And if yes, then Mr Aqeel, I would like you to know that I adore your company, I adore you since the day I read your novels. I didn't need your photograph, or your interview to get to *know* you. I knew you from your characters, from your stories, from the places you showed us, the people you made, the conversation they had. I knew every part of you even before I *met* you. But it was like a dream, when I actually got to meet you let alone talk to you personally. It felt like a face was given to the fictional character I had created. So don't think about why and how I am talking to you."

"Mmm, It's too much for me to take in at a time. Yet I have another question for you. May I ?"
"Yes, yes I am here to clear every doubt of yours."
"Is it platonic or something else?"
"Platonic! Aqeel, you have got it all wrong. You have no idea how many times I have practised talking to you. Whenever I read your novels or a short story I always picturised you narrating the story personally. If I could I would have stalked you everywhere and then screamed 'Marry me Aqeel Baig' wherever I spotted you. Your poetries, your stories were the starting point of a romantic tale *I* was writing with my dreams. I have spent years after years thinking about what you were doing, where you would be, how you were doing, how you looked and stuff and you are asking me if it's *platonic*? I thought it was obvious and my actions showed my likeness towards you but maybe it didn't." Her high pitched voice sounded so close and loud as if she was right in front of me and not kilometres away.
"It did Haniya, it did. It's just that I am not used to the love you are giving me. And I have spent years *loving* someone who didn't love me back romantically. They loved me but it was platonic. I was the only one who had feelings. So this time I just wanted to be sure that you were as much in love as I am. It's ensuring that you knew me from earlier, but I want to know you and when you came to my house I was delighted to have you. So can I make sure that we both have feelings for each other?" I fidgeted with my t-shirt.
"I'll write you a poem if you want. If that's, what'll make you believe in me."
"That would be amazing." I sighed with relief, a smile started forming on my lips. Knowing that love was at my doorstep and now that I had opened the gate, I could finally grab it.

I slept with content, in my dreamy pillow, which felt softer than usual, the weather seemed chilly and my bedsheets were warm. It had started raining outside, and the droplets of water that trickled down my window pane made me enthusiastic. This was a sign that this monsoon I wouldn't cry and run away from the rain, instead I'd look outside my window, make a cup of warm coffee and read a sweet poem.

I woke up the next morning with a fresh mind, when I looked outside everything seemed like it was pulled out of the washing machine. Clean and fresh, water washed every dirt, sorrow and doubt but left it piled in the middle of the road. If not cleaned manually it'd become sludge and get everyone's shoe dirty. It's the same with people, when their doubts are cleared some of it refuses to be washed away and accumulate at another place. This type of weather always left a mark, sometimes on the road, sometimes on people's clothes and shoes and sometimes on people's hearts. And it wasn't easy to wash the stain, I hope I wouldn't have to go through the pain of washing. So, I was going to be extra careful as however beautiful and romantic this weather seemed it always brought gloom. *To this new morning and new season, to the new bondings and relationships sprouting, I am wishing myself good luck.*

For the next few days, we chatted and talked over calls. Being connected with her online and offline had made it a habit. If we didn't talk for several hours in a stretch, one of us would remind the other of our existence and priority. It was going great, ever since she made it clear that we could be a *thing*. I was well assured that she was *the one* and yet I felt as if something was going to happen which would change certain things or elements around. It was a hunch, and I tend to be highly intuitive in these cases which made me fear that I might lose *her* or my own self.

But what was meant to happen, would happen. And we didn't have any role in it, it was like a river, once disturbed it would go on till the end until it gets mixed with another river or sea.

A week later on a sunday afternoon while I was chilling in my home with some leftover pasta and netflix. Something out of the ordinary happened. I didn't usually get any guests except Haniya, though it surprised me to see Alaia outside my door. I was taken aback, as I didn't expect her to come over. Although I welcomed her warmly, It was impossible to act rude to my only childhood friend. And there were other reasons too, how could one act rudely to one's first love? I was overjoyed to have her in my house, I didn't have any special occasions otherwise I would have invited her over. But now that she was already here, It was upon me to make it a memorable visit.

"Seems like you googled my address here. Sorry for not inviting you earlier." I pleaded.

"No worries, I am not a fan of formalities as you might know already. It's just that I had a lot of things to ask you and see if you missed your friend or not." She grinned.

"First of all, have you had your lunch yet? Cause I was eating my leftover pasta, though if you are hungry I can cook you a quick lunch."

"I have had a cup of coffee and a cookie since this morning, if you call it 'lunch' then I am all ok." She shrugged with an amusing smile on her face.

I made a one-pot biryani for her, but she couldn't stop talking while I was in the kitchen. She didn't have basic cutting and chopping skills so I just let her watch me while I cooked. Growing up, I loved eating but Dida knew only traditional recipes so it was upon me to learn and cook delicacies from different cuisines. That being a hobby, helped me alot with my days living alone. I could cook myself nearly anything, sometimes it turned out good and other times it came out *edible*.

Cooking and thinking went by together, it was a therapy to people like me. While for Alaia it was yet another boring household task, so she just peeked from above my shoulders and commented upon how I looked while cooking and how well I could pull off a three-piece suit. We gossiped about Dhruv being gay, and what we thought was a good book to read. She eventually got bored and sat in front of the TV to watch netflix. I thought she would pick us a nice movie, instead she put on a fashion show documentary and made comments on the dresses and how the model wasn't fit for the dress. How could they have made the show a little better for the spectators and how *she* had planned to hold a special show. I was getting bored. Too much of what I didn't understand. Though it was Classic Alaia, so how could I object to her decision? I couldn't do much and just nodded whenever she made a remark.

And before *she* could realise it was evening, we had spent hours together under the same roof. If my *teenage self* was here looking at us together, after years. He would have been content with just that. It was so soothing to catch up after years of being apart. We met several times in the past month though none of them felt as personal as this one. This one was special, it felt like old times, also it was less awkward. Alaia looked like she had a different purpose to come here and not just a friendly visit. Of course I had made it difficult for her, after coming into her life for a second time. Everything went in a different course rather than the ones we meant to take. She must have been worried for me, and for her. Being with me must have affected her work, the times when she helped me with the meeting and the interview.

She didn't complain, she never did at least to me. She just wanted to help me reach another goal of *hers* regarding my career. Sometimes I thought she was too concerned about her surroundings and that's just how she was. Cared too much about the people in her life, and too less about herself. I remembered her being the usual self she was back when we were in school. It wasn't that hard for me to make friends, I just needed one or two meetings and if our vibes matched we would become friends. It was a bit hard for me to start that conversation, but not unachievable. Although whenever I made a new friend, she judged them so hard and acted rudely to them if they talked to me a little impolitely. She used to chase them away, She was the biggest reason I had less friends. But I didn't mind it as long as she was there for me. I understood that having few friends was better than having unfaithful friends.

The silence which was brought by the magnificent sunset outside my apartment balcony was broken by her when she asked - " Are you dating Haniya?"

I didn't speak, instead I looked at her with great astonishment. How come she knew that I was meeting Haniya? Did she talk to her, or did she just guess?

HEARTBREAK

ALAIA

When he didn't refuse it immediately I knew there was a trace of truth in what I asked him. It surprised him that I knew, or found out about them. As if I caught them red handed, though there was no crime in dating. I should have felt happy for him, knowing that he was moving on and my presence didn't mean the same thing to him as it used to. He wasn't in love with me as he us ed to and a part of me wished he did. I wanted him to love me, see me the way he used to. The way he cared for me, listened to me, considered my decisions to be his last. How he prioritised me above any of his friends or classmates. If he wanted, he would have rebelled against my choices and thought about his own. He had the habit of telling me everything first than anyone else. But I think that habit was long gone.

It was getting awkward with his long silence and thinking, if he hadn't spoken in another second I would have brushed off the question. He replied with an innocent smile" We are meeting, yes. But we haven't gone much far."

If not for his smile and the pure joy I got knowing that it was not official yet, I would have asked him why had he invited her over so soon. But I stayed silent and gave him a small nod. With that I bid him a goodbye and came back.

I had to do something with my living situation. Or else I would end up losing everything I earned in my daily hotel bills. I was planning to shift in the bungalow once it was ready but due to some uncertain circumstances everything had to stop there. So I guessed I'd either have to buy or rent a place where I could live.

On monday I went back to the office, the tiffin boxes had become regular. It was strange how I was getting healthy food for *free*. I was glad that Kabir's mom wasn't that type of Indian mother who liked to make extra fatty food. This was the reason I didn't ask Kabir to stop. There was nothing bad in it, even though one could never explain why he was going that far. And why was *I* letting him do it? It could be because he was eager to save his place here, or was he just obeying his mother? Even though her mother didn't know me or had any reasons to take care of me, *his boss*. What could be their motive behind this? It may also be that they didn't have any motive and were just compassionate enough to provide food for a lonely person like me. In any case I was just grateful for whatever they were doing for me, and I wouldn't ask them to stop. I could perhaps do something better for them in return. I might help Kabir in learning more about business.

I planned on meeting Dhruv, as we had nothing better to do in the evening. We sat in a cafe and ordered some latte for ourselves. We mostly spoke about our work life, though there were some other exchanges too, he told me that he was getting engaged. I didn't even know he was dating someone. But seeing how the world was now, we didn't actively talk about each and everything concerning our personal life. Which served us good as, having people back bitch about you regarding your career, your relationship status was not fine at all. And when you were having difficulties with any of these in your life, it was fine to resort to loneliness. If it got worse, bringing elderly people in and talking to them, talking to your therapist, or a very trusted friend was the best option. I wouldn't recommend the friend part, at least from my experience because whoever I had met till date had proven to be a bitch. *Except one though*. Thinking of which I had only a handful of friends, including Aqeel, who were really sweet to me and never ever left me heartbroken. Others were Ammi and Marina. Now I only had Aqeel by my side. And I would do anything in my reach to protect that friend of mine. I would never let a girl like Haniya take him away from me.

I might be selfish, but yeah this was me. Haniya didn't deserve Aqeel, sometimes I felt like even I didn't deserve him. Earlier, I had treated him very badly, and I was gonna fix it. It would be Aqeel, who I'd be fighting for, and it was going to be worth it. I was SURE.

Afterwards, I left the cafe and said goodbye to Dhruv. I drove towards Aqeel's place. I didn't give much thought to it, and just mindlessly drove. As if the road was taking me towards him and not me. When I reached there, I thought of calling him and checking if he was home. When I called him, he hung up after two rings. I got furious as to why he hung up my call. Which wasn't even followed by an excuse text saying he was busy or something. So I went up to check. To my great surprise he was home and he had company. Haniya was there. He didn't seem happy to have me there. The surrounding took a bored and disgusted feeling which in my opinion came from Haniya. Aqeel might not be happy having me there unannounced as he practically hung up my call. But Haniya must have been pissed at me for showing up. She must be insecure now that *I* was at his place. She wouldn't be the centre of attention anymore. I wasn't bragging but Aqeel tends to forget about his surroundings and the people whenever I was with him.

It wouldn't be any different now. I was still his *ali*. And no one could take my place. And as I thought he greeted me warmly just the other second and then invited me inside. He even apologised for not taking my call. Haniya though with her innocent and charming smile sat there and greeted me hello, she looked mad. Or maybe It was my own reflection on her face.

I asked Haniya how she had been and she said that she was feeling amazing these past few days despite all the tragedies. I didn't know what the tragedies were. But given she had been spending her time with Aqeel, It must really be amazing. Growing up I didn't quite appreciate his presence, but after being apart for so long. I knew how much worth it was.

Aqeel made me a dalgona and black coffee for haniya and himself. Why was she sharing the same drink with him? And why was *I* the one who was left alone. Anyways I didn't care, and I shouldn't stress. She was just a nobody, while I- I went back a long way.

I might be acting like a judgy aunty, though I had full rights to check whether she could be a nice friend to Aqeel or not. Her intentions were way more than just being friends. Which was why I needed to keep an eye on her.

I was going to ask about Haniya but she questioned me first. "How did you *two* meet? I am quite curious about your story, we were talking about your childhood only, but Aqeel never mentioned when you both met." She gave me yet another soft smile. She must have known how her sweet soft smiles made me go mad. This was my second time meeting her, though it felt like we have had a rivalry for years.
"Oh,us? We were brought up together. I mean we were neighbours since the day his parents shifted in the flat just across ours." I shot my killer smile as a response.

She looked at Aqeel after she heard me as if I said something different from what she was expecting. Then she turned towards me and replied- "I thought you both were school friends but now that I know, it all seems obvious."

"What seems obvious?" I was curious to know what was going through her mind.

"Uhh, well we were just talking about you and Aqeel's childhood."

I was mad, mad at Aqeel as how he could just tell us about us to a stranger. He might know her but I *didn't* and I didn't feel okay sharing our precious memories. So with anger boiling inside me I turned towards Aqeel who was already looking at me with pleading eyes.

"Nothing too specific, just our adventures. Actually I had some old pictures and I was showing it to Haniya." He said to assure me indirectly that he didn't talk about anything too personal. I wasn't ashamed of what happened or what I did. If someone else was in my place, they would have done that too. I loved Uzair, not knowing that Aqeel had feelings for me. And because of this hidden feeling, my engagement got ruined. I *did* break our friendship, which was something Aqeel was afraid of the most. Though he very well knew the consequences and still did it on the day I was going to be engaged. I felt sorry afterwards and that was why I apologised. He was sorry too. And we were back to being friends again. I didn't want to bring up the past again and share it with someone who had no rights to have this much knowledge about our relationship. I was relieved that Aqeel didn't disclose the truth, otherwise it would have shown me in a bad light.

I hadn't had any dinner and now my stomach was growling. It came out a little too loud and embarrassed me. Not because it happened In front of Aqeel as we had shared many embarrassing moments together, but because Haniya was there too. I had no wish to look ungracious or mannerless in front of that beautiful witch. After hearing my stomach literally scream that it was empty, Aqeel stood up and walked towards his kitchen. I followed him there to have some words with him. I looked back at Haniya to see if she was watching us or not, but she was looking at her mobile phone. I sighed with relief as I really needed some alone talk with Aqeel. He had some food ready so he put them inside the microwave to reheat it.

"Thank you very much for not talking about us with *her*." I signalled towards Haniya who was sitting outside.

"Yeah, I know. I didn't think it'd be appropriate to talk about our past without your permission so I kept that bit a secret. Also because it'd make things difficult between us if I talk to her about my past love interest."

I was glad that he respected my confidentiality. But I also wished to become deaf. He thought that if he brought that topic up, he'd ruin his current relationship with her. Didn't he say that they were just meeting and nothing special. Now that I thought, It wouldn't have hurt me that much if he had *talked* about me. I would have understood his need to explain things to his partner, but he didn't tell us, about his first love because he thought it'd make things difficult for them. Did he just give her, his first priority? I used to be his first priority. And now I was not? It took like a few weeks for a girl so undeserving like her to snatch Aqeel's attention from me. She was too skilled for what I imagined her to be. I needed to step up my game or else I was done for. I would be left without a friend.

The only way to remind him about me was by giving him flashbacks of our past. So I stayed with him in the kitchen just like earlier and talked to him about how we used to run around my living room screaming on top of our lungs as we weren't pretending to be power rangers. How he always spent most of his time in my place, eating with us, sleeping with us and doing chores with my mother. He was the second child and first son to my mother, she always adored him. She sometimes jokingly said that she would adopt him if she could and he would burst into laughter saying that he didn't want a sister like me. I reminded him how he had always loved me, ever since he knew me. He never admitted that he wanted me to become his sister because he always had those feelings.

All my words seemed like it was for nothing, as he constantly checked over Haniya. Every few minutes he would look at her and try to talk to her. I tried to bring his attention back to me, to realise, he never *was* paying attention. Haniya and Aqeel both exchanged looks and as if they had a secret language, they used to communicate with.

Were the onions that made me cry? Or was I hurt? My eyes stung and tears started pooling, I tried my best to absorb them back inside my eye balls. But those stubborn bastards wouldn't listen and the next thing I know, I was bawling my eyes out. Aqeel didn't even notice. At that moment I realised How much I craved his attention, his eyes on me when I talked, his loyalty, his love. I grew with him, with his affection, he was ready to fight for me even though he could barely defend himself. I was accustomed to being taken care of by *him*. And now he didn't. Nothing related to me could budge the feeling he might have for Haniya. This stupid bitch had nothing better to do, so she decided to snatch the most dearest person of my life from me. Allah had already taken Ammi away and now *she* was doing the same with Aqeel. I wanted him to look at me the way he did when he loved me. I wanted to feel the warm gaze again and Haniya was being a hindrance. I couldn't do a thing to Haniya, as it would definitely hurt Aqeel and *that* would hurt me. I wonder what would happen If I had accepted his proposal and married him instead of Uzair. But Aqeel was too late, late to call me. I didn't want to be late. I hugged him from the back and cried. I wanted to hold on to him, and if I didn't someone would take him away from me. I could pass an eternity in that position, in that hug, in that warmth that radiated from him. When I hugged him, he *flinched*. Of course he would, I acted so suddenly. Luckily he didn't make any sound so that Haniya would know. I wanted to stand there, my face resting on his back.

He must have hesitated, as he stood still for a moment and then freed himself from my grasp. I wanted him to look at me with fondness, ask me If I was okay and then hug me back. Instead, his eyes were filled with confusion, when I looked at him after waiting for him to make a move. He didn't and then he asked me if I was missing my Ammi? Of course I was, though that wasn't the case right now. The person I was missing was *him*, and he was right in front of me. He grew up to be so fine, and yet every inch of me wanted the old person back. I wanted to tell him how much I wanted his love, but as if refusing to see me for what I was, he went away to check up on Haniya. I was crying but he didn't try to console me, and ran across the kitchen to see Haniya, as she dropped something. That was when I confirmed He had fallen out of love with me and he was falling for Haniya, instead. His concern, his attention, his affection, his compassion, his loyalty, he had written everything on Haniya's name. And I was left bare handed. Was it that easy to forget someone? Was *I* that easy to leave? It was all my fault, I shouldn't have turned my back on him. I should have gone after him and held his hands. While he was still in love with me, While he was still *mine*.

I couldn't stand anymore, my knees stopped supporting me. The earth pulled me down, I cried silently sitting there on his kitchen floor which felt colder than usual. A few minutes later he came back to check the food which was in the microwave and saw me on the floor. He helped me up and enquired what had happened to me, by that time my tears had dried and there was no proof so I lied about getting a dizzy head. He politely asked me to go rest in the living room while he set up the table. I didn't ask anything about Haniya and what happened several moments earlier when he rushed to take care of her. It was evident that she was a clumsy little girl and might have dropped something, intentionally to grab his attention. When I went to the living room, there was no one there so I looked around and found that Haniya was inside Aqeel's bedroom.

I hated girls who were younger than me, beautiful and had a cunning mind like a fox. Haniya was one of those girls, I was not even surprised to see her sitting on his bed. I went inside and layed down in the bed beside her. I had the best excuse to lie down as I said I had a dizzy head. Though I was there to disturb her, to take away whatever peace she had. She was putting a bandage on her hands, when I asked She replied that she accidently dropped one of the drinking glasses and cut her fingers as she tried to pick one.

"It was a small cut, really. I didn't need this." She said pointing towards the bandage. I gave her an assuring smile.

"Aqeel insisted that I put ointment, but when I refused, he put it himself. He had to check on the food which was why I am completing this bandage. I told him, these small cuts aren't that serious and would eventually heal. But he is too considerate." She blushed. Trying to hide the smile she was getting probably because of the care she got from Aqeel. I knew very well she wasn't used to such kind behaviour at all.

I couldn't say anything or you can say I didn't really have anything to say so I faked another smile. Everything made me want to hit her, or break everything in existence. I wished Aqeel hadn't got that letter, or never intended to reply to it. I wish I didn't write that letter in the first place or just stuck it below a drawer and forgot about it. Although there was nothing I could do to reverse the actions I took or the things that took place after it. All I could do to have my peace back was to take back what was mine. Take Aqeel back before I lose him forever. So I planned something. If I couldn't pull back Aqeel, I'd push Haniya away. So much that it gets harder for her to come back at all.

I

THINGS WE CAN'T EXPLAIN

AQEEL

I called everyone for dinner, while I fixed the tea table. I didn't have people around as much and that was why I never got myself a dining table. It was just me and I was fine that way though things are turning out pretty well now that I was surrounded by people. Haniya and Alaia came to the living room, Alaia looked fresh had she not told me she was dizzy I wouldn't even know. The sudden back hug from her was uncomfortable, not because I despised her touch but maybe I had grown a little unfamiliar with it. There was something different about the way she acted and talked to me. And I couldn't wrap my head around it. Anyways, there were and would be strange feelings associated with her, at first it was hidden love and now it was newness.

Haniya had a sullen face. It puzzled me what happened between the two, she was fine earlier when I had put ointment on her finger. Did Alaia say something to her? I didn't ask her, as I never got the chance. I didn't know for sure if it was because of Alaia, but I found her talking to Haniya in my bedroom while I clearly told her to rest in the living room as the bedroom was already occupied by Haniya. Though she chose to do what she found right. Alaia was a lot more chatty during dinner than usual times, god knew what took over both of them to act so strangely. I thought I could find out what was wrong just by looking at her, though Haniya never raised her head enough for me to look at her eyes. She finished her food and waited. Waited for what? I didn't know. I took their plates and other stuff to the kitchen. When Alaia thanked me for the food and the time we spent together. I asked her if she was feeling alright now and she replied with a yes. We bid our goodbyes as she had to head back home and rest, for the next day was going to be busy. Haniya on the other hand stayed back and I was grateful for that, as I wanted to talk some more. It was midnight already and I wished she wouldn't insist on going back. I wanted her by my side, although it would be difficult to explain it to her parents. What if her parents were conservative? and We were unmarried to start with. It would create a mess, and I'd have to figure something out soon.

It was after 10 minutes that Haniya spoke, she looked really sad and I wanted to know what conversation they exchanged when I was working.

"Did you ever *love* Alaia?" She asked, looking down at her feet.

This particular question felt like daggers passing straight through my heart and then they twisted. I knew just by this, what Alaia had done. She told everything to her, *she* was the one I was trying to protect by not sharing this detail about my life and now she had risked *my* relationship *with* Haniya. I felt bile rising up my throat, but something from inside my stomach said that it was alright to agree to my past. It was Past. " Yes." I nodded.

"Why didn't you tell me?" She made small knots of her stroll's edge, and kept fidgeting with it.

"It wasn't right by everyone's side. So I chose to just keep it to myself." I explained.

"I understand." She replied. I was so relieved to know that she understood. But that bit of relief didn't stay for long. As she spoke again. "You shouldn't have raised her hopes."

For the first time in hours, she saw me in the eyes, though there wasn't love. There was disappointment. "What do you mean?" I immediately questioned her, anxiety lurking behind my shoulders as shadows of my older self.

"What do you think she came back for? She was the one to write to you, am I right?" She fixed her gaze on me, and I would have loved it if it was not searching for answers rather than affection.

"Yes, yes indeed *she* was the one who wanted to reconcile and I didn't find anything wrong in it."

"She didn't just want to reconcile, Aqeel. She wanted you back." She broke into tears, when I tried to soothe her by rubbing her arms, she brushed off my hands.

"What did she tell you? How do you know what she really wants Haniya? And why do you think I *am* going to walk on her gestures?" I frowned.

"Besides I am not a toy that you can set aside for your different moods." I continued.

"I know-, I know you very well to understand that it's not your fault to begin with nor it is hers. But it is hard for me to decide where I belong.

She knew what she was doing. And I don't blame her for that." She said between little sobs.

"I don't know what happened, but I'll discuss this with Alaia, okay? Don't think that I will just leave you since my long lost love has come back. *You are the one who made me realise that I can still love.* You made me fall in love again, and this time it wasn't unrequited. Your worries are proof enough that you love me and I will cherish this love, Haniya. Besides, Alaia is my past, and I would do everything on my behalf to stay away from her."

My words did make her cry less than she was doing earlier. Though their conversation had already put the seed of worry inside her mind and I wondered if she could trust me around Alaia, ever again. Alaia's tone must have been different than what I would have chosen to tell her about our past. Which resulted in this kind of situation, where Haniya had started to doubt my love for her. I would have to consider keeping both of them as far from each other as possible. Or else they would break into another conversation which might worsen the whole thing.

I tried to reach Alaia but couldn't get through so I called her office number. I was surprised I even had it, though thankfully it came handy. I was expecting her, though someone named Kabir, possibly her assistant, picked up the call and said she was busy and I should call her later, maybe in two or three days. I didn't understand how people could be so busy that one would have to wait for two days just to talk to them about their visit earlier. I thought by saying who I was, I might get the chance sometime in the same day, though nothing worked. Well I guessed she really *was* busy and couldn't spare a minute or two for the one person in her life that stayed by her side all the time, even in the worst times possible. I didn't usually say this, though it was true. All her friends had abandoned her, or betrayed her at least once. If I weren't guilty for my actions I wouldn't consider leaving her all alone. I would still be by her side even if I wasn't in love with her. I still believed that there must have been a misunderstanding, or a change of tone when she told Haniya about us. She didn't have any reason to want me back, We weren't *ever* a thing, besides she didn't love me. And If she did, now. I wondered if I could love her back. As I was already knee deep in Haniya's love and It might take me just a few more visits and I would be drowning in it.

She looked impeccable with her hair down, eyes with a little hint of mascara, lips so beautiful that I could look at it for hours. And her smile, so welcoming that it engulfed me with its warmth. Her straightforward yet shy behaviour, made my stomach tickle. I felt like she was bold enough to ask me for love and coy enough to curl up like a flower petal when I looked at her. She brought out the extrovert in me and cared for the introvert too. She was always the one to understand what was needed at the moment and then discuss it with pure intentions. She was the one to embrace me just as I was, my true self. Through my literary works, she had been seeing me, talking to me, thinking of me. And I was unsure of her existence till that day when I met her in the studio. I will forever be thankful for Alaia, as we wouldn't have met if not for her. Alaia was the reason we met, she was the road that took me to the most beautiful place to exist in this world. And I would make sure she was not the one to ruin it. I didn't hold her guilty, though I wouldn't trust her completely with her choice of words.

It wasn't until two days later that I got the chance to talk to her. How surprising it was that she picked up my call after the chaos she gave birth to. Now it was upto me to explain it to Haniya, how strangely things had taken its course. I thought that Alaia might have discussed the scenarios a little differently, though now I was unsure of her intentions. After what I read in an e-article about me and Alaia. She must have done a private interview session in the course of the previous few days which was why it was hard to reach her. The article stated "Alaia the CEO and main designer of NXDE has finally admitted to have fallen in love. It comes to us like this, She must have been in love all along and was late to realise it. Alaia Mirza said to us directly that The renowned Author Aqeel Baig aka her childhood friend has her enchanted."

My eyes faulted, made the article look blurry through the bright screen showing my face and Alaia side by side. I stood there in my college campus under the flickering light of the men's toilet, speechless. I wanted to throw myself in the urinator beside me, or jump outside from the half broken wall of this so-called spectacular place I worked at. Everything looked ugly and I wished to die right there. What would I say to Haniya? How was I going to make things better? *Was Alaia really in love with me? Or was this a plan, a revenge plan against me? Why, all of a sudden she realised her love for me and told the media before saying a word to me?*

I wrapped up my work as soon as possible and took to the road. I very well knew where I was going and yet I was not ready to discuss it even with myself. It was just a google map search away and in 30 minutes I was there in front of the building. The building was not what I had in mind when I thought it was going to be the central office of the luxurious brand. For a second I thought I had come to the wrong address, so I quickly asked the people around and they said that I was at the right place. I had nothing holding me back So I stepped inside. The building was old and crusty from the outside as it was made around the 1900s by none other than the British. Though from inside it looked nothing less than a 7 star hotel. Maybe Alaia forgot to renovate the outer portion of the building or it was going to take place sometime in the near future. I asked the staff for Alaia and surprisingly they allowed me to visit her in her office right away. I believed I would have to wait as she appeared to be a very busy person and didn't have enough time to respond to my call and yet had time to give an intimate interview without considering my thoughts and beliefs. I was getting furious with every passing minute. How could she have fallen in love with me so suddenly and didn't even think of sharing it with me first? How dare she talk about such a thing publicly and never care for what I would have to say? Or did she purposely do it to make me feel the way *she* felt that time when I confessed to her in front of all the guests who came to attend her engagement?

When I entered her office room, I didn't consider knocking or asking for permission as she didn't do. There she was sitting and laughing with I didn't care who. She came to a halt after noticing me. She politely asked me to come inside and sit, requesting the person who might have been the one I talked to a few days earlier, to bring something for me to drink. She asked my preference, as she should have done before giving her statements to the media. But I refused everything and asked to be left alone with her.

Two minutes of silence followed after the guy left, and Alaia sat scrolling through her mobile. "So what is the reason behind your sudden visit? That article?" Her knowing exactly what I came for made me even more furious. "Why did you do that?" I asked, trying to not lose my cool.

" Listen Aqeel, I know you must be mad that I realised it after so many years. But believe me I thought it was just my guilt, after leaving you, after turning my back from your love. I had the idea that I was in love with Uzair and he was too. Though he was nowhere near love, all he wanted was a bride to make his mother satisfied and I was a pawn in his game. It took me a lot of time to realise that I had *always* loved you, in some way and losing you was the worst part in my life. When these interviewers asked me about if I was dating someone I would have brushed the question away. However I wasn't able to this time, Your face kept reminding me of the love you showered me with." Bullshit.

"Alaia, I have no words for what you are feeling right now. Maybe this is the aftereffect of meeting me. But I'll tell you, this can't be love. You can't love me, and even if you do. I don't know If I can. I am falling in love with someone else and I can't ignore her." I blurted out.

"Are you sure she is in love with you? As I am not, she seems exactly like Uzair. Fake promises, lies, false hopes and everything. She is just after your money, your fame. How can a person fall in love with someone they have only met a few times and because of work. Can't you see? No, actually you are too naive to realise it. As you were late to realise that you should have confessed to me way before. If it wasn't my engagement that day. I would have heard you, considered your feelings and then acted accordingly. I would have never told you lies."

"You just can't judge someone based on other's actions, Alaia. Besides I am very sure she is in love with me. Have you met her? Have you talked to her like I did? What Uzair did to you, might have been a reaction to my actions. Or maybe you are right about him. Though I can assure you Haniya isn't like him. She is *not* after my money or fame. She has loved me even before knowing who I was. She has loved me through my writings, where I have expressed myself entirely as I am" I was getting emotional, tears had started welling up in my eyes. I wasn't supposed to cry, in front of Alaia, the girl I had loved my entire childhood. The girl who was confessing to me right now that she loved me and yet I was not sure if I did or could do it. The girl I would do anything for, and yet can't think of leaving my current love interest.

"See, she is in love with your characters. What you have written is your characters and It's very common for readers like her to fall for fictional characters. I would suggest you stop thinking about her, and yeah I have talked to her. From which I have gathered that she loves the way you write, she loves the way you manage being what you are and stay humble. Just like any other fan, she is all over you. But has she seen you in your worst? Has she been with you when your mother left? No! She wasn't. And guess who was. *I* was and I will be. I am deeply sorry for not respecting your affection towards me, it was just too awkward at that time. But now, I understand and I am ready to embrace it. Give me a chance, will you?" She tried to reach for my palm, which rested on her desk. I quickly took back my hands and rested them on the arm rest of my chair.

"I don't know. Seriously, If you have realised it, I am glad. Still I can't give you anything right now, for I have already put my heart for Haniya. I can't love you anymore, Alaia. For I have fallen for someone else. And thankyou for staying by my side, no one can ever equal you. Your position in my life is intact if that's what you are worrying about. So please, take your words back from the media. Say something that can undo everything." I left after delivering these words for It was getting impossible for me to stay there.

MY LIFE, MY FRIENDS, MY RULES!

ALAIA

If I was going to make Haniya run, I had to claim Aqeel first. I didn't have an exact plan to do anything but I had an interview lined up for the next day. It was for an article, the yearly one which recorded my progress as a business woman and inspired others. I usually got questions on my dating life though I didn't respond to any of it. But this time when the interviewer asked me, I thought about the possibilities. I wouldn't actually have to actively seek his attention, one rumour would be enough to piss off Haniya. So I took my chance this time and enthusiastically shared my feelings with the interviewer. They acted as if they had just won a lottery. I intentionally emphasised on the 'I' when I told them that *I* was in love with him. Because Aqeel had just suffered a huge media backlash and If I said anything about him being involved with me, it would cause him another one. And I couldn't afford to have him angered, it was *him* for whom I was doing all this.

Anyways, what chance did Haniya hold against me? She was a newbie. And when the whole town would know about me being in love with someone, people would hardly remember anything about Haniya. Ironically, people didn't know much about her friendship with Aqeel. And after this, they'd only remember my name alongside his.

Now it was Aqeel I had to handle. I just need to remind him about *me*, and suggest he should focus on *me*. Because it was me, *always*. When he showed up in my office, I was surprised, though it was expected. Like, I knew what the consequences were. I tried my hardest to convince him that I was in love with him. That was my only option, but he was adamant that he had moved on from me and was now in love with Haniya. I knew this conversation wasn't going to go in my favour so I immediately texted Akriti, she was a journalist. She had been contacting me constantly for a statement, a comment, a mere gesture to show where I was headed in my life. So I asked her to come to my office immediately along with the paparazzi. Aqeel and I argued for another half an hour, when he started to make his way out. I got anxious, because I wanted the media to catch us together. Though now, time was ticking and I wondered if the paparazzi had arrived yet or not. I wouldn't have done something like this, but Aqeel was making things hard for me. He was arguing with me because of that new bitch in his life. So I had to do it the hard way.

Aqeel stood up and walked outside, I followed him outside to see hundreds of people accumulated around my office entrance recording us, LIVE! I bet Aqeel was anxious, there were sweat beads starting to form on his forehead, he glanced towards the media and then towards me. He knew *I* betrayed him. If they were here just for the photos, or a word from us. Aqeel could have easily escaped, but now when they were recording us live, he *froze*. He stood there like a statue, people jumped up and down to take a look. With so many cameras and lights around, the pedestrians got curious and took out their mobiles too. More cameras to add up to the lot. One small mistake, and we could ruin everything. I regretted calling Akriti here. She was well prepared. I was afraid I had put Aqeel in the worst situation ever. People wanted to know why we planned to meet here in my office rather than at a restaurant, were we in a relationship? Did Aqeel say yes or not? I heard Aqeel sigh, I needed to step in. Of course he didn't have any words, and if he had, my plan would have been a major failure. Before he could say anything or muster up enough courage to deny the rumours. I walked past him, and stood in front of all the cameras. These cameras never intimidated me, I was made for the spotlight. Though today, I had to take a deep breath before opening my mouth for those hundreds of mics to record me.

"Aqeel hasn't given me a word yet, as he needs some time. For now My love just stands unrequited. We are just friends and would like to take some time alone so we can talk about our future." And with just that I signalled Akriti to go away with everyone else. Others still tried to ask Aqeel about his opinion but he kept his silence. I was relieved that at least he had *enough* faith in me to let me talk after what I did. Though as soon as the paparazzi left, Aqeel left too. He didn't say a word to me, not even a goodbye. Well, my wish was fulfilled. I knew it wasn't going to be that easy, he was going to be upset for a while. But I knew very well that I could bring him back anytime.

I went back inside and ate the lunch Kabir brought me. Since the day he joined his mother has been sending me lunch. I think she adored me, of course she loved fashion and perhaps she was thankful of the job I gave to Kabir. He worked really well so I guess he was permanent. Earlier, I had asked him to look for an apartment and take my father's suggestion too. My father tried to persuade me into living with him until I got married, though I was not planning to marry anytime soon. So he helped Kabir choose an apartment which was near both my office and my father's place. And now Abbu could come check up on me anytime of the day, unless I was at the office. He could come there too, but he didn't think it was wise to disturb me. Well, I'd be shifting to my new place in a week. I only had a few luggage to transfer and some things from my office. Though having an apartment wasn't enough I had to get furniture. Some of the furniture came with the apartment, and we shopped the rest online. These things kept me busy for the previous two days along with that interview. Now I was left with the aftermath of my decisions. I had to find a way by which I could make Aqeel understand my intentions. Though I could hardly understand my own doings. It seemed a little too much, to get back my friend.

I remember my childhood home before I shifted my parents to abbu's current apartment. Aqeel used to live in the same building. Everyday after finishing school, he used to come directly at our place. He would spend a few hours with us and then went back to have lunch at his own place. He would bring us some of the food Dida cooked, as long as I remembered she was a really kind person. After my mom's cooking I only ever liked dida's. But now, I was left with none of them, and all I could do was enjoy the food a stranger cooked me. The hospitality Kabir's mom was showing me was unmatchable. I should visit her one day, if Kabir was okay with it. The people I had lost to time, to my impatience couldn't be brought back. But the people I still had, I would cherish them forever. Which was why I was so pumped up to get my position back in Aqeel's life. I would do whatever there was that needed to be done. Even if my ways were a little questionable and mean.

I was busy having my lunch and daydreaming and breaking a rule *I* made. As I failed to realise that Shruti was present there, she had knocked a few times before coming inside. She said she came over to show some of the new designs her team members were working on. I asked her to leave the samples on the table and that I would check them after lunch. Though there was more she wanted from me. "Can I ask you a personal question? I don't mean to disturb you during your lunch but I won't get any more chances so…" She gave me those puppy eyes and I couldn't refuse. "Shoot! Before I change my mind." I said "Do you actually *love* Mr Aqeel?" She asked. "What?" I almost spit out the food. "I am sorry to intrude, this is your personal matter. But I am asking you because I have seen Mr Aqeel with that Rj at a cafe and they seemed like a couple to me." She nervously gulped "First of all it's none of your business, next I know he is seeing Haniya but nothing is permanent." I remarked. I realised how loosely I was handling my employees, that they had started behaving as if they were family and not just employees.

"I am sorry again, it was not my place to speak. Though as a friend and not as an intern/ employee I would suggest you to not force him into loving you. People leave when they are forced to do what they don't wish to do. He didn't seem to like all this chaos." She continued with her opinion about something she knew very little of. "Enough! off you go now." My blood was boiling, not because Shruti had overstepped her boundaries, she did, but what angered me more was that everything was true. Aqeel must be hating me now. For all the years I had been alone, he had been alone too. I might have dated a few guys here and there but he stayed single. I didn't know the reason behind it, he could have dated or married. And yet he didn't, and in all these devastatingly long years, it was the first time that he had shown interest in a woman other than me. Which hurt me like needles. I couldn't bear it. I knew I was hurting him, but I was doing all of it to bring him closer to me. Wouldn't he be happier with me? His first love rather than Haniya, a fling? We could even marry each other, travel the world, he could write and paint and teach and cook whatever pleased him and I could work, I could design, Clothes and our life alike. Marry? Yes, I could be so much happier with him as my partner, as Ammi suggested. As Abbu did even now. And If Aqeel had any problems, or did I, we would work on it together. Besides, I was not going to change anything after a teenager decided that My friend, My childhood companion, was upset because *I* confessed to him about *my love. Fake confession.*

I was tired after the day's events so I packed my stuff and got ready to leave. As my assistant, Kabir was driving me home. I went outside and saw that he and Shruti were having a conversation, they were batchmates so it was a regular. I signalled him to come with me. He hurried off towards me breaking off whatever they were talking about. I told him I was to head home early so he should go and get my car.

After a few minutes he showed up in the front driveway. I pulled a shotgun as usual, as I hated leaving him all by himself in the front. He was my assistant but he wasn't obliged to drive me, it was a driver's job. Also because I enjoyed our banter. Though today, something took over Kabir, maybe it was Shruti's influence. He talked about my apartment and some work that was due, about my father and all. I didn't suspect anything as he was doing my work and he had the right to discuss it with me. But when he brought up today's events. I was starting to get curious. Maybe Shruti told him something about our conversation and he was planning to finish what Shruti had started. Maybe they ganged-up against me? It could be true. They were college students. Don't all of them do that? Make little groups and protest for their rights? But in this case they were protesting for what? Aqeel? Did they even know him? If they had, they would have known why I was doing this.

He straight up asked me " Did you call them? The paparazzi?" He then added " It's very common for people like *you* to do that, whenever there is something you want to brag about or a new piece of information you want to deliver. So did you do that intentionally?" He asked, carefully shifting his gaze from the road to me and then back at the road.

"Are you accusing me of putting *my* friend in an awkward situation?" I questioned back, instead of a reply. I didn't owe him an explanation, nor did I owe anything to Shruti. "I am not accusing, I am merely asking. If you don't intend to answer I'll assume it's a yes." He said, while his muscular and veiny hands moved on the steering wheel. I couldn't help but notice them. Wasn't he supposed to be a boy? Then why were his features so *manly*? I shook my head to remove these thoughts before answering him. "Why are you doing this? I mean what does it matter to *you* if I did call them. I am doing this for him." I stated.

"Accept it. Accept that you are doing this for yourself. I will try as much as possible to not cross my boundaries though as your assistant I am worried for you and your reputation." After a pause he went on again "It was me, not Shruti who saw Aqeel with that girl. They really looked happy and then this happened. Today too he looked tense and worried about all of this. He is your friend, and I think you would want him to be happy instead of brooding upon this chaos. If the paparazzi knows, or your friend opens his mouth in front of the people. Your name will be ruined. You will be called out for creating this mess, and snatching Aqeel from his girlfriend." He nodded as if agreeing to himself. I very well knew what might happen, if people get to know what I was doing with Aqeel and Haniya. But they'd also understand that I was in love with Aqeel for which I was ready to go to lengths. Aqeel would realise it and maybe he'd consider leaving Haniya for good. On the other hand, I thought I was going crazy, considering the side effects of my actions. I should have known better, I should have warned Akriti before calling her that I meant no harm to Aqeel's name. He shouldn't have faced this all. The media and their competitions… All of them were fighting for the latest spicy news, scandals and downfalls of people like me. I had caused a great deal of difficulties for Aqeel these past few months so I had to come up with a plan which was less risky. I didn't even know why I needed to do this. It should have been easy. I was his childhood sweetheart, but it seemed like Haniya was successful at replacing me. Aqeel wasn't paying attention to me anymore. Why did he have to realise that he needed a partner after all these years of confinement? Couldn't he try again? couldn't he consider proposing to me again? trying his luck for the second time. When I was at his doorsteps, well technically my letter, still he could have thought that 'oh my god, my love is coming back in my life, she remembered me and I should try confessing again. What can go wrong, maybe she'll ghost me for another 5-6 years but I'm used to it so it shouldn't hurt much. I can wait for her to change her mind and finally see me as a perfect partner.' I know he wasn't a pick-me teenager, but couldn't he?

But no he didn't think like this at all. In Fact he thought 'Oh so my crush has finally reverted back to me with kindness and I must look elsewhere for a not so worthy girl who loves reading romance books written by me where the character doesn't get a happy ending and dies in a car accident.' I sound so bad, when I said all this. But this was exactly how I was *feeling*. Why wasn't I given a second chance? *Was I not worthy enough of his love?*

And with a whoosh I was back in the reality of this world. Car Accident. I zoned in. Kabir was panicking, he had hit someone. Maybe, or was about to. I didn't know what happened but we were out of danger. I was so observant in my own mind that I didn't even realise anything. And when I looked towards Kabir, he was stepping out of the car. He had stopped the car mid road, people complained from behind and honked several times. I was still unaware of what exactly happened. As I peeked through the window, *there* he was picking up a small puppy. I put the pieces together, the puppy must have ran in front of our car. Kabir must have hit the break at the right time and the puppy was saved. People looked at the scenario and continued complaining saying that he shouldn't be blocking the entire road just because of a puppy. Something snapped in me. I opened the door and went out.

"Hey! You. Stop honking the car right away or I'll break your window glasses."

"You should consider talking to your *boyfriend* and tell him to clear the road. We don't have forever to save this roadside trash."

"Mind your words or I'll break your bones too. Who are you to call this harmless animal 'trash'? It is *you* and your mindset that is trash. Wait here, till it is rescued or you'll be the one below my car." I threatened.

I heard Kabir calling my name from behind. He was holding the puppy in his hands who was smothered with mud. I went back and sat inside the car. Kabir came inside and sat, still holding the puppy in his hands. I stretched my hands towards him for the puppy, as he was the one driving, so I should be the one holding the puppy. Our hands brushed and it coloured my hands brown. Kabir took out his handkerchief and wiped his hands clean so that he could drive. All the while, my eyes didn't move an inch from his veiny hands. They were too distracted and what he did just a while ago was impressive. When he glanced towards me, I flinched. I had to look normal, as if I wasn't just eying his hands. I fished out some napkins for myself and placed it on my lap so that the puppy could sit there without getting my dress dirty. I started cleaning the puppy and my hands, trying to look busy. Thankfully Kabir wasn't suspicious and started driving.

"Why did you scold that illiterate man so much?" I jumped when he suddenly asked me that. A small smile tugged on his lips.

"As you mentioned, he was *illiterate* and deserved that scolding. How could he dare to name this cute little thing 'trash'." I nudged the puppy's nose with my own. Kabir told me that there were some older dogs who were chasing him, which was why he came in front of the car. The mud was ruining my white shirt, the napkins didn't help much, but why would I care when I had such a pretty thing in my hands? I looked at him, and he was scared. At first the dogs chased him and now he was in a stranger's hands, he must have been scared. Was Aqeel scared too of what I might do next? Was he nervous that he would lose Haniya if he tried to save me and lose *me* if he tried to stay with Haniya? These thoughts kept eating at me and made me dizzy. It was then that I felt two gazes on me, first the puppy who was trying to understand who I was and the other was Kabir's.

For a second, my heart jumped and then tumbled back to its place. This guy right beside me wasn't good for my heart health. He was looking at me, maybe he *was* for a few minutes. I opened my mouth to say something but couldn't. When I looked around we were in a parking lot. My new apartment's parking lot. We had reached. And I failed to realise my surroundings, again. I felt Kabir watching me, still.

"Are you okay?" He looked really concerned.

"No" I almost said. I almost let the tears from my eyes roll down, but then held it back. "Maybe" I replied.

"Should I call your dad? You don't look okay. You were quiet all the way, in a way where you looked dead. I tried to talk to you a few times but you just didn't respond. I am sorry if I made you think a bit more about this situation. I shouldn't have stepped in at all, it is your life and you can do whatever with whoever you want." he said.

"No, it's okay. And don't call my dad or else he'll get worried."

"Fine, I should leave then. Will you take care of the dog or should I take it with myself?"

"I'll take it with me." I said and he replied with a nod and then stepped out.

"WAIT!" I called him. He was just about to take a right turn when I stopped him. He turned towards me and then waited. I walked towards him with the puppy in my hands. " Can I pay a visit to your place? I mean I have wanted to meet your mother for a little while so…" The sun excruciatingly painful to my eyes made me squeeze it into tiny slits.

"Of course you can. My mother will be delighted to have you home." I sniffed and pulled back the tears forming in my eyes and nodded. It wasn't the sun, but I could always blame it. "Tonight then, I can have dinner there, *if* you are okay with it."

"Yeah, yeah sure! should I come pick you up?" He asked, rather politely, in a gentleman's manner. Was he capable of doing so?

"No no , that won't be necessary. I can drive there. Just tell me the address… and thanks for today." I didn't know why I thanked him but looking at that puppy's face, I was less troubled.

DINNER AT KHAN'S

Alaia

Within two minutes, Kabir texted me his address. I never knew he lived so far from here, it was an hour ride by car. After dropping me off, he must have travelled by bus. He could use a car, maybe I should lend him one. He worked for me so it shouldn't be a lot. After I said goodbye to Kabir, I headed up to my apartment. I was mentally and physically tired and as always a good shower would fix me. So I took the puppy with myself and gave it a nice wash. After coming out of the shower, I gave some chopped veggies to the puppy. Unfortunately I didn't have any dog food, how was I supposed to know that I was bringing one home? If Ammi was here, she would have been furious and by the next minute, both me and the dog would be sitting outside. She didn't like bringing dogs home, but cats were fine with her. That's how Aqeel managed to have a pet cat for a while before she died. Dida only liked farm animals, like goats and chickens in the house. She always had one pet around. But never allowed Aqeel to bring inside a cat, so he hid his pet in our place. I was not fond of cats, though they weren't much trouble. They would just find a place and sit there all day or run around Ammi and Aqeel. I never bonded with that cat so when she died, I never felt sad. In fact I was relieved that I wouldn't have to clear her litter box. Although it was worse for Aqeel, he cried for a week straight. Though dogs had always been my favourite, but I never came across having one as a pet. Now when Ammi was not around, maybe I could have one. She wasn't here to complain that dogs were filthy and she won't be able to pray without cleaning every inch of the house first. I didn't pray, so I need not to clean every bit of the house. *This dog* was free to roam around everywhere, literally everywhere. He could even come to my office, and I would be delighted.

Along with the address Kabir had told me the time, 8 pm he said. I usually had my dinner around 10-11pm. But I'd have to respect the host and their time. By the time I had cleaned myself and was cozied, it was already dark outside. And I would have to leave an hour before the scheduled time so before that I had an hour to get ready. It was going to be my first time at

Kabir's place so I must dress nice and decent. Ammi always, always urged me to wear a traditional salwar suit whenever I was to visit a family member's house to show my respect. Kabir's mom was not my family but she was to Kabir, who I was attached to as a boss. Also I belonged to one of the most successful and beautiful clothing brands to ever exist. The pressure was intense if one couldn't figure it out.

I browsed through my wardrobe, which wasn't that big as I only got to wear my clothes twice before they went out for charity. So I had a handful of clothes that stuck with me throughout, some of them were Ammi's. I couldn't find anything similar to my thoughts, and this wasn't the time where I would get to show my creativity. I had very little time. And the majority of Ammi's wardrobe was at Abbu's place, which could have contributed right now.

Nonetheless, I got an amazing idea. I did my makeup as subtly as possible and took the dog with me to Abbu's. Thankfully my place was near to his. I reached there in 20 minutes, He was surprised to see me there but I had little to no time to explain it to him. So I straight up went inside, dropped the dog in the living room where Abbu was enjoying his Cricket match along with his buddies and some popcorn. I dressed up and said goodbye to Abbu. I asked him to give some food to my dog and that I would pick it up later. Strangely Abbu didn't ask me anything about where I was headed and why I was wearing my Ammi's peach coloured embroidered saree? The blouse was a little tight, but the saree looked fabulous. I must have gained weight or else Ammi and I were nearly the same size. As Ammi always said, I looked good in a bun. I made a loose messy bun not because of the aesthetic but because I was running out of time.

Wow! Why was I trying so hard to impress someone who was already so impressed by me? By someone I meant Kabir's mom, as he said she adored me. I need not have prepared so well, it was just a friendly visit. I was not used to wearing a saree so the fall kept coming off. I couldn't afford such distraction while driving the car so I tucked the loose edge of the fall at the other side of my waist. Draping the saree wasn't a problem for me, as I had done it so many times before, for others but today I couldn't find any safety pin. If I had, this fall wouldn't keep coming off. I was afraid of having a wardrobe malfunction and embarrassing myself in front of everyone. But I had to focus on the road. My nervousness made the roads and turns look longer and frequent than it was. Half of the time I was worrying about being at the wrong place, or taking a wrong turn.

Even though I had the google map opened in front of me, I had to stop and ask pedestrians about the location several times. At last at 8:30 Kabir asked me about my whereabouts and I told him about my situation. It came out that I *did* in fact take a wrong turn and then I was moving in a circle. Nervousness can do this to you, Kabir told me. I remembered how I used to scold Aqeel everytime he got lost. He wasn't good with directions, and I was afraid I took this trait from him. I now realised how much I was influenced by him. Anyways Kabir guided me towards his house through call, till I saw him waving at me. He asked me to park right in front of their porch, and I did. It was a two story house, he told me they lived in the ground floor and the upper floor had been rented out to someone else. It was a nice and cosy place, there were sea shells hanging from the door frame. Kabir told me that his mother was inside her room getting ready, so he gave me a small tour until his mother arrived. After entering through the front door, there was a living room cum dinning. With a dining table in the middle, a sofa set at the far right corner with a tea table in front of it. Other than that they had Three bedrooms, one belonged to Kabir's parents and one to him. The third one I guessed was left for guests. And then there was a huge kitchen facing the dining table and a bathroom at the left corner. There was a staircase too on the left corner of the house, which led to the other floor and the terrace. But the tenants used the staircase outside the house, a metal one. To keep the privacy intact, of course.

It was my first time there, but the place looked homely and peaceful. There was minimal furniture but it looked aesthetically pleasing, everything was covered with a white crochet piece of clothing. The designs were old fashioned, though it radiated love and care. Not at all like the furniture I had in my new apartment. Which were expensive and new but looked cold and distant to me. My attention was fully towards the interior, and I had no idea where Kabir's was. I think it was on my *waist*. Which was visible as I had the fall tucked in. I looked at him, slowly checking me out while he explained to me about their house and when It was built. Who would tell this shameless guy that I didn't care about the house now when I saw him checking me out without a care about this world. I snapped my fingers at him, to divert his attention towards my face. "It's rude to stare." I retorted. "Sorry!" he smirked. "You can compliment me if you want, just don't stare. It gets on my nerves." I suggested. "You are a compliment to yourself." he bit his lower lip to suppress another smirk. What? I mean, I knew I was beautiful but this was something new to me. I couldn't help but chuckle. "You don't have to flatter me, you are a permanent employee. Don't worry about your job, I hate fake people." I said. "I thought you liked people who sugarcoated their words rather than tell the truth. Besides, I didn't say it to flatter you. I said what was true to my eyes." He smiled. "Ah, that. I didn't mean it in that way. Yeah, I like people who *know* how to talk to their superior, but I didn't say that I liked people who licked their dust." I said. He chuckled a little before saying "Sorry for being so intrusive this afternoon. I didn't mean to. But I just felt like you did this for a reason that didn't include love. If you did love him, you would have preferred to share it with him first. Anyways, it was not my place to suggest anything as I barely know your situation."

"Yeah, you shouldn't have said anything. But you did, and now you can't go back in time to fix it. You know, your words affected me alot and I started overthinking about it. But then I realised that this was my and Aqeel's problem. I know him, and you don't. So I need not have worried myself that much." Deep down, I knew I was wrong. And yet I was ready to be the vamp, if it meant that I'd get my friend back fully to myself. Yes, I was being possessive. So what?

Kabir's mother came out of her room by the time we were done with the tour. And oh my god, she looked *gorgeous*. I did imagine her being pretty looking at how *handsome* Kabir was, but this much? She wore a simple salwar suit and had her hair in a braid covered with the loose edge of her dupatta. But she looked really pleasing to my eyes. She wasn't what I had imagined exactly, I thought she would be the chirpy kind of woman. Though she looked far from that, she looked decent and welcoming.

Something in the air made me greet her with ' Assalamualaikum' and not a hi/ good evening. It felt like a decade since I had greeted someone like that. Ammi used to insist upon greeting elders and youngsters equally alike. But since she was dead, those etiquettes were also long gone. I almost felt like I was looking at Ammi, the dressing sense was entirely different but the aura was similar. Ammi was more into embroidered, and bright coloured clothes. Even though She used to wear Salwar Suit, it had to be the best and eye-catching. But Kabir's mom was the type of person who would choose comfort over style and simplicity. At that moment I was proud of her, looking at her own style, she did a good job at styling Kabir.

Also I got the hint that she didn't get to fulfil her dreams and had to respect the society by wearing decent clothes. Ammi was exactly opposite, she would fight for her style and her own opinion. She wasn't the type to get under someone's shoe.

Rozy aunty, I had asked Kabir about her name, asked me to sit down and gave me a cooling welcome drink. "Sorry to make you wait, I thought you would come late as you might be busy. So I used that time to get ready, well just had to change into better clothes thats all." She said with a nervous smile.

"No it's completely fine, I got a nice house tour. I have to say your house really is pretty. My Ammi would have given anything to stay in a house like this."

"Well the credits are for Kabir's dad to take, I never ever lifted a hand. All these tapestries, croquet covers were made by my mother-in-law. And my husband didn't want to let go of it. The house itself belonged to my Father-in-law. So you can say that we are merely taking care of their property."

The conversation carried itself from the sofa to the dinner table, Kabir was mostly silent. He nodded once in a while to agree with his mother, and when his mother told something embarrassing about him he would laugh it out. I talked to her without worrying about anything, as she didn't seem to be the judgemental kind of person. Instead she was really cool to discuss the latest trends, fashion, work and food. I was regretting the fact that I didn't take anything as a gift to present to her. She had been looking after me for so long now, sending food regularly and stuff. I thanked her for her hospitality to which she dismissed saying that I was like a daughter to her and she would continue to look after me as a mother. I couldn't be any more thankful than I already was. I realised that she didn't think of me as someone very special that you needed to impress or something. Rather she was really calm and it looked like I was just meeting a relative and not the mother of one of my employee's.

I remembered one time, Kabir had told me that his mother wanted a daughter. Maybe she was just treating me like her actual daughter. I felt at home, and not intimidated at all. I had thought that she did what she did to secure Kabir's job. But now I knew, she just liked what I did for a living, which was something she had imagined for her daughter and son. It was surprising how people who cared for you, looked out for you and actually supported your career didn't differentiate you among others. They won't praise you for your achievements, they won't say oh my god! you are so hard working and talented' straight to your face. Rather they'd stand behind your back to support you, they'd encourage you towards a better future, they'd mock you a little but also they'd hold your hands throughout the journey. They'd talk about your achievements behind your back, they'd proudly tell everyone how good you were. Perhaps, Rozy aunty was one such person, she didn't say a word of praise for me or my looks.

"Why have you tucked your fall?" Rozy aunty asked. Due to the recent happenings in my life, I had become an absentminded person. "Oh! I couldn't find a safety pin in my dad's place and the fall kept slipping from my shoulder so.." while we shifted towards the sofa after finishing our dinner. Aunty was preparing some dessert, while she asked me about my saree.

Later she took me inside her room and taught me to fix my saree to fall on my shoulders using a hairpin, brooch and other things that could substitute for a safety pin.

"Is this saree from Singhania's?" She interrogated me.

"Yup! Straight outta my mother's collection." I smiled, feeling proud of my mother's collection.

"It's really pretty, I could not even imagine wearing it."

'Why so?"

"My mother-in-law would never let me wear anything but a Banarasi saree. And now that she is not alive, I have become old enough to just wear decent clothes."

"Well, what does a saree have to do with being old? Look Sarees are a never ending trend and forget about people who bring you down. You have gotta wear whatever you want."

"Leave me as I am, Kabir is getting bigger and bigger. Will it look nice if I start wearing attractive clothes at this age? my husband would want the opposite. I am glad that he didn't push me to wear a burqa, I had nothing against it and I know we should cover ourselves but still."

"Fine, I'll not force you but I promise one day, you'll have to wear clothes of your choice and not others. I'll make sure of that." I gave her a mischievous grin. "By the way aunty, sorry for inviting myself over. But I really wished to meet you in person after how you took care of my lunch and other things. I mean, I used to have take outs and usually dined in restaurants for dinner and skipped meals because I didn't have enough time or cooking skills. Though you saved my diet by providing me with packed food. No one would do that for a person like me. But you did." I said.

"Hey! It's okay. I was upset at Kabir for not inviting you over. I am glad that you were smart enough to do it yourself. I asked him a few times, but he told me that you would be busy and wouldn't wanna come. He should have known better. I wanted to meet you for a while now, after you kept him at this job. He could never get this job on his own, if you didn't give him a chance. He doesn't care about his degree at all, and only goes to the university because I asked him to. Who does that? He could have retaliated and said that he wanted to go to a business school instead of Fashion. But he was dumb enough to obediently follow my wish. When he told me you were helping him learn about business. I couldn't be more grateful to you. You know he tends to be a little sacrificial, and doesn't care about his own." She kept going on and on about Kabir and I heard her with a smile.

After our mother-daughter gossip, Aunty insisted Kabir drop me home as it was late although it was past duty hours and Kabir need not do anything. But her being a stubborn mother, she didn't listen to me. And Kabir had to step outside the cosy little corner of his house at 11pm in the night. I asked him to take me to Abbu's place first so I could change in my usuals and pick up that puppy. It was in dire need of a name. Kabir drove me there, I said it would take me only 10 minutes before I'd be done there. I would have asked him to leave but he wouldn't have any transportation at this time of the night. It was around midnight, though he said he would manage. But I didn't want to cause him more difficulties than I already had. So he followed me to Abbu's place, where Abbu urged that I stay there just for the night. He wished me to spend some time with him. I couldn't say no, or you could say that I was forced to say yes by Abbu and Kabir, both of them. So I stayed there, and asked Kabir to take my car. He would come again the next morning to take me to the office.

Strangely Abbu promised me that he would not talk about my marriage or blind dates at all. We sat near the balcony in the late monsoon wind, sipped some green tea and talked. About Ammi, stars, weather and my mood lately. He was well aware of the situation, he didn't question me though. Merely warned me to not hurt Aqeel for the second time. I myself never wanted to do that, we already went through alot. It was strenuous to even get back where we stood now. Abbu knew of my guilt, of my desperation for the friendship we had forged. He admitted that he was getting old and ill, he was never the guy to do so. He would always say, he was young and fit. He did look young and fit, though now when he mentioned. I saw that he had gained weight, he looked swollen at some parts of his body. He had always worked out and maintained a good diet. Maybe he was worried about me, I was not going very smoothly on my path at this time. Or it might be that he just forgot about his health and let loose playing cards with his friends and watching Cricket. We chatted till 3 am in the morning and then went to sleep. I slept in the spare room which he had prepared for me hoping that one day I would show up. I tried sleeping but couldn't, the visit to Kabir's place proved to be a little soothing. Still as soon as I was out of there I was back in my old mood. I kept thinking about stuff, Aqeel, Haniya, Rozy Aunty and Abbu. I had some people I could count on, friends or nemesis; they still existed. There were others too, who I barely mentioned, Marina, Shruti, Kabir. They worked for me, but they had my back and I knew it. I paced around the house, looked for some snacks in the pantry, and fridge. Found some Namkeens and Liquor. Strange. I didn't know when, but Abbu picked up drinking. Maybe to soothe his lonely heart or to give company to his friends. This explained now, about his health. I should have known better, should have came here before. Should have talked to him, comforted him as I was not the only one to lose a dearest one.

It was around 5 am, and I was still awake. Found some really nice pictures of our family trips, which we had enjoyed together all three of us. There were my childhood pictures too and 8/10 of them had Aqeel on it too. Sometimes smiling, sometimes hiding and other times looking at me. Then I heard something, maybe a clatter. I thought that my puppy woke up, he had been asleep throughout the time I was there that night. I checked for it but no sign of him. And again I heard something, my name. Abbu was calling me. His voice was in pain. Barely audible as if he used all his energy to call for me. I ran towards his room and saw him lying down clutching his chest. He was in pain, and I saw a relief in his eyes as he noticed me. I went towards him and inquired what had happened. I knew he was in pain but what kind of pain? I had no idea. Or you can say I didn't want to admit it just now. I hoped for it to be a minor ache in the chest, because of gas. But then he was struggling, to even draw a breath. I asked him if he had any medicines. I looked for it but all the drawers were empty. Helplessly I called for the ambulance. I didn't have my car, nor could I have carried him down alone. It seemed like an eternity before the ambulance came. I prayed while I tried to soothe him, comforted him. Checked everywhere, gave him a tablet which was meant for gaseous problems. Hoping for a miracle that something would make him hurt less. But nothing helped, at last the ambulance came and took us to the hospital.

'Oh Allah! I know I had neglected you, but please spare my father. Please don't take him. You already have my mother, at least leave my father with me. I know I am not a good daughter but please forgive me, just this time.' I clutched my chest, my eyes burning from the salty tears. I couldn't lose another parent. This was all my doing, if only I looked after him, stayed by his side after what happened to Ammi. No, this couldn't be happening. Allah won't do this to me. Allah would forgive me for I had neglected him long enough. But I was still a human, a child.

Nothing seemed to help, I needed someone. To stay by my side, I couldn't handle my father in this position alone. I called Aqeel. Once, twice and the numbers piled up to twelve calls, and he didn't pick. I understood, he had blocked me. Of course he would, *I* had snatched his chance to be with the person he really wanted to. I was the worst person in this planet right now.

My last option, I didn't expect anything. He was merely an employee, my assistant. I called him and he picked just after the third ring. I was relieved, and nervous too.

"Good morning, what do you need at this hour?" He asked me drowsily.

"Kabi...Kabir my father..." I broke into another sob.

"Hey, hey. What happened to your father?" He was now alert.
"He is in pain, his chest is aching. I hope it's not a heart stroke." I sniffled

"Yeah, it might just be because of gas. Don't worry. Have you called the ambulance?"

"Ikr! it must be because of gas, I gave him a pill to ease his pain. But It didn't help. I am headed to the hospital right now. Can you come?" It was not a question, I wanted him to come.

CONSEQUENCES

AQEEL

Was this how the Universe was going to treat me? Strip every ounce of love, every person I loved from my life like this. At first my parents, Alaia and then Dida. Now I was on the brink of losing that one person I found after so many years of being alone and unloved. I was not mad, nor upset with Alaia. I was simply ashamed of her. I knew she was lonely too, but wasn't this too late? What did she think I would do? run after her like a dog chasing its master? I had loved her deeply, but through the years that love ripened and then decayed as there was no one to pluck the fruit out. After all these years, she came back. Hoping for what? that I would fall in love with her again? I'd embrace her, after the humiliation we both had to suffer? Her engagement got called off, with a person who didn't even trust her enough to question me. He just left her, because of me. What did I have to go through? I lost the one and only friend I would have trusted over my life with my silly confession. I was like a tea cup, which was getting filled with her love daily. And then one day, the limit was crossed, I couldn't watch her getting engaged to someone unworthy of her. Not that I thought I was worthy enough, she was the sunshine of our life. And I used to stay under the shadow casted by her brightness. I loved it there. Though that day, I gathered enough courage to come under the light, and got burned by it. I ruined every possibility, and then I was left alone. With no family members by my side. She had me to blame, And I had myself who was the sole cause of those events. I lived with the guilt for years before finally acknowledging that there was nothing I could have saved. If I had chosen any other day, things would have ended up the same. Her getting angry at my confession, then yelling at me for misinterpreting her casualness. I knew I got ahead of myself, took her frankness, sunshine behaviour as the cause of my disaster.

Should I still be sad? Should I have written her an apology letter?

I did, Many times. Through my poems, through my stories. Which she never read, never appreciated. Should I have loved her still? so that I could finally get a happy ending with the person *I* cherished the most? Why did the world have to go through its phases? Couldn't the fruit stay fresh for an eternity? so now when she said she was ready to embrace it. I could let her pluck it. I doubt it though. That she loved me. Nonetheless, there was no other reason she would do this filthy act.

I tried calling Haniya many times, but she didn't pick it. I waited outside her studio but no one let me in. It was her command, and I couldn't gather enough courage to show up at her doorstep. I left messages and emails, I spammed every account I could have my hands on. Though it seemed like she didn't care. Why would she? She had warned me about Alaia. She had told me that Alaia was coming for me, that she *wanted* me back in her life. I had thought of something else. I thought Alaia wasn't that type of person, though I was wrong. Now my curiosity lied in her, Why was she doing this? What did she really want with me?

I gave up. If Haniya was going to hear me, this wasn't the time. She needed to prioritise her decisions too. Either she could ghost me and leave me for her own good or she could support me while I dealt with this mess created by my own friend.

People kept tagging me everywhere, so I changed my privacy settings on Instagram and twitter. But I couldn't stop the news, this was the time I regretted not having an assistant. Or a lawyer. Anyone who could have helped me out of this. I overestimated my own skills. I couldn't deal with the media, the people, the accusers, the fans and Alaia, alone. I needed help. But in times of need, everyone happened to be busy. Not that they were excusing themselves out though. Haniya was upset and Roop was busy with his own wife and family problems. I didn't have anyone to count on, other than them. And I was not going to take help from any of my colleagues, not in this life at least.

It was getting stressful so I put my phone on Airplane mode and hid it inside my closet. It was dinner time, but I couldn't even swallow water so forget about eating the oats chilla I made. I put it in the fridge, as it might come handy at odd hours when I'd get hungry. A good cold shower might help relax my rather tense shoulder and forehead muscles, so I went inside my bathroom and let the shower run. I was still halfway shampooing when the doorbell rang. If I tried calling out to whoever was outside, it would not help as the sound would barely go outside. I increased my pace and washed my head. The person on the door must be an impatient being as no matter how fast I tried to wrap my towel around, that person kept ringing the bell. Then a thought crossed my mind. What if we were on yet another emergency? Or it could be Haniya. I was already a clumsy person to start with, but when put under pressure I forgot how to function normally. I didn't want to die nor did I want Haniya to wait outside my apartment as a clueless person. But my stupid brain was malfunctioning, and the towel kept coming off. I couldn't be naked infront of Haniya, nor anybody else. I used a cloth clip to hold the towel in place and ran towards the door when it rang for the 6th time, while trying to not expose myself even more. I fixed the towel tighter when I was at the door. Then after a long deep breath I opened the door for her, thinking she would yell at me for not responding faster. But the last bit of enthusiasm and happiness was drained out of my system when I saw her instead. Ezra, *My Sister*. WHYYY???

I looked at her with surprise. She was surprised too, not because she expected someone else like me but because she had seen me after a decade and I was half naked. I didn't invite her in and almost closed the door on her face because I couldn't deal with her now. Not when my own life was turning upside down because of someone I used to love. But Ezra, like a spoiled rich kid she was, shoved me and entered my apartment without my permission, almost tumbling because of how heavy her luggage was. Did she run away from home? And what did she think she was doing by coming to *my* place? She didn't even remember me, didn't contact me for years just like mummy and now she had the audacity to show up here. I looked at her, and didn't even bother to close the door after me. I wanted her out, I couldn't have her around me.

"WHAT ARE YOU DOING HERE?" I questioned, forgetting about my clothes.

"Can't you see, I am here to stay for a while." She replied.

"And why do you think I would let you do that? Who do you think *you* are?" I pointed at her. My patience and calm disappear into thin air by every passing second.

"*Your sister*, whom *you* abandoned." She protested, hands on her waist. Typical woman.

We didn't realise that we were practically yelling at each other and the front door was open, still. Saroj Aunty who worked at Roop's house as a maid came out of the house to check on us. And to say, the scenario wasn't quite pleasing to her eyes, half naked me with a girl over at my place at such an odd hour, as she murmured complains before shutting the door again. I'd deal with her later. I closed the door before any other neighbour of mine decided to come check on us.

I went inside my bedroom, changed into pyjamas and quickly came back.

"*I* didn't abandon you, yall did. All of you. Mummy, papa and you." I frowned.

"We didn't abandon you, you chose to stay there with Dida. I had nothing against her, but I had to choose mom and dad over her. And you chose Dida over everyone else, Bhai." Her eyes widened, accusing me for all that had happened.

"Don't call me that, 'Bhai'. You don't deserve to. No one else does. You can't just come here and claim me." I warned her. She kept her luggage aside, and settled down on the couch.

"I am not *claiming* you, You are already *ours*. You have always been and we don't need to say it out loud. Besides, I have just come here to help you, to be by your side. Like you have never been for me. You don't know how it is to live without a brother you know you have." She was calmer now.

"Okay... so do you think it was easier for me to live without everyone else? I don't even have Dida anymore."

"Which is why *I* am here, Bhai. I am here for you. Mom sent me here, to look after you. With everything going wrong with you. She wants me to help you, and I *too* want to stay by your side at such difficult times."

"Well, tell her that I am thankful but I don't need anybody's help. I have survived all this long alone and I can go by just fine. So just Leave, okay? I can't deal with you right now."

"If you think you can get rid of me that easily, then you are awfully wrong Bhai. I have come here for a mission and I *will* make sure I come true to my expectations." And with that I knew she wasn't going anywhere, she got that stubbornness from our mother. If she said she was going to do something, she would surely do that even if the universe stood against that. That was the same attitude my father fell for my mother and till this date my mother had him wrapped around her pinky.

Well I figured she was going to be hungry after travelling for 2 hours. I was still an older brother to her, despite the problems between us, I still cared for her, a little, maybe. The traffic of Kolkata would beat Mumbai's after some years. I reheated the oats chilla for her, she made a disgusting face after seeing the oats chilla and said "Can't you make something more appetising? I am meeting you after almost a decade and this is how you treat me?"

"Can't you keep your 'Mummy ki pyari beti' in your pockets? I am your brother who you forgot about so don't even try to order me around" I left the chilla on the tea table while she sank on the couch as if the earth was pulling her down and into the core. I knew my couch was comfortable. While she was going to stay over, It was going to serve its purpose as a bed. As I couldn't just drag her out of my apartment *this* late at night. No matter how much I despised having her around when my life was a mess. I didn't want them to think that I was a failure. What did she want with me anyway? What did it mean she was here to help? Why would my mother care for me now when there was nothing left to be cared for? Anyways I pushed aside every question that formed in my head as there was a huge responsibility on my head now. This girl, I even forgot how old she was and how she was going to help me. I counted the years on my fingers, when I went for the second time and my digits were still not enough I figured she was old enough. 23, exactly. The same age as Haniya. I looked at her side and she still hadn't touched that chilla so I figured that I had to make something else. "What do you want to eat?" I half-heartedly asked her. And with just that she smiled the most sunshine smile one could and my heart melted. She then showed me one of my instagram posts. "Make me this, do you have all the ingredients?"

I looked closely and it was the fettuccine alfredo I made six months back. "How did you even find my instagram?"

"You are making it sound as if you are an undercover agent and I won't be able to find you. Besides, I have been following you for years now. It's just that you didn't notice and never bothered to block people you didn't know. You know that by making your account private doesn't ensure your privacy if you still have followers who are unknown to you." She raised her eyebrows in question.

"Don't talk about privacy when you have disrupted mine by showing up here." I couldn't help but laugh. I missed it. The sibling thing. It didn't matter for how long you have been apart, it was all the same. I hadn't spent much time with Ezra when she was growing up. Mummy and Dida had their differences. When Mummy got pregnant with Ezra, I was 6 and that was the time when the differences started growing. Mummy wanted to live separately, Papa tried to stop her but no one could. I loved Mummy but not more than Dida, so I stayed. I had Alaia that time and her presence made everything look small. It didn't bother me that my sister and I were going to have different houses. Growing up those differences that separated Dida and mummy, infected me. I started taking sides and then in the next few years. I was as distant from my mother as the moon is from earth. Ezra and I met a few times each year but that also stopped after a while. And here she was now, at my couch lying down as if it was her den.

I made her the fettuccine alfredo she wanted, thanks to my pantry that had nearly everything. After that I asked her if she needed to wash up. She said yes, so I motioned her towards my bathroom. Till then I made the couch as cosy as possible for her to sleep, and switched on the Ac. I didn't know her preferences, so I just lit one of my favourite scented candles for her. Washed the dishes and cleaned the table. After that I waited for her to come out of the shower. Ten minutes had passed and she still didn't come out. When I went inside my bedroom to check on her. I saw that she was already out and was now lying down on my bed. The sheet was tossed over her and she had circled herself with all the pillows and cushions possible. I was dumbstruck. WHAT IN THE HELL!!!??

"Oh, bhai can you switch off the lights for me?" She pleaded.

Arms crossed over my chest, I stared at her.

"WHAT?" She asked.

I went towards the bed and took a pillow. Threw at her with as much force as I could.

"Bhaii!!!" She screamed.

"What do you think you are doing by taking over my bedroom? I made the couch a cosy corner for you and you are here in my bed. Where am I supposed to sleep then?"

"Go sleep in the cosy corner you set up for me. I am not going to sleep on a couch. *You* are and you will be for the rest of the days I am here."

"Ughhh, I hate you!!"

"Hate you too Bhai, and switch off the lights please." She said while snuggling in.

I knew there was nothing else I could do so I did as she asked. But I wasn't going to let her be at peace, so I switched off the Ac too and escaped. After a few seconds I heard her curse. I rolled my eyes with disgust, but I did curse too, sometimes, rarely.

I slept in the corner I made for her, thankfully my scented candle wouldn't be wasted on her now.

Next morning, I woke up pretty late, at around 11 am. I had a class at 12:30. But since I had my phone inside my closet I didn't hear the Alarm. Ezra was still asleep. I carefully took out my phone so that I wouldn't wake her up even though I wanted to scream and disturb her while she slept. But that would be worse, as I would have to deal with her first thing in the morning.

12 Missed calls from Alaia. Shit.

Maybe she realised her mistake and was trying to apologise. But then a notification popped up on my mobile screen. Live news from the SSKM hospital. The headlines said- " Well- known Fashion designer and owner of NXDE Alaia Mirza's father died out of heart stroke."

A sudden ache in my head made me fall back on my bedside. What was that? Fake news? No it was real. I called Alaia. Busy. So I called Kabir. Busy.

I changed and then grabbed my car keys as soon as possible and then out. I texted Ezra to order something for breakfast or make something in my kitchen as there was an emergency while I walked towards the parking lot. She didn't need details.

FRIENDS FOR LIFE

AQEEL

I thought about what must have happened with Mr Mirza, while I drove towards the hospital. On normal days, I wouldn't mind the traffic but since I was in a hurry, it made me furious. I didn't know the reason behind my impatience, if Mr Mirza had died there was nothing I could do now. He wasn't alive anymore, so he didn't need any help. Just mourners. I was worried, not for him but for his daughter. Mrs Mirza was long dead and now *he* was gone too. Knowing the reason behind his death wouldn't do anything. I wanted to know how *Alaia* was. Even though I was mad at her. I couldn't leave her like that, all alone just like me she didn't have anyone else too. When I reached there, I asked the nurses and other staff about her. They all motioned me towards the morgue. They had shifted him from the ICU to the morgue until all the formalities were done and the dead body was claimed by the family members for the funeral. I saw a large crowd in front of the morgue and in the lobby, mostly *media*. I brushed past everyone until I could see her. There were some distant relatives and friends of Mr Mirza who were being interviewed. I looked past them, and there she was. In Front of the body, she sat with her head well rested on Kabir's shoulders. Tears cascaded down her cheeks, while she held on to her dad's fingers. Someone bumped into me as the crowd increased, it didn't hurt me but out of pure habit an ouch came out of my mouth. She noticed me, and immediately she was on her feet. I looked at Kabir and he looked sad too. Almost tearing up, was it because he got close to Mr Mirza or because he was sad for Alaia's loss? I didn't know and didn't care. Alaia walked towards me as if she was *dead* too. Small and slow steps, one at a time. She didn't have any energy left inside her. Her father had died, the only family member she had. The relatives and distant families didn't matter. Mr Mirza's death didn't trigger any sadness in me but seeing Alaia in pain took my peace away.

To lessen her efforts, I walked with quick steps toward her and when I finally reached her. She grabbed the hem of my shirt and pressed her head against my chest. Those little sobs changed into a loud cry. I hugged her and comforted her by massaging her back. I let her cry as long as she wanted. She didn't speak, just cried. I took her towards the benches and sat with her in my arms. It was about half an hour later that Kabir came with coffee, for all of us. Alaia was still in shock and unresponsive. Kabir told me what had happened. I cursed under my breath as I couldn't help her during that intense time of need. I let my anger get in the way. If only I had picked up her calls, it could have saved her dad. We could have reached the hospital before death could reach Mr Mirza. Though thinking about it, or regretting my actions wouldn't bring him back to life. And if death was in Mr Mirza's fate, we couldn't have done anything to save him. That's how it worked, one couldn't change their fate. What was written would happen despite our protest, the only thing we could do was pray. So I prayed for his peaceful afterlife, and thanked Kabir for helping her.

2 hours later, we exited the hospital. Alaia had filled all the forms and cleared the checks. I helped load Mr Mirza's body in the hospital van. A lady came to give Kabir company and together they organised the funeral back at Alaia's apartment. I rode there with Alaia, she was doing better than before, but not nice. Both I and Kabir went for the burial, and left Alaia with the relatives. The rituals lasted till late evening, and some of the relatives were still there. Some of Mr Mirza's friends were present there too. They all gave Alaia their condolences, and prayed together. I figured out much later that the lady who was with Kabir was his mother. Alaia introduced us, that was when I realised, they knew each other pretty well. Kabir had brought take out so we ate together. It was hard, watching Alaia in that condition. She could barely eat anything. Kabir's mom requested her to eat a bite, but she refused everything. I wanted to embrace her, and give her comfort but I couldn't, in the presence of all the people. I was just a friend and not a blood relative, people would judge Alaia for being close to a male. So all I did was to say the same thing as Kabir's mom. And to my surprise Alaia agreed to eat. As if there was something going on around me of which I had no idea. But was sensed by Kabir's mom, she asked me to feed Alaia. I did, and maybe that made Alaia a little less upset as she ate. I was so grateful to Kabir's mom for that, as I wouldn't have figured this out myself. I realised Alaia needed me, or you could say that *she* wanted me to stay by her side. So I stayed the night there with her, Kabir and his mom left us alone.

The next morning, it felt empty, the realisation hit me like a bulldozer. Alaia wouldn't have a father from this day onwards. While for me, my parents were still alive and healthy with the grace of Allah. I was just too angry and self absorbed to look after my family. But Alaia lost both of her parents and she wasn't close to any of her relatives. For now *I* was her only family and Kabir was very generous being just an assistant to look after her so well. I figured I should tell Ezra about everything, so I called Roop as I didn't have my sister's number. Amazing. Roop went to my flat and connected me with her. She got angry as I didn't inform her earlier and even left her all alone in my apartment. I apologised for my lack of care towards her. Maybe all this was happening to teach me that I *should* look after my family too and Alaia was a part of it.

Ezra told me she was on her way to Alaia's place, she didn't know Alaia much but she felt a connection with her through me so she asked me for the address. Kabir showed up with breakfast, while I was still brushing my teeth. I wonder what was the thing with this guy? why did he keep coming back? I mean he was kind and considerate, but he should know that it was not his responsibility, right? I was beyond grateful for all the stuff he had been doing for us, for Alaia. But shouldn't his work be limited till the office?

Anyways, I woke Alaia for breakfast. And again, she refused to have anything. So I did the same thing as the last day. I asked if I could feed her, after a few moments of thinking and contemplating, she nodded. So I fed her those fluffy chole bhature, Kabir brought. Alaia asked Kabir if it was made by his mother and he replied affirmatively. Maybe Kabir and his mother were a little too involved with Alaia. Should I be questioning that now? Or Should I focus on bettering my own relationship with her?

Eventually Ezra came there too. It surprised me, seeing that she brought some of my stuff as *she* thought I was gonna stay at Alaia's place for a while. It had my tees. Pjs, medicines and toiletries. But she kept something hidden from me in her hands. Which she handed to Alaia.

"I thought this was yours, so might as well give it to you." Ezra told Alaia. I wondered what it was, so I asked Alaia to show it to me. When she opened her fist, it was Haniya's hair tie. I snatched it immediately and wore it on my wrist. Ezra's eyes widened and Alaia was just confused. I didn't want to explain anything so I left the room and took the breakfast plates with me to the kitchen. Ezra followed me there, and sat on the counter.

"You shouldn't take other people's stuff and give it to people who it doesn't belong to." I placed the dishes in the sink.

"If not Alaia, then who does that hair tie belong to? I know you damn well and you wouldn't have a girl over at your place."

Should I tell her? "It's Haniya's" I must have forgotten this hair tie, while showering. But I hadn't forgotten Haniya, she was still my precious. I started washing those dishes to avoid eye contact with her.

"And who is this Haniya?" Ezra asked me curiously.

"Umm, it's not official, but we are seeing each other."

"Oh! Good…"

"What?"

"I said good…"

"Yeah, I got that but what is good? That I am seeing someone?" I placed the lathered dishes separately.

"No. It's good that it is not official."

"If you have got any problems with me seeing Haniya then keep it to yourself, I am not listening to someone who just showed up."

"I don't have any problem with her, for god's sake I don't even *know* her but what I am saying is that you aren't supposed to see anyone."

"And why do you think it should be that way?"

"Well, let me get things straight, bhai. I came here to resolve things between you and Alaia. I have not known Alaia but mummy *has* and according to her you should be accepting her proposal."

I rinsed out the dishes and placed them on the rack.

"I don't get it. Why does mummy think that *I* will need *your* help to get things straight with Alaia? You are just a kid, at least to me. Besides I am not accepting Alaia's proposal as I said I am seeing someone else. Things don't happen this way, people don't just get to show up in your life and own it. And to start with, she didn't even propose to me. She made that statement to the media, and she'd have to take it back as I am not going to entertain these things."

"It's okay Aqeel, you don't need to accept my proposal." Ezra and I both turned back to see that Alaia was standing right by the kitchen door. "I am sorry for messing with you. I shouldn't have told the media about my feelings towards you. I should have said that to *you*. Though, now I am not sure, if it would make any difference"

Alaia left the kitchen, her eyes sparkling with unshed tears. I followed her to her bedroom, where she sat on the edge of the bed with her face covered with her palms. I stood in the entrance not knowing if I was welcomed inside.

"Look, Alaia. I know that your feelings are valid and I don't have the right to say that *you* can't feel this way. But I was finally moving on when I got your letter. Then we met again, and I thought that maybe we could reconcile as friends and this would be our happy ending. I could get away with my life however I wished and you could continue your life without any guilt. I thought maybe, what I did, what happened was long gone and now I could find love again. And I swear to god, I thought the same for you. I hope that you'd find a nice person, you'd get married and have a peaceful life with a fantastic career. But never in my consciousness would I have thought that the person you'd love would be me. This would have been true if I was still that teenage boy who was in love with you, I would have wanted *you* to love me back. Now, I just can't imagine this."

"Do you think I wanted this? No, believe me Aqeel I wrote those letters so that *I* could apologise for my rudeness towards you. That's all. I didn't even hope that you'd reply to me, let alone agree to meet me. But after meeting you, I realised how much I missed you. How much I missed the old you, the one who loved me and cared for me above everything else. It ached me to see you with other people. Isn't that love? I want us to be back together like old times. I want all your time for me. I need you to look at me the way you used to when you were in love with me." She was crying by the time she finished talking. I couldn't watch her cry like that, crumble down like an old rusty building. It was all because of *me*. I believed I was incharge to taking care of her, so I went and sat beside her. Stroked her back with my palms and gave her water. "Who told you that I am leaving? I am here to stay. We don't have to be romantically involved to love and embrace each other. We can be friends, just like old times."

"But then you'll not be mine, you'll belong to someone else. I want a hundred percent of you and not just a fraction."

"No one can fully be yours. We all belong to people in certain amounts, certain fractions. Believe me, even *I* don't own myself. You have to understand that I have already shared a major part of me with Haniya." I kissed Alaia's forehead to provide her comfort even though I knew my rejection would weigh it down.

"It's okay, you don't have to justify to me. I have known you for years. I know I can win you back easily."

"What I think is that you need to rest." I didn't have a reply for what she told me.

"Maybe, but I just woke up. Are you trying to get rid of me by asking me to sleep all day?"

"No, I am just trying to look after you." I gave her a small smile to convince her to rest. She needed it to recharge from the loss she had to suffer. Besides, I didn't want her to waste her time on me. I was not mine anymore, I couldn't just hand myself over to her.

"Lie down and rest. Don't think about me. Think about your dad, and pray for his peace."

"Yes, I will." She replied with a deep sigh. I gave her a nod and then closed the door after me so she could rest for a while. She was already upset about her father and now I had done my part too, at upsetting her. I felt like, whenever I came into her life, I ruined it. I was starting to think that it was a bad idea. Replying to her letter was one thing but I shouldn't have let her come back in my life. I could have ignored it by saying I was still mad at her for rejecting me. I could have played victim there, but I simply chose to accept her apology.

I went back to the living room, Kabir had left for the office and Ezra was sitting there alone. I sat beside her hoping that she wouldn't restart that conversation.

"You got a call" She handed me my phone which was buried somewhere in the sofa. It was Haniya's call, so I took it outside on the balcony. I looked back to check on Ezra and she was giving me the side eye. I mean WHAT?

"Assalamualaikum"

"Walaikumsalam, so you finally decided that I was worth *one* phone call?"
"You are worth more than that, Aqeel. But for now you'll have to deal with a phone call only" A coy smile played along my mouth after hearing about my own worth.

"I tried to reach out to you millions of times, but you didn't respond. Look, I am very sorry for what happened and I am doing everything in my power to resolve things with Alaia. Once she is stable enough to hear me out, I'll convince her to sort this matter out with the media and then we can-"

"I didn't call you to discuss this Aqeel. I am not hoping for anything between us. Alaia loves you and deserves you more than *I* do. I was just an admirer all along, you don't have to talk to Alaia in this matter. I called so that I can sympathise with Alaia's loss. I know you are there with her as you should be. She needs you right now, please say sorry to her on my behalf and give her my regards. And for me, I'll be happy with your memories and the time we spent together. Please don't think about me and give your time to her." And with that she ended the call. Didn't even wait for my reply. I was going to say that *we* could make things official between us once I settled things with Alaia. But it looked like Haniya wanted to end things between us.

'When things don't go your way, understand that something even better was decided for you by Allah' Dida used to say this. But I didn't agree with it. The only good thing that could have happened to me was Haniya and now that particular person refused to stay by my side.

GROUP WORK

ALAIA

After Aqeel left, I laid down in my bed hoping for a sweet dream to take over my consciousness that would haunt me with Abbu's absence. Now that I looked back, I barely paid any attention to Abbu. I neglected him after Ammi died and gave all of my time in building my career. At that time I thought that was the right thing to do, and I would make both of my parents really proud. I thought I did a great job at making this label a success but I failed miserably at being a daughter.

I couldn't sleep given the fact that it had only been an hour since I woke up this morning. So I thought of praying as it was already Zohr and I didn't wanna miss it. It had been years since I last prayed so I forgot even the basics. When Ammi was alive, she scolded me for missing my Salahs but now when she was not there I had completely abandoned Allah. I used whatever knowledge remained within me and searched the rest up on the Internet to pray. For another hour I just cried and made prayers for Abbu's peace and Akhirat.

"Wakeup Alaia, you are going to be late for school" Ammi yelled from across the room. I pulled the sheet over my head, and covered my ears with a pillow to avoid Ammi's scolding. "Wake up!" She snatched my sheet away and turned the ceiling fan off. Being stubborn the way I was, I continued sleeping in the summer heat. Another yell from Ammi and I was awake. Except I wasn't in my childhood room. I was in my new apartment room and Ammi was *nowhere*. The window curtains were open and the room was filled with the last rays of the setting sun. I realised after a few seconds that someone else was in the room too... I looked around and found Kabir standing beside the bed. Waiting for me to come back to earth. "Uh, I am sorry I must have fallen asleep" I straightened out my hair and checked for drool on my face, thankfully there was nothing. I realised I had become extra conscious when I was near Kabir. While in the presence of Aqeel, I was very calm and cool. I thought this was because I believed Aqeel would love me in every condition. But I needed to make an impression in front of Kabir, it was ridiculous, how I behaved sometimes.

"Oh, it's fine. You needed rest." He said.

"Why do yall believe I need more than 10 hours of sleep to rest? I slept perfectly fine last night. I wouldn't have slept but I think I got tired after praying."

"You'd do fine with just 5 hours of sleep but given the situation we just want you to feel fine. And maybe what's lying ahead of you is tiring and problematic."

"Why? Did something happen?" Fingers crossed, I hoped nothing worse had happened.

"Yeah, I went to the office this morning and everything was *wrong*. Do you remember we had a client who gave a wedding order?"

"Yeah man, I completely forgot about it. What happened with that dress they ordered?"

"Well since you weren't available and we were due for delivery today, the other designers completed the dress on your behalf but the client wasn't impressed by that. I tried to talk to them but they insisted on talking to you."

"There isn't anything I can do now, except ask for an apology." I was already upset because of how bad of a daughter I was and now this. It made me even more anxious.

I called the client and till I waited for them to pick up I paced back and forth around my room. Kabir brought a glass of water for me, and God knows I was so thirsty, that it felt like a dessert in my throat. I quickly grabbed the water, thanked Kabir and put the phone on speaker.

After the fourth ring, someone picked up. My hands trembled while I initiated the call "Hello, Hi this is Alaia Mirza. Am I talking to Ms Shireen!?"

"Yes, yes you are. I was hoping to get your call."

"Uh, I am so sorry. I heard what happened with your dress but let me assure you my designers have done an impeccable job and it won't disappoint you." I lied there, I didn't even know how the dress looked after they gave the final touch. Initially *I* was supposed to complete the dress as asked by the client.

"You are not getting it, I saw the dress myself, today when I personally went to pick it up. I was so excited to try my dress out, but it completely ruined my mood. See I know that your works are fabulous which was why I chose your label for my wedding dress in the first place. Though the dress was nowhere my expectations. I am not going to wear that piece of rag, it lacks elegance, modesty and style. And asking for a refund won't get me a new dress before my wedding so I want you to redo this dress for me."

"I wouldn't have let this happen if not for my father's sudden and unfortunate demise. Believe me. I know my work ethics and I try to be as punctual as I can be."

"I do know about your situation and I am deeply sorry for your loss but I just can't negotiate with my wedding dress."

"Well you just have to trust me on this and give me a few more days and I'll deliver the dress on your doorstep."

"Alright but remember that my wedding is just three days later. And I know you wouldn't wanna risk your reputation so I'll trust you just *this* time."

"What do you mean, *risk* my reputation?"

"Well, you know that the media is going to cover my wedding, and you wouldn't wanna see me say shitty things about your label."

"Are you *threatening* me right now?"

"I don't want to, but can't really help if you are being irresponsible. I am simply looking out for you as you wouldn't want people to say that you are compromising your work for some personal problems."

"Well then thank you for looking after me, but you don't need to worry. I'll complete the task I took in my hands." I hung up the call. It had started giving me a headache. Kabir was right beside me, so he heard everything.

"Are you okay? Do you need anything?"

"Yeah, can you please get me a coffee? I think I might have a headache."

"Sure" He started to walk out of my bedroom when I remembered about the puppy.

"Wait!!" I yelled. He turned around to face me. "Yes?" He asked. "Kabir…can you do me a favour?" I asked. "Favour? It's my job to help you." He replied with a smile. "No, I mean. You are already doing so much, besides it's not related to your job. I completely forgot about the puppy you rescued that day. He must be in my Abbu's flat. Can you please bring it here?" I requested. "Yeah sure. But it would be nice, if I take it with me. I don't think you'd be able to take care of it all alone. You are in too much distress right now. Take this time for yourself. Also, you'd be working on that dress. So it's best If the puppy is with me. Give me the keys, so I can pick it up." He said. I gave him the house keys and some cash. He refused the cash saying he didn't need it. But I insisted that he take it. He was doing more than he was supposed to be just an assistant, and I didn't know any other way of showing my gratitude. He'd get his salary as usual, but what he was doing was worth more than that.

I went inside my bathroom to rinse my face with cold water. I wasn't expecting it to be *that* cold, that it enhanced the headache. I came back and lied down. After a few minutes Aqeel came with two mugs of coffee. I took one of them. He sat beside me, the same place Kabir was sitting earlier.

"Kabir told me what happened with that client of yours. How are you going to fix things?" He asked, worry shaping his brow in a frown.

"I already had a rough idea of what I was going to do with the dress, but things took a very bad turn." I looked down at my coffee, trying to hold back the tears.

"Yes, but what I am asking is how are you going to work on that dress? You aren't supposed to leave the house for a few more days. Call it religion or custom. I don't know the actual reason but this is your grieving period."

"Sorry for interrupting, but we can do it from home." We both looked up to find Kabir standing by the door.

"I mean, I can help get your essential stuff here and you can work on it while still grieving your dad." he added.

"It can work, we'll help you finish the work." Aqeel said while squeezing my arm for assurance.

"We can also take Shruti and other's help if you need."

"Yeah, maybe you are correct. I shouldn't worry when I have yall." I smiled knowing that I could trust these people with my life and they would save me.

Aqeel and Kabir both went out leaving me and Ezra behind. Aqeel went grocery shopping and Kabir went to the office for the second time that day to bring all my stuff and the dress. Some relatives and friends came to meet me, or say sympathise with me. I barely knew anyone or forgot who they were as it had been years. The last time I met them was at Ammi's funeral. I had received a ton of wedding invitations since then but I always ignored them. After talking to these people I got to know that my Abbu used to be in touch with them and he went to every wedding and every function he was invited to. These people loved Abbu or maybe they were just really good at pretending. I was doing the same, I put on a fake smile to greet these people. I didn't want to show them how badly hurt I was and why I believed it was all my fault. They didn't have to know everything, every mistake I had made till this date. So the pretending game between us kept on for hours. Ezra kept me company, and ordered take out for these people while I chatted with them half heartedly. Sometimes I hated the fact that I was an extrovert. I couldn't even excuse myself by saying that I couldn't communicate well.

It felt like an eternity when Aqeel came back with groceries. He greeted everyone and headed straight to the kitchen. I followed him there leaving everyone to bicker amongst themselves.

"What are you doing?" I asked.

"Making some dinner for everyone. Kabir said his mom will make us dinner but I just couldn't ask her to do it for us every time."

"I mean it's good that *you* are cooking, I love it. But it's not like she was doing a favour for us. She loves cooking and feeding people. She has been cooking my lunch regularly. At first I thought She was doing it to impress me but turns out she is just a pure soul with a big heart. Kabir gets that from his mother, the caring and nurturing behaviour." I admitted.

"Sounds like both of them love you."

"Kabir's mom? Yes. But Kabir? No, he doesn't love me. Why would he? I mean he is just my *assistant*. His mother is different, you know, she thinks of me as her own daughter." I chuckled.

"I know that he is just your assistant, but look at him, going to lengths for you. Might be respect, I assume he is a fashion student right? He must be fascinated by your work to help you so much with your dad's funeral and everything."

"Yeah maybe, do you know he was the one who worked with my dad to find this apartment for me? I was passing my days in hotel rooms. Abbu asked me to live with him but I ignored his advice as he would *again* ask me to get married. I wonder *if* I had agreed with him, he could have been alive. I could have known earlier about his condition and could have taken him to a better doctor. Did you know he was drinking, and had a heart condition? I didn't. He never told me and I never tried to ask him about his health."

"Things could have turned out to be different, but we'd never know. So don't think about what could have happened, all you need to do is think about your present. And why didn't you listen to your dad? He could have introduced you to potential guys." He said with a goofy grin.

"I wasn't interested in marrying back then." I said.

"Are you *now*?" He interrogated.

"Yeah, if the guy I am interested in, agrees. Then maybe I can think about marrying and settling down." He laughed at my words, not knowing that I was being serious. I wasn't sure about my feelings towards him, I barely believed my own words but if it was *him* I could think about marriage. I let him cook and went back to meet the guest. After a few more hours Kabir came with all my supplies and the dress. Shruti tagged along.

"Looks like we are having a sleepover." Ezra said excitedly.

"Sleepover and work," Added Shruti, with both her hands fisted to show thumbs up.

I couldn't help but smile at their enthusiasm. "Are your parents fine with you staying at my place?" I asked Shruti. "Yeah, I told them I was working overtime. They were happy as I am taking my job seriously." She smiled. "Alright, let's get to work then." I suggested.

"But first dinner." Aqeel announced from the kitchen.

"Yes!" Everyone said in unison. We were starving, after eating just takeouts all day.

We formed a circle on the living room floor. I had a dining table but it was made just for two people and we were *five*. During the move in, I made sure my furniture was as minimal as possible. I never imagined people coming over so it didn't look like a problem to me. Now, we were having to eat on the floor, anyways it felt *homely*.

Everyone was *too* tired to work as they weren't the ones who took an extra long nap this afternoon. So they went to sleep. My apartment was a 2BHK flat, from which, one was my bedroom and the other one was being used by Aqeel and Ezra. I didn't know what to do with Shruti and Kabir's sleeping situation but they figured that the sofa was comfortable enough for them to fall asleep. For a day or two I changed my bedroom into a workplace. I worked on designing the idea I previously had and removed the items I didn't like, added by my employees. It was around four in the morning when the design was finally on paper and the dress was ready to be redesigned by me. I took a break and prayed the morning prayer, then went to sleep.

The next morning I woke up because of hushed whispering outside my room. I went to check outside and saw that everyone was awake and having a conversation without me. They were trying very hard to not make any noise but when four people were talking at a time, it was bound to be noisy. They stopped talking when they saw me staring at them, confused.

"Continue whatever yall were doing. I like it." I found it rather cute.

"Well we were discussing breakfast, I said I'll make it but everyone seems to want a different thing." Aqeel said while shrugging and then he put his hands on his waist like a disappointed mother.

"What are the options?" I asked.

"I want egg toast, Shruti says she'll have anything, Ezra will have garlic bread and Mr Aqeel wants oats." Said Kabir.

"Hey, you don't have to add 'Mr.' Just call me Aqeel." Argued Aqeel, feeling old amongst these youngsters. "Aww, someone is feeling old." I pouted. And everyone laughed at that, we all earned a frown from Aqeel.

"Ezra, good choice. I want Garlic bread too." I pointed towards Ezra. At last everyone agreed on garlic bread so Aqeel went in the kitchen to make it.

"I am coming too" Ezra decided to help Aqeel. It was the right thing as she didn't have anything else to do and Aqeel was cooking for us, alone.

After breakfast, Shruti and Kabir started working on the dress. Since we were busy, Aqeel made multiple rounds of coffee for us and made sure that we were well fed. Ezra was a nice person, I didn't know much about her, but she seemed like a thoughtful person. She was just like Aqeel but with an extroverted personality. She maintained our will to work and kept us entertained. I realised I never really asked Aqeel about Ezra, when did she come and why? I knew their relationship wasn't any good but seeing them bonding over these events made me feel content.

Since the client wanted a modern wedding gown which was modest, I added a waist length jacket to cover the arms. Adding sleeves would give it a simple and basic look, which my employees had done. So I removed the sleeves and made it a sleeveless dress. I kept the dress simple, but did some handwork on the jacket like crystal work and hand embroidered the bride and groom's name on the back. Both the dress and the jacket were ivory white so to spice up the dress I dyed the ballet length veil an ocean green colour. Shruti helped me with the crystal work and Kabir dyed the veil for me. While we worked, Shruti and I discussed work and Kabir had his headphones on. Once in a while he hummed along with the song, and it made all of us laugh at him as he was a terrible singer. But he didn't have to know that.

I took my time to sew the jacket and then do the hand embroidery. This dress wouldn't just be worn by the bride but she'd *own* it. We had done the colour analysis test on the bride before and we'd figured that she'd look gorgeous in that shade of green. We worked overnight to complete the dress and thankfully it was fully ready just a day before the wedding. My mourning period was over but Aqeel said that I should rest so he offered to deliver the dress. Since he wasn't an employee, I asked Kabir to go with him. I would have gone myself as I had promised I would, but after working for two days straight I was really tired and the offer looked tempting. Kabir and Aqeel both drove to the client's house with the dress. I had instructed them everything about how the dress was supposed to look and what they were supposed to do if the client still complained. But luckily the client was impressed by the outcome and accepted the dress with a huge grin. The remaining payment came even before the guys came back with the news so I was relieved.

Our group work didn't go to waste and I was able to save my drowning reputation. This achievement called for a celebration, but just when the work ended I was filled with sorrow again. Sorrow of losing someone who would have patted my back for my hard work. I remained inside my bedroom all day, sobbing. I couldn't help it. Everyone came one by one to soothe my pain but nothing helped. I was able to save my work but I couldn't save my father who had supported a silly wish of a 10 year old kid who wanted to become a fashion designer. I wouldn't be able to see his proud smile, If I *ever* played dress-up again.

FEELINGS

AQEEL

To live peacefully in this world, meant you'd have to be perfect at one thing - Pretending.

Haniya broke something we hadn't even started yet. I was planning to make things official while she ended things between us officially. Could I even blame her for that? My childhood best friend told my potential girlfriend about how I was *obsessed* with her and why I became the reason behind her failed engagement. Then she went on and told everyone about her feelings, literally everyone. All this must have made Haniya insecure about whatever we were going to start. I didn't even know the whole conversation that went on between these two women. I needed Haniya just like I needed my daily insulin shot. Within a short period of time ,she became irreplaceable. Something about her, made my restless heart calm down. She relaxed me, I didn't get nervous around her. It was *nothing* like how I felt about Alaia. Alaia was my adrenaline dose, she made me anxious in a way, a cold coffee would do first thing in the morning. She made my blood rush through my veins, and my cheeks went red every time I used to see her. The puzzling feeling I got whenever she touched me, felt like firecrackers inside my stomach. I felt all the butterflies people talked about. But with Haniya, it was different. She was like the feeling one gets after coming home from a very long trip. I felt like I belonged to her. She radiated a warm energy around her, which smelled like freshly baked bread. She didn't even have to try, but she made everyone happy just with her presence. Besides, what I had with her was mutual. While with Alaia, it felt that we wouldn't *ever* have mutual feelings. When I loved her immensely, she loved someone else. Now when she said that she was in love with me, I didn't feel the same way.

I had to pretend I was fine, all the time I spent in Alaia's house. She was mourning her dad, I couldn't just share my own sorrow with her or show any signs of sadness. It would have been rude, towards her. Plus, if I told her that Haniya was breaking things off with me she would have jumped at the chance. But I was not going to let go of Haniya *that* easily. She was just worried that we wouldn't be able to stay happy when Alaia was here. Or maybe she was worried that I'd choose Alaia over her. Alaia was one of my dearest people, but I couldn't choose just one. I wanted both of them, one as a friend and another as a partner. Alaia would have to compromise her feelings for me, and I was not doing this to get back at her for what she did with me back in the old days. I genuinely wouldn't be able to love her ever again. When I had feelings for someone else.

I stayed by Alaia's side as she needed me. I tried to comfort her whenever she felt down, which was mostly everyday. Though I knew she'd get better, she had far more problems in her life to deal with right now and just not her dead father. That is what happened in this life, you lose someone very precious but you can't lose yourself by wasting your life after them. Alaia was stronger than what I had thought. She was sad, but amongst that sadness she worked day and night to fulfil her client's needs. No wonder, her employees like Shruti and Kabir looked after her. Though I had felt something else too, Kabir acted a little differently with her than other employees.

On our way to the client's place Kabir and I talked. At first it was just small talk, I hated to admit but I had gotten better at small talk. When you meet new people almost everyday because of your job, you get better at things you didn't like. Kabir was pretty chilled out like he was talking to a friend and not someone he met just a few days back. Then the conversation took a smooth turn towards his job and Alaia. I got to know that he was learning business by working with Alaia and him being a fashion student was just a plus point. I asked him if he had any girlfriend but strangely he said no. My colleagues should have been there to hear him. Not everybody needed a partner to feel happy. But who'd want to waste their precious time by trying to explain this to people? I surely didn't. I knew myself and the reasons I stayed single for, but I was a little curious about Kabir. If I judged him by his looks, he seemed like a f-boy, but I knew very well to not judge books by their cover even though they sometimes made sense. I asked about his reason for being single.

"I couldn't find a girl." He replied so fast that it seemed like he had his answer memorised. Of course, people must have asked him this question a million times, like they did to me. As if it was impossible for a guy to stay single and be happy.

"Ehh, that's a pretty bad reason. There are many girls out there, you could even date Shruti." Nonetheless, I was a curious being too. I mean, he could be happy, but why stay single when you are at the peak of your youth? Also because he had the *looks*, girls must have been going crazy after him.

"Haha, she is nice but… not my type."

"Okay, then what's your type?" I asked, curiosity bubbling in my chest. I had a feeling, which was why I was keen into figuring out his interests.

"Mmm, maybe someone who is passionate about what they do. I like career oriented girls."

"I see…What about Alaia?" I purposely asked this question as I knew there was something going on inside his mind related to her. The way he cared for her and looked after her even though he didn't owe her anything.

"Yeah, yeah she seems like the girl I am talking about but.." He stopped mid-sentence as if weighing the words he was about to say out loud.

"Hey, Listen. I am not implying anything here. Don't worry." I dropped the topic as I might have made him uncomfortable.

"No, no it's okay. Though there was something I wanted to ask you too."

"Go ahead."

"Are you going to accept her proposal?" I furrowed my brows at the question. I looked at him and then outside the window. I didn't know what I was going to do. Accepting her proposal meant, I'd have to forget Haniya and if by chance I rejected her. This time it would not only affect our friendship but it would be responsible for her defamation. I didn't want to cause her any difficulties nor did I want to cause one to myself. There were two options in front of me and none of them looked good.

"I have no idea." I replied, still looking at the last monsoon shower of this season.

"Sorry. I don't think I have the right to say anything but I know how much you have loved her." He swiftly changed the gears and drove towards our location. I was surprised not because he told me what he knew, but because I knew it myself. How deeply I had loved her once and now I was thinking whether leaving her would be less painful or accepting her?

He continued saying, "I have been to a few of your library sessions."

Those sessions were rare, but whenever I felt down or had a writer's block. I went to the public library and recited some of my poetries. Those who have heard me recite, must know about my actual feelings behind those words. Those people didn't know that I had written those poems or novels, they just knew my *pain*. The pain I projected through them. "Oh, sad. Sorry you had to bear all that." I chuckled.

"You don't have to say sorry, I enjoyed it alot and others did too. I am not the type to read but I loved those words. They taught me what love actually feels like. Sometimes romantic, sometimes painful. And now that I know you wrote all that for *her*. I have to say you must have loved her the way no one could ever have."

I was tearing up, my past would always be with me like a sweet memory of a candy. It gave me what I had right now, nothing would have been mine if I hadn't embraced it. If only I had given up on everything, forgot about her like an ex you don't want to remember. I would have died slowly, I would have evaporated from the surface. But it kept me going, because I was never ashamed of loving her and a part of me always *knew* I wasn't the guy who'd get the girl. "How did you know it was about her?"

"It's very obvious. Your characters resemble her in a peculiar way where they are her but not exactly."

"You must have observed her very closely to know the true person behind the veil."

"Maybe. Do you mind if I give you a free advice?"

"No, please give me. Your advice might save me from this hell." I laughed again, even though I was serious.

"The girl you are currently with, is very nice. I don't know her but I have seen you with her. And she seemed to make you very happy." He said.

"Right? I knew it." I beamed with joy. We reached our location and that conversation ended there. On our way back we were so happy after a successful delivery that we forgot about everything.

PERKS OF BEING WEALTHY

Alaia

As soon as the dress was complete, we had checked for any alterations and then it was ready to be packed. Shruti had helped me pack the dress and Kabir along with Aqeel loaded the dress in my car. Shruti left for the office and others for the delivery. While Ezra stayed back with me and helped with cleaning all the mess we had created. That was the time when I realised that I needed a maid. While we were busy working on the dress, Aqeel helped clean the house and cooked for everyone else. But I should have arrange a maid who would do all this work as I was no good.

Ezra and I talked about random stuff like movies and clothes that were currently on trend. I found out that Ezra was somewhat like a curious child. She asked too many questions and sometimes it was hard for me to answer all of them. Just like Kabir.

"Can I ask you a stupid question? I am just too curious." She asked while folding my fresh laundry.

"Shoot."

"How much did you get paid for that dress?"

"For that dress? It was around 10 lakhs."

"10 lakhs???" Her jaw almost fell to the floor.

"Yeah, it isn't much you know, if you compare with the other brands." I chuckled after her response and fixed my bed which was more of a trash bin.

"Are you saying 10 lakhs isn't enough? Man..I would have bought a house with that much money. And people are investing that much for a wedding dress?" She was impatiently typing something on her mobile while talking to me.

"As I said, it isn't much. People are spending multiple crores at their wedding which hardly lasts for 5 years. Besides, all that money doesn't actually make it to my bank account. Most of it goes to the suppliers who provide us the fabric and other materials which are sometimes imported. Plus this dress was a customised one, that's why I charged this much."

"Sorry, but I just googled your net worth. I could have just asked, but it seemed too intrusive. Is it really 20 million?"

"Unfortunately yes."

"No offence, but you are being greedy here. 20 million is A LOT."

"Ezra, my dear. You have no idea how this industry works. My label touched the height of success two years back and it's still worth 20 million, and you are talking about Indian Rupees and not dollars. Given the demand and the product I provide, I should have become a billionaire by now." I knew very well that it would take me more time to get what I wanted. I was trying to be on demand and charge less than most of the label's average price rate. So I must be patient with my work and do as it was planned.

"Hold one, I just googled bhai's net worth and guess what? He has a whopping net worth of 2 million?? I guess everyone I know is rich, except me."

"Hehe, anyways, I didn't ask what you were doing? As in your career, except googling our net worth."

"Ahh, me? I am working part time at a cafe."

"And, what are you studying?"

"I dropped out." She scratched the back of her neck.

"What? Why?" I didn't expect this from her, not from someone who was related to Aqeel. He was so studious and his sister dropped out? But I guess, we couldn't compare these siblings. They grew up very differently and in distant surroundings.

"Studying was just not for me." She made a funny face and I couldn't help but laugh.

"Mom and dad refused to support my luxurious lifestyle and asked me to get a job, but with my qualification I was not eligible for a single job so a part time barista was all I could become."

"Are you satisfied with your decision?" I was concerned about what would become of this kid.

"I am, for now, but seeing how much y'all are earning, I am *terrified* with what I did. Looks like I have to do something about it. Shall I look for a sugar daddy?" Her whole being was excited with just the thought.

"Oh my-" I slapped my forehead, feeling disappointed in Aqeel's sister. I always thought that Aqeel wouldn't be able to do anything in his life with the not-so-concerned behaviour but his sister was next level.

"Chill! I'm just joking. I'll see what I can do." She said,

We were still not done with our conversation when those two *delivery* guys came back from their errands. They were tired after working so much, and they hadn't even rested so I asked them to go and sleep.

Ezra and I continued with our chatter now with some soft drinks, the guys had brought while on their way back.

"Well, You didn't tell me *when* exactly you came. I didn't hear about you from Aqeel at all. I thought you guys weren't in touch."

"You are right. We weren't in touch which was the main reason I came back. I told Bhai that I came here for a mission. Which partly included you."

"What do you mean?" I asked.

"As you know that things aren't great between my parents and Bhai. And I was very disturbed with that, all my life, I have wished all of them to get back together like a normal functioning family. So when I dropped out, I had nothing better to do so I thought why not try and talk to bhai. Maybe I'd be able to talk some sense in his mind. Mom and Dad wished the same as me, they are waiting for Bhai to come back but he just won't listen. Also I saw that there were issues between you and him. I have heard alot about you and bhai's childhood memories from mom and dad. They told me *how* inseparable you both were. It was getting hard for me to see him all alone, you know. So I thought maybe I can help y'all. That's all, and I just randomly showed up the night before your father passed away."

After listening to her, all my concerns vanished away. People didn't become successful with just their careers. In order to become a successful person they have to be loving and sympathetic with others' problems. I was only good at my job, but looking at this girl I had come to realise that life was more than just your career. She was doing great at her life, without even achieving anything yet. She had a loving family and a brother who was concerned about her but won't tell. She cared about everyone in her life, even me. I was touched with only her words, no wonder she was Aqeel's sister. They both had a way to touch people's hearts with their words.

"Can I ask you for a favour?" I asked her.

"Yeah sure, tell me what it is about."

"Please take care of your brother, like you are doing now. He won't tell you, but he misses his family too. He won't accept that but you'll have to understand it yourself. It's just that there are misunderstandings between your mother and him. If you can try and resolve those, everything will get better."

"I can't do that alone. You'll have to help me. You'll have to try harder to get his attention. I'll pray for both of you, and about mom. I'll clear all the misunderstandings between them, slowly but definitely." We both smiled at that.

I asked Kabir to take a few days off and rest. Aqeel and Ezra left for their own lives and couldn't wait for me to finish mourning my dad. I eventually started work the other day. Everything was back to normal for a week. But then two weeks later, news channels got an anonymous tip that I was living with Aqeel. I figured it must have been those so called snakes, I meant relatives. Those snitches were being so sympathetic and nice, only if I knew what they were planning to do. Now every social media app, news channels were flooded with the news that Aqeel and I were in a live-in relationship. I hoped that Aqeel didn't think it was *my* doing. Or else I would be done for. This time though, Aqeel took it very lightly and called me to ask if I was doing ok. He was concerned about me, If I would be able to handle all this chaos or not. I knew we weren't immune to rumours, but this was too much. Responding to any of these would have been a waste of time. So I paid the news channels to stop these rumours. In the world of Social media, there was always some drama going on, and this would end soon. So I didn't bother any of them. And just as I thought in a matter of one week. The news about me and Aqeel stopped trending and some other rumour about a drug scandal took over the internet.

My place felt suffocating with no one to share my thoughts with. I was living alone all these years but somehow I felt even more lonely now. My dad had passed away, and the few days I got with all the people I had started to care about, were making *these* days a living hell. I tried to stay at the office as much as possible. I even started a new routine. I was consistent with my prayers, I was sleeping in time and waking up early for gym. And guess who else was going to my gym? Aqeel. In my opinion he wasn't the type of guy to hit the gym. When I asked the reason behind this new change in him he said that someone had advised him to start gyming because his health was deteriorating. I wonder who this person was? as he never heard me when I asked him to do the same. It could be Ezra. Anyways, I was glad we'd meet more often now when we shared the same gym. And the rest of the routine was pretty much the same. Kabir's mom continued to send me lunch boxes, and sometimes they were accompanied by dinner too. She was visiting me once a week, I had nothing to complain about as I loved her company. My house was deserted most of the time so when there were guests coming over, I got overly excited about welcoming them. She even taught me a few simple recipes when I insisted as asking for lunch boxes was getting embarrassing. She told me it was fine, and she'd still send me those as I would have less time to prepare myself a good lunch. But I told her that I'd manage to prepare meals once a week so I don't bother her much.

Whenever I met her, I felt like I was meeting my own mother. And the scar left by the passing away of both my parents faded a little each time.

Dhruv called me last night and invited me to his wedding. Last, when I had met him, he was talking about his engagement which was privately done a week later. And now there was a big fat wedding awaiting for us. He was so excited about his wedding, it took *3 years* for his family to accept his relationship. I was beyond happy for him, he had been my only friend in this industry so far. He didn't ask me to bring my family along, as he knew there was no one left. Instead he invited Aqeel separately and asked me to make sure he came. He told me I was allowed to bring any of my friends, as he wanted to share his happiness with everyone. And I knew exactly who'd be going with me.

MORE STRONGER THAN EVER

AQEEL

I wanted to stay there with Alaia for longer. Wanted for her to know that I was still there for her and I would be, even if everyone else left. But If I had stayed, she would have gotten the wrong idea, and I was grateful for my choice as what happened after my stay at her place was ugly. The false news which got ignored after a while would have gotten proved. People would start talking about our relationship again, as they didn't care if her father passed away. They wouldn't care if I was there to comfort her, as for them a guy and a girl could never be platonic.

I came back with Ezra, she was still staying with me. And I didn't wanna agree but I was actually loving the fact that she came. It was not enough to compensate for the time we had been apart but it was doing fine by me. And she was insisting that I meet mummy and papa. A part of me wanted to meet them as it had been years, but another part of me wanted some more time to think through things. Whatever differences Mummy and Dida had, was between them. I got agitated easily being the witness of all the quarrel and arguments between them. But still, I couldn't go back and meet them, at least not this early. I didn't even know if I was welcome there, or if it was all Ezra's plan. In all these years mummy didn't try to reach out to me and now all of a sudden she wanted me to come back. This didn't seem normal to me. Were they alright? What about their health? Being their one and only son, I had never really tried to reach out to them too. I never asked Ezra how they were doing, and after perceiving the loss of Alaia, I was becoming concerned.

I was afraid they'd fire me as I was taking too many leaves these days. Fortunately they didn't, as I had a strong alibi about my friend's dad passing. And as of now everyone was treating Alaia as my girlfriend. This was going to go as long as we didn't clarify things out. Anyways I was able to save my job, because of the chaos I wasn't able to write any notes so I had to pull a few all nighters for that and for the pending chapters I needed to write according to my out line. Finally I was back with full force at my job and this time I'd try to be more disciplined. Haniya was being considerate of me, as she accepted my calls and even texted me a few times. It wasn't like earlier, we weren't being very cosy with each other, nor had we flirted for a while. But it was fine, as long as she was talking to me. It was proof that things weren't officially over between us and that there was *hope*.

Another week passed and It was getting hard for me to convince my heart. I couldn't wait anymore, so I went to Haniya's studio. She was on-air at that time which was why I had to wait an hour before she came out. Would I be over-exaggerating it if I said she was amazed at seeing me there. Fans always visited Haniya, there were a bunch of people waiting along with me. But she came straight towards me, didn't even look anywhere else once she noticed me sitting there in the lobby. For a while I felt like a special person, who was getting a special treatment from someone who was special themselves. Others hadn't recognized me until I came forward, and once they did, it became so noisy inside, that my ears went deaf. I wasn't expecting people to know me let alone ask for my autograph. I acknowledged it much later that it was more for all the rumours and less for my novels. I was famous but for all the wrong reasons now, it felt like people forgot who I really was. All they cared about was rumours. Some people weren't even sure what the actual stuff was about but they still lunged towards me with their cameras. The studio staff forced them out and shut the doors. I tried to keep my calm, but internally I was feeling dizzy and my mouth felt dry. All the while, Haniya held my arm as if I was a child who might get hurt or get lost. This was when I knew she still cared for me. And who was she compromising everything for? After we made sure all the people had left, we went to a nearby cafe, now with disguise. We had to be extra careful as to not stir any more problems, this was Haniya's idea. I *wanted* people to catch us together, create a new rumour and I'd delightfully admit it. I was ready to shout at people that I was dating Haniya, but she asked me not to. For whom?

We took seats at the corner where no one could see us, as requested by Haniya. I was curious as to why she was doing this? Why did we need to hide our relationship after almost breaking up? But she said- "You have to understand, this isn't right. We can't do it."

"What can we *not* do?" I was extremely annoyed.

"We can't be in a relationship."
"Why can't we? We both *like* each other. Right?"

"It's not only about us. It's about her too."

"And why do you care for her so much?"

"Because she is your friend, Aqeel. And you loved her, she loves you. We can't just shove our relationship on her face." She was quite annoyed at her own words.

"We are not shoving our relationship on anyone's face, we are thriving against all the odds. She knows Haniya, she knows that *I love you* and not her. And she still wants me to be with her, and I can't do that. I didn't force her at that time and I won't force *myself* now." And just so easily I had confessed to her.

"You *love* me?" Her eyes glistened with fresh tears.

"*Yes* I do, and I will continue to love you. Please don't make me do what I don't want to." I took her hands from which she was wiping her tears, and did the same for her. She continued to cry and I held her hands trying to explain to her that staying apart from each other wouldn't help. And I deeply missed her when she wasn't around.

"If you love me Haniya, then be with me till the end. I will convince Alaia, I'll do whatever it takes for me to make her understand who I love. And if she doesn't understand my love for you, then I'm afraid she'd have to forget about me. We have survived this much by being apart, I can manage my life without her if keeping her means I'd have to lose you."

"Stop!"

"WHAT?" I asked confusedly.

"Stop talking about her." She sniffled.

I couldn't help but chuckle. Wasn't she the one taking her side and now she didn't want to hear her name?

"I love you too." She whispered.

It felt like I was drowning till now and I was just saved. The relieved feeling I got, after her confessing that she loved me too was above every other feeling. Our happy moment was interrupted by the waiter who brought our orders. I almost cursed at him, yes I was *that* pissed. I hated being in a public place, if only we were somewhere private. What would I have done then? Kissed her? Damn yes, If *she* confirmed then.

We silently drank our beverages and watched other people chattering before Haniya was done sniffling. I found it immensely cute, ughh!! I wanted to go somewhere else so badly. I asked her if she wanted to come home with me but she said she had a family dinner that day and some relatives were coming over. So she had to leave, anyways it would be too rushed if we did anything. Things weren't pretty around us and we should focus on making things better. Once things got settled, I'd go talk to her parents. If they accepted our relationship then we'd take it a step ahead and if not I'd just have to kidnap her, haha. Just kidding.

THE WEDDING

Alaia

It was almost after a month and the wedding day had finally arrived. I liked fall, much better than monsoon but I missed summer so bad. I picked out an outfit from my own collection. It was a white cocktail dress, at first I had no idea what to wear at the wedding but I took Ezra's suggestion for it. She went back to her mother's but came back after a week. I must say, I loved these siblings. It was a nice thing that I got to meet Aqeel almost everyday, but he had been keeping secrets with me. Whenever I asked him if he was free, he said he was not. But I think he was meeting Haniya again, he never stopped. Though I was so busy myself, I couldn't spare enough time for him. Otherwise I would have done something to stop whatever was going on between them. But there would be an amazing opportunity for me. I hated to do this but, Aqeel wasn't paying any attention to me lately so I just had to grab his attention. I decided I would propose to him, and ask him if he'd marry me. I even bought a ring for him, when I went to buy myself a pendant. I knew he wouldn't say no to me If I approached him *romantically*. I'd become the type of person he'd like, to make him fall in love with me, *for the second time.*

I ironed my dress, selected the jewellery and the footwear. I put all the stuff in the cupboard drawer near my desk. I had some last minute work to do on the design for my new collection. I usually painted the designs to see how the colours would look with the design so I had some open paint bottles on my desk. And while trying to find my flat brush I accidentally spilled all the paint on the cupboard beside it. Some of the colour seeped inside and onto my dress.

"Oh fuck! Shit, shit."

I panicked and felt nauseous just with the thought of my dress getting ruined. I immediately washed it under water but since it was a darker colour over a lighter cloth, the strain remained there. I looked at the time and it was 3 hours before the event, except I had an appointment in a salon half an hour later.

"Not today man! This shouldn't have happened today. How am I supposed to fix this dress or select another." I grumbled and sat on my bed holding my head in my hands as if I was going through an existential crisis. Actually I *was*. I couldn't think of anything so I called Kabir. I had become so dependent on him that I called him several times a day. If I needed new stationery, I called him. If I needed my schedule to be checked, I called him. I wanted lunch, so I called him. And he fucking responded to me *every damn time*. I mean even though I was his boss, he wasn't obliged to do everything I asked him to. I wondered if he was doing it for a bonus or if he actually loved working for me. Or was he- no he couldn't possibly be in love with me. He did flirt with me a few times but there wasn't anything like that between us that would give him the wrong idea.

Anyways he picked my call right away, and I asked him for some advice.

He told me he'd bring me another dress so I could relax and go for my makeup and hair. I didn't know what and how he was going to arrange another dress for me as I put all the other dresses on sale. And yet I trusted him with that. I went to the salon as planned and got my hair and makeup done neutrally so that it would go with any kind of dress. I took the jewellery and footwear with me too. Kabir arrived at the salon fully dressed for the event and carried a huge bag with himself. The stylist who was getting me ready pulled out the dress for me as I still had some hair rollers on and my makeup half done. It was an ash blue georgette saree with hand painted half daisies on it. It made me think of summer, the summer I liked *so much*. The summers I spent with Aqeel, those beautiful and vibrant days. It was not just a saree for me but an emotion. Only this day I was sulking for summer officially ending and here was a saree that brought back the fresh feeling of the season. It was odd during the current season but I loved it. It was light and easy to manage. I thanked Kabir maybe ten times for bringing me that. But where did he get this from? It was so pretty and elegant that I melted. The thought of *that* day crossed my mind. When I had gone to meet Rozy aunty, Kabir's mom, he was openly checking me out. Did he like me wearing a saree? Did I look good in one? I didn't have any curves to flaunt while sporting a saree. But did he like it anyway? Though why did it bother me this much? He could like me, many people did. I got fully ready in another half an hour. My short and curly hair with the saree on, gave the whole look, *retro* vibes. If anything, the disaster that happened with my cocktail dress made my day. *Whatever happens, happens for a reason.*

Kabir and I drove to The LaLit Great Eastern Kolkata, the wedding venue together. On our way there, I asked Kabir how he managed to find this gorgeous looking saree for me on such a short notice. He told me it was his mother's and she had decided to give it to me the day she saw me on a saree. So this saree was a gift from her, and not because Kabir liked looking at me in a Saree? Perhaps he didn't like me. I shouldn't care. But this guy right here, made me insecure for the first time in my life. I was not used to, not-being-liked by guys. Maybe I was wrong about him, and I shouldn't think about him that way. He was my assistant and was just doing his job. I ruffled his hair and thanked him for the present. And he squirmed under my touch, I wonder what was that for? I withdrew my hands as I didn't mean to make him uncomfortable. After reaching the venue, I took the present I had bought for Dhruv, a rolex watch and Kabir took out the bouquet he brought. A giant collection of different roses, looking at all those flowers I wanted one for myself. I didn't realise that I was gazing at the bouquet like a lost child inside Starmark, when Kabir literally plucked one out of the roses and gave it to *me*. It was a pink one, I took it from his hands confused as to how I should react to that gesture. It was as if he knew what I was thinking about. He adjusted the other flowers so no one could suspect one missing. I had no idea what to do with that rose, so I just held it in my hands. But Kabir as always came to rescue me and helped me put the flower on my hair. I had met many guys, dated a few of them, but none of them made me feel so confused in my own body. I felt butterflies in my stomach when he gave me the flower, and another wave of them when he came closer to fix the rose in my hair. WHAT DID HE WANT? WHY WAS HE DOING THIS? WHAT WAS HE THINKING? DID HE LIKED ME OR DID HE NOT? I couldn't wrap my head around the fact that he was so chilled out and his breathing didn't even falter for a second. And here I was in a turmoil of my own thoughts. Why did I want him to like me? Why did I care if he didn't like me like other guys? I had Aqeel to focus on, so I was going to propose to him tonight. And he would accept it. Aqeel would accept my proposal, right? He was still securing the flower with a pin when Dhruv came outside to welcome his guests.

"Hey Lovebirds!" He teased me.

"Dhruv!" I screamed back at him to which he raised his hands in surrender. My mind was already a mess of thoughts, and my body felt like a betrayer. Reacting to a guy, who was mannerless, kind, flirtatious, passionate, hard working and handsome. When I put it down, I realised there was just one thing that was bad about him. His manners...which was impeccable towards others but just a little childish and frank around me. I avoided looking at Kabir, as it would make both of us feel Awkward. We entered the venue and to the enormous hall.

Guests had already arrived, the big hall looked smaller for the amount of people who attended the wedding. On one side was the huge stage meant for performance, I heard Dhruv invited his favourite indie band to play. On its opposite was the special table made for the Newly wed couples. Dhruv and his partner ditched the traditional marriage ceremony and just got married to each other at the court. And they were now going to celebrate their wedding with all the people they loved and also the ones they didn't. Half of the people who were attending this wedding were against this marriage but they were here as they just couldn't miss this lavish party.

Dhruv introduced me to his groom, who was as handsome as Dhruv himself, just a little shorter. But what's height gotta do with love?

I wondered If I was in favour of same-sex marriage or not. I had mixed feelings but I was happy for this couple. I hoped their marriage would prosper and that they'd live happily till the end of their lives.

There was no theme to the party, as Dhruv wanted everyone to enjoy their own kind of theme. Everyone was dressed to their best, and I was getting uncontrollably excited to ask for everyone's outfit. Even the aunties who were over 60, came in sexy gowns. Sure the confidence of people who were associated with this industry was *crazy*, in a good way though.

I took rounds around the tables, greeting people I knew and introducing myself to new people. The performances were yet to start so we engaged ourselves in clicking pictures. Aqeel arrived a little late along with Ezra. And oh my god, they looked so pretty. Ezra wore a hand-embroidered suit and Aqeel was in *Kurta*?

"Looking like a snack huh?" I teased him.

"Oh please don't!" Aqeel said looking embarrassed.

"I was talking to Ezra but yeah you are looking handsome too." I nudged him with my elbow.

"Nice try, but I am definitely not looking like a snack. Your compliments suit Bhai more than me. He is glistening in that kurta I chose for him. And look what he chose for me." Ezra complained.

"What? This suit is so fucking gorgeous, what are you saying? I love it on you." She indeed was looking cute.

"Really? I'll only believe you if you introduce me to Sid, I heard he is coming to this wedding. Oh my god, I can't meet him looking like this. I chose a knee-length black dress for me but Bhai didn't let me take it and instead bought me this dress." She was such a child. She kept complaining about how bad she looked in a suit and that she could only impress Sid if she was wearing a dress. I mean she gave me top delusional vibes, as everybody knew Sid was an F-boy and broke so many hearts. If he didn't have that good looking face, he wouldn't have gotten any work in this industry. No talent, no efforts, but a fuckable face, that's all it took for bollywood and its fan's to go crazy. No, I had nothing against Bollywood, but they needed to step up their game.

I didn't need to introduce Aqeel this time, as everybody came running towards him. He politely greeted everyone and talked to them. Occasionally he looked towards me, and that meant he either wanted to escape from that conversation or he was just looking at me because I looked *pretty*. Well if it was the latter then I'd be blessed tonight as I brought the ring alone with me in my clutch. I'd propose to him as soon as I get some alone time with him. That was when I remembered that I had handed my clutch to Kabir and then forgot to take it back. I called him but he didn't pick up so I texted him to bring my clutch. So rude of me to forget about the person I came here with, I got so busy with other people that I completely abandoned him at a place where he *barely* knew anyone.

I stayed with Aqeel and Ezra talking and taking pictures. We ate starters and drank cocktails, Aqeel didn't drink nor did he allow his sister so they both had Mojitos. Ezra was pissed because Aqeel was acting way too protective towards her and she wasn't having any fun. So I helped Ezra escape and busied Aqeel with other topics. People just weren't ready to leave his side, one of the producers who attended came to Aqeel and decided for a meeting about a book adaptation. I hoped this meeting wouldn't end up like the previous one, I hated being the person who forced him into it. And just finally when people were going away, my blouse decided to loosen itself. It was Kabir's mom's blouse so it was a little loose on the shoulders and I had hand-stitched it to secure it. But the stitching came out and one of my sleeves was falling over my shoulder. Aqeel noticed it before I did, so he asked if he could help. I let him. There was an extra pin which was used to secure the plating, I gave him that pin so he could pin the sleeves and make it tighter. I must have had the worst fate today, as photographers who were clicking pictures for the magazine, clicked us in that intimate position. "Fuck!" I mumbulled.

"Sorry sir and ma'am, I didn't mean to come in between your intimate time." He said it out, louder than normal. And it grabbed everyone's attention. Everyone was staring at that exchange, when Aqeel broke his silence.

"It's okay, but do you always click pictures of others without asking for permission? Which magazine are you working for? Who gave you this much freedom and audacity?"

Dhruv came upfront by clearing the crowd that had gathered in such a short time. "What happened?" He asked looking concerned

"Alaia had a wardrobe malfunction and I was helping her with that while they clicked her pictures in that position without evening asking for her permission."

"Are you okay Alaia?" Dhruv asked me and I nodded as a reply

"I'll ask them to delete the pictures so don't worry about that. And yeah they won't work for the magazine anymore I'll make sure of that." He said.

"They must be going extra lovey dovey with each other when the photographer clicked their pictures." "These kids won't even decide if they are dating each other or not and then would openly show their affection." The crowd mumbled on their own. And I became furious, how dare they talk about us like that?

"Excuse me?!!" My temper shot up.

"It's true, has Aqeel even asked you out yet? Or he is too busy using you." One of the aunties who I thought was cool interrogated me.

"What the fuck are you even talking about? He is not using me okay? He stayed with me because I just lost my dad." Aqeel held me back by my arm as I was lunging over that woman.

"And has your grief faded away so soon that you are celebrating with your boyfriend?"

"Ugh this is too much, I can't handle this." I broke off from Aqeel's grip and headed out. On my way I collided with Kabir who was bringing my clutch with him. And the clutch fell down on the floor right near where everyone was standing. The ring box came out. The woman who was just accusing me for being shameless picked it up and examined it.

"So I was right, he is indeed using you Alaia. See you are trying so hard to please this man and he is not even committing to you." She commented.

I looked at Aqeel in shock, I didn't want it to happen this way. I wanted to propose to him in a romantic way so he would even consider my proposal. But this blunder had to happen right now.

"I was going to ask him today." I said it more to Aqeel and less to that woman.

"So do it, go ahead and propose to him. We were waiting for this to happen for a while now. Let's see if he'll accept it or not." She challenged me with something I was afraid of. I had no idea what he would do. I never wanted to put him in this kind of situation but now it has been done.

I looked at him again, but he was looking at the floor. Probably regretting his decision to come here.

"Hey, don't steal my spotlight dude. Do it fast and get over it." Dhruv asked. Of course, he didn't know about my situation nor did anyone else. They knew what they saw.

I moved forward towards Aqeel, my legs were trembling so much I could barely stand properly. I prayed to Allah for a good fate. Whatever he says or does will affect both our reputations. So I hoped he would say what I had expected to hear from him when I bought this ring. Tears started forming in my eyes, I tried to hold them back but they just won't stop. I took smaller steps, for me and him. I needed time to gather enough courage to do this, and for him to think through things. To decide what his answer was going to be. Ezra came beside me and took me to him, carefully but faster.

"I am sorry Aqeel." I whispered, he remained silent. And that's when I started crying, tears rolled down my cheeks one after another.

Ezra comforted me and cheered me up as everyone else was watching us.

I straightened my back and raised my head to look him in his eyes. "I love you Aqeel, I love you." and presented him with the ring. I couldn't ask- 'marry me' because I was unaware if he even loved me back to marry me. Then there was a pause, I held my breath as did everyone.

"Bhai say something, say that you love her." Ezra requested Aqeel and I continued to cry because he could either accept my love or leave me in ruins.

"I do love you too Alaia, my friend." He replied and I looked up at him. His teary eyes said something different but he took the ring box from me and urged me to put the ring on his finger. I quickly did what he asked, even though I couldn't believe in what he said.

FAILURES

Aqeel

Everything was a blurred image, as if I was an alcoholic trying to sober up on vodka. I didn't know why and how I did what I did. It felt right to stand up for the shattering reputation of my friend. So I stood, I gave my voice to the silent prayers of the one person I wouldn't wanna see cry because of me. I said yes to Alaia's confession out of necessity. I believed she was shocked too, as I was so sure about not being in love with her until it was her dignity which was in line. After I said my answer and we exchanged the rings, the crowd cheered for us as if they weren't the ones who were degrading us for being close to each other. The party resumed with even more enthusiasm as ever and the band performance started. We played our roles well enough to fool everyone including ourselves. There was a weight growing in my chest, and so was it for Alaia as I assumed. I thought she would be happy after all she came with the ring, so she must have planned on proposing to me. And everything happened in her favour, it didn't matter how much it would affect her as she was used to it. But something in her silence throughout the party made me think twice about her situation. Was it guilt? What was it that made her unhappy so much that she didn't even speak to me after that. I hoped she had an explanation behind the ring, if it wasn't for that we might have gotten away with the situation much easily. And I wouldn't have to do what I didn't want to. What would I tell Haniya? Will she understand that I needed to save Alaia from this situation by saying yes to her proposal? Did I make the right move? Or have I ruined everything once again?

We didn't have dinner, after everything went against us. Food wasn't the right choice after such a disaster. We silently left the venue after meeting the couple for the last time this evening. The valet parking staff told me that my car's tire was punctured and that they'd send me the car later after fixing it. So I started looking for uber, but Kabir came and insisted that we go with them and that he'd drop us before going to Alaia's place. I would have said no, but Ezra too wanted to go with them. She was jolly after my little engagement with Alaia. She liked her more than Haniya, but maybe she'd have changed her mind if only she met her.

Ezra and Kabir had softened to each other, maybe because they belonged to the same age group. There wasn't anything romantic going on between them, as Kabir was invested somewhere else. Me and Alaia weren't the only people who were sad, Kabir too was suspiciously sad. I figured he had taken a liking for Alaia, and this drama made him upset. Honestly I liked him, and he would actually be good to Alaia, he was. Unfortunately Alaia was blind towards those feelings and I could sense that she was completely unaware of what was going on inside his head.

I wondered how people could be so ignorant to the love they received from people and only run towards what they thought was love. I hoped she realised that I couldn't marry her when I was in love with someone else and that there was someone who loved her so much to sacrifice their love without even getting to confess first. I felt bad for Kabir and for myself. I once was in his position. If my suspicions were wrong or right, it was yet to be decided. But for now, I believed in what was right before my eyes. The look in his eyes clearly hinted at sorrow, sorrow that dawns upon a person in love.

Ezra pulled a shotgun and left me in the backseat with Alaia. She kept on searching for songs to play for our ride back home, as it was going to be long. Alaia's destination was the closest and Kabir's the last so Alaia would get off before us and Kabir would take the car home. After a brief few minutes, Ezra chose the song 'Perfect' by Ed sheeren. It felt like a torture to my soul, and Alaia gave out a deep sigh. I felt like choking Ezra but I calmed myself down. She did it purposely, her naive mind must have thought that we were grateful for the latest events and couldn't wait anymore to celebrate our love. But you were wrong Ezra, I couldn't wait to die as life was getting messier by each day.

The next day as expected, the news broke out that we got engaged during Dhruv's after marriage party. For everyone this was good news, or maybe not. But I got a lot of wishes for our life ahead together. But my only wish was to die and leave this planet for good. As one doesn't accept a proposal and then call it quits the other day. If I did anything like that, it would raise more questions, and more problems for the both of us. Nonetheless, I was sure for one thing, me and Haniya were over. There wasn't anything to explain now, it didn't matter how much I tried when in the end I chose Alaia upon her. She would be hurt deeply and I would want her to understand, but how was I going to face her after this? I failed to prioritise things and people. There wasn't much left for me.

Another week passed, with us being depressed and silent about it all. No one reached out to one another, people made our edits and our names were trending together. Nothing mattered anymore, as life was duller than it had ever been. Haniya called and texted me multiple times, but I just couldn't bring myself to pick it up and face her. I was being a coward, or maybe I was always one. And as a result she appeared in my house one afternoon with some pastries.

"You can have those once in a while, you know that right?" She smiled.

Yes I could savour the sweetness of her presence once in a while if it didn't hurt her more. I served the pastries and made some black coffee for us. And waited for her to say something or anything, as I was out of words.

"You don't have to be this silent, it's making me feel awkward about my visit. Should I leave?" She suggested.

"No, no, absolutely not." I blurted out.

"Then say something, talk to me."

"I don't have words."

"Then talk with your eyes, it speaks a lot, even more than your poetries."

I couldn't even look at her properly. I wonder how I was supposed to talk through my eyes? How does this even work? "I..umm. I am sorry Haniya, I am so so sorry. I couldn't stand up for ourselves against her." I took a long breath.

She took the coffee mug from my hands and put it on the tea table. Then I held my hands with her. "Look, I am not mad. I love you enough to sacrifice it for your good. And maybe Alaia loves you more than I do, besides she needs you as her support system. I can't ask you to leave her and come to me when I know you care for her."

"I do care for her but I love you even more and I can't have a future if it doesn't include you. And you are saying that she loves me, what kind of love is this where she doesn't respect my opinion? If she weren't famous and people weren't talking about us, I wouldn't have taken this step. But I can't ignore the fact that this decision is killing me. It's all for that damn confession I made years ago. I know I ended up ruining her oh-so-great relationship with that dumb guy but she doesn't get to do the same with me. Is she really in love with me or just getting back at me with this revenge plan?" I took a long breath after that as I said all these words in a single breath.

"Aqeel.. It's not about revenge at all. Maybe it took years for her to realise her love for you. She must have felt something in your confession and never forgot about it. Now when she has the opportunity to get you back in her life, she is using it all. I know this makes her look bad, but when you love someone deeply you want them to be yours anyhow."

"Then why don't you do anything? I am a coward, I am not able to leave my friend but you can ask me to stay right? You were so concerned the day when you heard about our history and yet you are ready to sacrifice me this easily. Don't you realise that I need you to be possessive about me. If you are willing to leave me, how will I be able to fight her? There is no point in fighting, if you don't fight with me." I was nearly shouting at her by this point.

"Listen, I am ready to fight for you. Do you think I don't want you to only belong to me? I want you all for me, but maybe I am just delusional enough to think like that. I might be your biggest fangirl, but you are the only fanboy she'd ever want in her life. I can't snatch something from her that is not completely mine."

"The difference *is* that I want to be completely *yours*. And I want *you* to own me, yet I can't do that if you continue to push me away."

"Who is pushing who away?" Ezra came out of her room (previously mine) while rubbing her swollen eyes.

"Ezra, this isn't the way you come in front of your guest. In your pjs…and why were you still sleeping?"

"So I am now a guest?" asked Haniya.

"Bhai, what am I supposed to do on a sunday afternoon? Anyways, introduce me to your 'guest'." She quoted the word 'guest' with her hands.

"I am not a guest." Stated Haniya.

"You are when you don't want to be in my life. And Ezra, this is Haniya, you should greet her even though you are the same age. She should be greeted."

"Okay, please don't get offended. It's not like I don't want to be a part of your life, it's just that I am who I am and she is Alaia the perfect Mirza. How am I supposed to compete with her?"

"Yeah, you are correct. Alaia is way too perfect and gorgeous. But don't degrade yourself so much, it doesn't suit you." Ezra advised Haniya.

"Ezra, whose side are you on? Mine or Alaia's?" I interrogated her.

"Of course I am on Alaia's side, Bhai. Why don't you just marry her, when you are already engaged?"

"Oh yeah, I forgot. You guys even got engaged. I mean, that was a tragedy the way it happened. I saw it on instagram. But how will you even back out from that? There is no way we can be together now." Said Haniya.

"So what? Should I give up now? That's what you both are implying? If it wasn't for her honour I would have rejected her. I was trying to explain to her how I can't love her but she wasn't ready to hear me out."

"Yeah maybe, see there is no other way. What are you going to tell people? That she is madly in love with you but you are not, though you care for her and accepted her proposal even though you never wanted to marry her. You can't explain to other people how complicated your situation with Alaia is and the reason behind your abrupt decisions." Haniya clarified.

"These are the reasons I kept myself anonymous for so long. See how being famous is causing so many problems for me. If only I hadn't responded to her letter or agreed to meet her. And then the meeting with the producers. All these made my real identity come out and now it's the biggest problem I have in my life. I can't even post a picture of us because people know that I am dating Alaia, which I am not. But they have the proof. This goddamn internet has made my life a living hell."

"Stop complaining, some of us don't even have a job and you have a big fat bank account just because your novels are famous, your love stories are famous, whose inspiration was 'Alaia'" Ezra quoted Alaia's name with her fingers. These kids and their obsession with quotations and the internet.

"Well, I worked for those 'famous novels' you are talking about and if you want a big fat bank balance then you should consider working." I quoted the words with my fingers, and couldn't believe in myself.

"Anyways, Aqeel I don't think you can solve this problem without causing damage to Alaia and yourself. So better follow the path in front of you and believe in Allah. He'll do what's best for you and for all of us. Besides I am satisfied by just being your fangirl" She ended the conversation with that and left.

She might get satisfied with just that, But I couldn't. I was not going to marry Alaia at any cost, and I'd find a way to break this engagement. I got an idea, so I called Kabir and asked him to meet me.

We planned on meeting outside, because I didn't want Ezra to get involved in all this. She wasn't even on my side so there was no need. He came in Alaia's car, she must have given it to him for use as he drove her everywhere. We went to a nearby market area where there were some food trucks. So we explored some of them and tried new food items. I didn't want to start the particular conversation so soon so we kept jumping from one topic to another. It was his day off so he was quite glad that we both came to hang out. While we ate, he kept talking about how Alaia would love a certain kind of street food and hate others. I laughed externally, but internally I kept thinking about how much he liked her. My initial reason behind this meetup was to talk to him about Alaia, and now I was sure how I was going to carry it out. My first question was- "Why do you think Alaia had that ring with her that day?"

"Isn't it obvious that she was planning to propose to you?"

"Yeah, but why was she upset then.?"

"Maybe because it didn't happen the way she had wished for."

"Mmmhm, I get that! and why were *You* upset that day?"

"Me? No, I wasn't. Why would I be?" He continued to lick his ice cream which dripped all over his shirt.

"Oh please, who are you trying to fool, someone who has written romance novels for a living? I was suspicious and asked your type and now it's confirmed how sad our engagement made you."
"It's not what you think?" He tried to convince me.

"It is exactly what I am thinking and you don't have to deny it. See I didn't want to get engaged nor do I want to marry her. Whatever feelings I had for her faded away with the passing time. I am doing all this because she is my friend." I paused for a few seconds and then continued.

"I think you should express your feelings out loud. Not because I want to get away from this relationship, that's partly the reason but I genuinely think that you'd be good to her. And she deserves to be with a guy who actually loves and admires her and not the guy who is trying to protect her as a friend. We are better off as friends, but she won't listen to me. You can change her mind, you can make her believe that it is you who she needs."

"And do you think she'll come running to me if I did confess to her? No."

"I know, it's Alaia who we are dealing with. But you have gotta try atleast once. And I'll try to persuade her into believing that this relationship we have isn't the one she should be in. So will you try?"

"Ah, I'll have to see. I don't know, If I can even ask her out. Let alone dream about her accepting it." We both laughed.

"It's a long shot, but it'll be worth it believe me." I added. He nodded to that.

IGNORANCE

Alaia

Of course I didn't want things to happen the way they did. But now the more important part was that I was engaged to Aqeel. He put the ring on my finger in front of all those people and the media. It was difficult to process any of it, though it would sink in a few days. I didn't know if Aqeel was okay with this but he must have thought something before committing to me in front of everyone. He must know that there was no going back from here, and personally I would like to think that he meant what he said. Yes, he definitely meant it when he said he loved me. I could say this because I had seen how much he cared for me. He didn't hesitate before lending his hand for help whenever I was in trouble. Wasn't this what love was actually about? Plus his love had always been selfless, he always ended up sacrificing himself when it was about the people he loved. But I won't let him do that again, when he'd be with me. I'd sacrifice if needed but he shouldn't always be the one doing it. He had been alone all his life, but I'd stay by his side from now onwards. I'd love him enough so that he won't be lonely or sad.

I didn't talk to Aqeel as I was planning a surprise for him. My proposal didn't go as planned and I was pretty upset that he had to hear from other people before I had any chance to explain about the ring. Yet I had expected him to call me and talk about what happened, he didn't. Probably because he was shocked with my direct moves or maybe the things those people said got to him. Anyways, I had planned an engagement party for us and I was sure he'd love it. He just needed some time to get over the Haniya situation.

I was talking to the event manager about our venue and other arrangements when Kabir barged in my office with flowers. They were the same as the ones he gave to Dhruv.

"Kabir!! Knock on the door before coming in" I mouthed. And he went back and knocked on the door for my permission, I nodded so he came inside. I told him to wait as I was still on that call. He kept looking around the room and fidgeting with the flowers. Sometimes he fixed his hair and sometimes his t-shirt but never once did he look at me. I guessed he was nervous, the question was why? I finally got off the call and asked him to sit. But he just stood there like a mannequin. For a second I thought he was one but I was mistaken. He took long deep breaths so I realised the matter was serious and important.

"Hey!" I waved in front of his face so I could grab his attention and with that he snapped. "Back to earth Mr Kabir, what's the event?" I inquired.

"Yeah, yeah I am sorry." He sat on the seat across from me and was silent again.

"Look If you don't tell me what you came here for, I'll have to ask you out as I have many many jobs to do."

"Yeah, you seem pretty busy. But who were you talking to, I thought I managed all your events and stuff."

"Yup, you do. But for this particular one I'll have to manage it myself"

"What is it about? Another fashion show?"

"Well I thought to keep it a secret but since I know I won't be able to manage it alone and I would need your help at some point, and there isn't any harm If I tell you. So, the thing is that you know about what happened at that party. We didn't want it to happen, I thought it would be romantic when I proposed to him but, no. So I am planning my engagement party and it's a secret you have to keep from Aqeel because it's a surprise." I told him with much enthusiasm.

"Ohh...so you are planning a party, I see." All the colour faded away from his face and he looked as if someone had just rejected him.

"Anyways, are these flowers for me? I love flowers but have never received them from anyone. If it wasn't you I would have thought that you were hitting on me." I took the flowers from his hand and smelled heaven in it.

"What if I was actually hitting on you?" He asked hesitantly

"What? Umm, it would be strange if you did that as you are my assistant and there is an age gap between us. Plus I am engaged to Aqeel, you know." I tried to say, even though my heart was racing like never before. *After all this, he was proposing to me? Did my proposal to Aqeel affected him this much? That he was proposing to me now? So, I guess he did like me? But why not before? Why now?*

"And what if Aqeel isn't really into you? And when did you start caring about the age gap and work problems?" He pointed it out. I never cared for such things. It was a failed attempt at making him believe that we shouldn't do this.

"Excuse me, watch what you are saying. If Aqeel was any less interested in me he wouldn't have accepted my proposal in front of all those people. He isn't the person to give false hope and besides I never cared about age gaps, that's true but that doesn't mean that I'll actually be with a guy who is smaller than me. I prefer mature men, someone who is older than me." Another attempt. Kabir was mature, irrespective of his age. And I remembered the times he made me feel differently. But it was all worthless in front of Aqeel.

"I don't mean to pry, but have you talked to Aqeel after your engagement that day? Have you considered asking if he was doing okay or if he was happy with what happened? No, you haven't and I would advise you to do that before surprising him with another major bomb."

"You don't have to think about me and Aqeel that much, do you understand? Now if you don't have anything to say apart from what I should or should not do about Aqeel and my situation, you can go away."

"Well I initially came here to present you with these flowers, which you are so fond of. And to tell you that I was indeed hitting on you as I really really liked you. But since you are busy planning your engagement party without a groom to start with, I don't think you have enough time to spare me. Also, I'd like to tell you one thing. I wouldn't care about you, but I do as I had been told by someone that you don't do so for yourself. When I was working with your Abbu, to find you a new home. He told me that he was putting his trust in me. That I was a mere assistant, but he thought I was capable of taking care of you. So he asked me to. And I can't go back on the word I gave to him. You like it or not, I'd care for you and I'd continue liking you." He stood up and left without a second thought.

Well that was strange, my assistant was thinking about me 'romantically' and I had no idea. Technically I had, but it was too strange to believe in it. Though what he said was true, I do not have time for him. People like him go away as quickly as they come in your life, but with Aqeel I was sure he was the one to stay. But one thing Kabir said stuck with me, what if Aqeel did what he did just to shut the people up. I needed my answer, before losing it all. Besides, Abbu was worried, which might have been the reason for his concern towards me. I called Aqeel and told him my plan without even listening to him first. I wanted to see his reactions, well hear it.

"Are you out of your damn mind?" He replied. Not the reaction I was expecting.

"Woah, what happened? Aren't you happy?" I asked, knowing very well where this was going.

"Happy? For what Alaia? You're ruining my life?"

"No!! What? Aqeel, tell me you meant what you said that day to me that you loved me."

"I hate it how many times I have to tell you, Alaia, that I am not in love with you. What I said that day was true, but I added 'friend' after that. I love you Alaia, but as a friend. You are a great friend and I love you deeply to care for you. And what I did that day was to save your honour, I never meant to exchange those rings. I loved you romantically in the *past*, now this is our present. I hate to push you away, which is why I have been tolerating all this for so long. But not anymore, I am not going to marry you. In Fact I was going to return you this ring one day when you'd be ready to hear me out."

"So you knew that I was going to propose to you and you accepted my proposal even though you didn't mean to do that?" I had started crying because this felt like the biggest betrayal to me.

"Yes, because I couldn't bear to reject you in front of all the people. Which is why I had to accept it."

"And what would people think if we break up now?" I asked. Not willing to accept it yet.

"People will think what they'll anyway, what I am saying is that I can't care about people anymore. I have my own life Alaia, if I spend all my time after caring about people and you. I am afraid I'll die out of suffocation."

"What do you think will happen to me, if you leave.?"

"You are not a kid Alaia, I do hope you understand that you can't keep me forcefully. And about you being alone, you are not alone. I'll always be by your side as a friend, besides there are people who are deeply in love with you. If you allow yourself to see beyond us, you'll be able to realise who I am talking about." I didn't have to think much as I knew who the person was. I hung up the call, as I failed. I had ignored every word of Aqeel where he told me he didn't love me, but today I couldn't ignore anymore. He was pretty clear he didn't want to be with me. He wants to be with Haniya. As much as I wanted to curse her, I couldn't. She wasn't the one in fault, I was. I thought that Aqeel still had feelings for me as he did in our past, or I could make him fall in love again. But that wasn't the case now. I had lost the power I had upon Aqeel, lost the love I craved all these years. If only I had valued his presence, his love, his care towards me in the past. I wouldn't have to see this day today.

I packed up work and went back home. It felt utterly silent and dead to me. I thought I was taking care of him, when I was only pushing him further away. Maybe If I hadn't asked him to go to that meeting, people wouldn't have spread rumours about him and no one would have known about his identity. In my journey of trying to get close to him, I ended up making him hate me even more. He was kind enough to let me come back into his life, and I didn't understand the basic etiquette of being a friend. When he was in love with me, he cared for me and never forced his love upon me. It wasn't until my engagement, did he open his mouth. And I? I tried to take him away with me from everyone else. I hate the day he met Haniya, but it was I, who introduced them both. If that didn't happen, Aqeel might have reciprocated the love I said I had for him. But all this was making me question my own feelings. Did he hate me that much or did he love Haniya a little too much? That even *I* couldn't take her away from him. Was it my repulsiveness that led to this? Should I have cared more about his feelings back then, for him to respect my love now? Do I even love him? Or was it just jealousy that grabbed my attention towards him? I wonder how he'd react if he gets to know that I called the media the very first time our relationship rumour got out. I knew that Kabir and Aqeel were in contact with each other, as there was no other way he would know that someone was in love with me. Kabir expressed his feelings just today and then Aqeel told me on the phone about how I should give time to other people who loved me. Was it Aqeel who encouraged Kabir to propose to me? He wouldn't have done it on his own right? He knew how I loathe immature people. He knew that there should be a barrier between us na?

I laid down on the bed, in my work clothes. As I had no energy to go take a shower or change. Normally I would do a skincare routine, but I couldn't care more about my appearance now that Aqeel didn't love me. I wondered If I loved him or the fact that he loved me was more pleasing to my heart. Knowing that someone intensely loves you, makes you wanna dance, sing and care about your appearance. But now that I knew he was completely over me and there was really no hope left for me, what do I do? Where do I go? My lunch was still in the box I packed it in, as I had lost the appetite. I felt like I was a sloth and had no energy to even move. Was guilt bigger than grief? When Abbu died, I worked more than I did in normal working days but now when I was going through the consequences of my own rash behaviour, I couldn't even lift my finger. Walking felt like a battle to me, when I had to walk up to the front gate of my office for the cab. Kabir vanished after our argument, I wondered where he was. Was he hiding because he thought he had made a mistake, or crying because how casually I rejected him? My brain faltered to make any more thoughts as sleep engulfed me in its darkness.

I woke up the next morning, my whole body was aching as I had overslept. I had scars on my face and neck because of the jewellery I was still wearing from the previous day. I slowly stood up and went to the washroom to freshen up, and in the mirror I saw a strange woman. I didn't know her, her face was swollen and eyes were watery. Dried up tears and drool was all over the face and the shirt she wore underneath her now crumpled beige customised jacket. I stared at the figure for a while, trying to recognize the person behind it and all I saw was a woman too arrogant to see the fault in her own self. Fresh tears formed in my eyes, as this was who I was now. Not the famous fashion designer everybody knew, but a person who misunderstood someone's love and care for granted. One doesn't get love that easily, they have to cherish the love they receive and give it ten fold back, then only they become capable of receiving love. I always thought that my parents would stay with me forever, as if they weren't mortal beings. I had thought that Aqeel would love me at all given time and circumstances and I wouldn't have to do anything in order to make them feel the same way.

Love for me was a forever thing, but it comes out that love can end the very moment you forget about giving it back. I tried to keep Aqeel all for myself, and now he was with everyone except me. He wouldn't even understand that I was drowning in this quicksand of emotions.

After washing my face, I stood under the cold running shower for what felt like an eternity. I hated cold showers, but today it was awakening. I came back inside my room drenched in water, as I hadn't even cared to discard my dirty clothes and wear fresh ones. Then again I stood in front of the mirror and slowly took off every piece of clothing and examined myself. No part of my body felt like it was anywhere near death. Everything was fresh, delicate and strong except my eyes. They looked very old and were pleading to die. I shook my head and threw the thoughts away. I couldn't die, couldn't think about it. This wasn't me. I liked facing my challenges, and so would I do it again. I started searching for clothes when the ping sound of notification came from my mobile phone. I went upto my bed and grabbed my mobile. It was the warning notification that my phone was about to die as it was out of charge. So I immediately put it on charge, something grabbed my attention. An email from the organiser of my engagement party. I opened it and it said that they successfully sent all the invitations which were due today.

"Fuck!" I was supposed to cancel the event, as what was I going to say at the event? That my fiance gave me my ring back and now we weren't together?

I called the event manager and asked if they could cancel the event. They said it wasn't an issue to cancel the event but I'd just have to pay the cancellation fee as they worked hard for it. The actual issue was the invitations, what would I tell them? Why were we cancelling the party? People would surely raise questions as to what was going on between us and that would affect my sales. I was already behind my game, I was constantly working but couldn't come up with a new collection for this season. There was only one month left before I had to create a winter collection. This wasn't me, I would have done it earlier and it would have already been through the critics review. But now, my personal life is all over my professional life. One wrong step in my personal life and I'd end up ruining my career. People were expecting more than I was capable of providing right now. The event manager told me, It'd be smart to postpone the event by making excuses about my health and stuff. So I asked them to do it on my behalf and send an apology email of event postponement. I went back to searching for clothes and wore whatever seemed decent. I didn't have enough time to take care of my looks today, so I called an Uber and went to the office. Surprisingly Kabir was there before me. Not to work but to resign. I was halfway inside my cabin, when he came from behind and handed me his resignation letter and my car keys.

"Don't think that I am trying to leave you, I am only resigning so that this work obstacle between us doesn't bother me." He held me by my arm and whispered in my ear.

"WHAT DO YOU MEAN BY THAT?" I shouted

"That means Alaia Mirza, that I am going to keep trying to change your mind. And maybe one day you'll understand that running after a train once it has already left the station isn't going to be fruitful. Also that I care for you and can love you enough, so that you'll forget everyone else." He came closer and stroked the back of my head from his other hand. For the first time he came so close to me and my body betrayed me by sending shivers from the place he touched to my whole body. I stiffened my body in response to his touch, No I didn't break free. As his touch was warm and welcoming, not cold and weird. I couldn't process any words as a reply to his frankness with me. I was not even his boss anymore, as he signed his resignation. I remembered this wasn't the first time he came close to me, there had been multiple times earlier. But I didn't feel the same way, I didn't feel it to be anything beyond a friendly gesture though now the story wasn't the same. And I could swear I had smelled him too many times, when we drove in the same car, stayed overnight in it and worked with each other for hours. But this time it was different. As if he started smelling extra nice, even though it was the same scent he always wore.

LAST SHOWERS

Aqeel

It was really late at night, around 11 pm when I came back home. There was an event in my university, I was not the kind of person who would attend these. But when you are a VIP guest in your own University, there isn't an option to avoid it at all. When I came back, I found that Haniya was leaving. I was genuinely surprised to see her there, so I almost went and Hugged her. But my overthinking brain had already calculated the pros and cons of doing that. I asked her to stay the night but she said it wasn't appropriate to do that and also that I should focus on Alaia, even though I remembered the night we spent talking and talking in this same household.

She left without even saying anything as a goodbye to me. Was this how she was planning to behave now? All I was asking for was that I wanted to be with her, she had feelings for me too but was still insecure.

I asked Ezra what the matter was, and she told me about the invitation she and Haniya both got for the Engagement party. "I hate it when she does things in her own way and doesn't even bother about asking people first." I threw my backpack on the sofa and lied down using it as a pillow. Ezra went and grabbed some water for me.

"Haniya just came to congratulate you for the party, but she said she wouldn't be able to attend it as she is moving out." Ezra explained. I sat up immediately after the second shock of the day.

"Why? What happened? Is she moving out because of me? Why did she leave without saying anything to me, then?"

"She said she didn't want to worry you more. And that she got a really nice job which requires her to move out to a different city. It was a sudden decision and tonight is her flight to Jaipur. She is going away, Bhai. Although I really wished for you to marry Alaia. I am reconsidering this myself. And also the event has been postponed for now. We got another email saying that Alaia is ill and needs some time to rest."

I patted Ezra's head and left. I needed to go after her. Only If I could match the timing. I knew the guards wouldn't let me past the gate and I could only stop her If I managed to get there before her. I kept calling her while walking towards the parking lot. She didn't pick up my calls or saw my messages. I drove towards the airport, when my car ran out of fuel in the middle. Yes, exactly what needed to happen when I needed it the most. Calling an uber wasn't an option, as it would take a lot of my time. And time was the most precious to me then, so I took a taxi to the airport. Paid more than it should have been paid. Ezra kept calling me and I kept rejecting it as I was trying to connect to Haniya. I reached the airport and checked the flight timings for Jaipur. The boarding time was 12:55 am. And right now it was 1:20 am. I asked the guards to check whether someone is yet to board the flight, but they told me that everyone has already boarded the flight and it would depart at 1:30 am according to the time. Ezra called me again, but I ditched the call and tried calling Haniya again before her flight took off. She didn't respond to it. I got a text from Ezra - "Hey, Bhai picked up my call! Did you meet her? Sorry I lied."

WAIT. WHAT? What did she lie about? I needed to know so I made the call. She picked up my call in an instant.

" Did you meet her?" She interrogated

"No, She must have boarded the flight. She isn't picking up my calls, can you call her on my behalf please? The flight is going to take off at 1:30 am. Please make the call?"

"Hey, hey, sorry! I lied. How could you trust me so much when I am the last person who should be trusted. Haniya is home, she is not going to Jaipur."

"What? And why did you lie to me? This isn't the time to joke around, Ezra." I shouted.

"I know Bhai, I am sorry. I only meant for you to chase after Haniya so you could go to her. See I know I was on Alaia's side, but I might have changed my mind. Haniya is what you need, and not Alaia. She is too pure and kind, and I wouldn't wanna see you with anyone less loving."

"Can you tell me where she is now and why she is not picking up her calls? Call her and tell me right now."

I was relieved to know that she wasn't leaving, Ezra's lie almost gave me a heart attack. I didn't know what I'd do if she moved out. Would I be able to change her mind and make her come back here? I was not sure, Though if that was the case I would do my best as I wouldn't be able to live peacefully without her. A few minutes later Ezra texted me that Haniya wasn't picking up her calls either. So I had only one option left. And I was impatient enough to not wait for the morning to come. I didn't care what she would think or her parents would think about me. I made up my mind that I would see her tonight. So I texted Ezra back and told her to take care of herself as I was going to be late tonight. I had no idea how I was even doing all this as I was extremely tired after the event. But I still drove towards Haniya's place. I vaguely remembered her description of her location. So I asked around to some pedestrians and in the tea stalls. They didn't know much about Haniya, but some people recognized her father so I asked them where they lived. And I finally found the apartment building. I talked to the guard and asked him to call Haniya's intercom. Thankfully she was the one who picked up, for a moment I was scared as to what I would say if any of her parents received the call. The guard then asked Haniya if she knew me and she asked the guard to let me in. I was still afraid of what I'd do when I met her parents, but strangely she was home alone at this hour of the night. I hadn't realised it was 3 am already. Haniya casually let me in, and I looked around the empty house to make sure there wasn't anyone before hugging her. This time I let my heart rule over my mind. It was sudden, but the hug assured me that she was here in front of me and not on a flight to somewhere outside Kolkata. I then took a few seconds to just admire her, My one arm holding her waist and making sure she was as close to me as possible and the other hand caressing her cheeks. She looked curious and concerned but she let me have my moment. And hugged me back.

"Why didn't you pick my call? Are you mad? Why are you doing this to me, Haniya?"

"Uh, I might have lost my phone on my way back. And no I am not mad nor am I trying to ignore you. I just think that it's best for you to focus on Alaia right now as you know she is ill and alone. Did you check up on her?"

"No, I completely forgot to check up on Alaia as Ezra lied to me that you were moving out to Jaipur So I went to the airport thinking I'd be able to stop you."

"You went to the airport? At this hour? It's an hour's ride, Aqeel?"

"Well, you were behaving so strangely with me and then I believed Ezra. Anyways, I am grateful that you are not moving out." I kissed her forehead, still not letting her go.

"Technically, I *am* moving out. We are shifting to a new place, which is closer to your place. My parents are currently there, and I stayed back as I still had some packing left to do. Though it seems like I won't be doing it anytime soon."

"Why?"

"As someone is being too possessive of me right now and has been holding me for what seems like 10 minutes. But I like it, a little too much actually." She expressed. I blushed when I realised the time but it only made me want to hold her for longer and she smiled.

"The event is going to be cancelled." I stated.

"Wasn't it just postponed as Alaia is ill?"

"Yeah, but I told her that I'll give back her ring. So there won't be any engagement party, for now."

"And she agreed to that?"

"She'll have to. Because I am not going to marry anyone except you." I looked at her sparkly brown eyes which were immersed in mine. My eyes went from her eyes to her beautiful and soft lips. The hand which was holding her chin now grazed her lower lip.

"Are you proposing right now?" She asked, in a low voice.

"I might be. And I am only taking yes as an answer."

"And I'll only say yes if you kiss me right now, right here." She challenged me. My heart started beating at a higher speed than it was before she made this demand. I would have thought about the pros and cons if my desperate lips hadn't planted themselves on hers. The old memories of being afraid of ghosts at this time of the night as I watched a horror movie would now be replaced by a blissful memory. Everything was a blur, I don't remember when I passionately kissed her. Was it really me? I didn't even know If I was capable of doing it, but this was Haniya. She made me fall madly in love with her, so much that I forgot who I was. I had no idea when and how we ended up on the couch. We cuddled all night before sleeping in each other's arms until the sun came up and filled her living room with bright sunlight. It woke both of us, but we were only happy to have found each other. If it was my teenage self, I wouldn't have gone past the hug. It would have been too much to me, but thinking and weighing things wasn't an option when I was with Haniya. I felt carefree and new, when I was with her. And for this, I would gladly choose Haniya over everyone.

It was still early so we went back to sleep in her bedroom. I woke up at 10 in the morning because of the alarm. And Haniya wasn't beside me, nor anywhere in the room. So I went out in the living room and found the room empty. The couch we made out last night wasn't there anymore. And all the other furniture was gone. Haniya emerged from the main door which was left open for the people who were shifting the things.

"Hey, you are awake! Good morning." she grinned and came for a hug. I warmly accepted it and kissed her cheeks. I wondered how it would feel to stay by her side in a similar house.

"Good morning to you too, my love." I exclaimed.

"Hmm... so I have got a nickname too." She giggled.

"You'll have a number of nicknames if you only say yes to my proposal."

"OH, I thought I already said yes." she said and I remembered that she had given me a condition yesterday. And I had fulfilled it. That meant that she was finally letting me have her.

I smiled like a fool, but had to control myself in front of the people who continued shifting things.

"Will you miss this house?" I asked her

"Indeed, I spent all my childhood here. Though it was much awaited, you know moving out. As if we continued living here, or I continued living here, I wouldn't be able to get over the death of my bully. So I am fine with moving out. I need to go out and explore new things. New people."

I nodded as I remembered how I sold the flat I spent my childhood in a few months back. A person must let go of the past, or else they won't be able to escape or move on. So we did. We got distracted by one of the staff who accidently spilled the contents of one of the cardboards boxes. And came out a bunch of old books from that box.

"Sorry, I'll pick it up right away." The person apologised to Haniya..

"Oh, it's okay. Be careful." Said Haniya.

I noticed something in the books, so I went to check on them. When I picked a few of them, Haniya came and snatched them away from me. "Wait! Let me see what you are hiding."

"No, it isn't something interesting. We just need it to go to my new place." She waved off the question and started walking towards the staff.

"Haniya, are all those my books?" I asked, eyes widened with shock. She stopped midway the room.

"Why do you have every single edition of my books, Haniya?" I asked her in a suspicious but teasing way.

"Uh, maybe because I am too obsessed with the writer?" She inclined her head to one side and gave me a mischievous smile. And I couldn't help but smile foolishly. I thought I was only capable of loving someone, never really expected love from the other side. But I was not stupid to ignore the love I was finally getting from someone. On the other side though I had completely turned a blind eye towards Alaia. The thing about her love was- that it was possessive, unkind and would trap me inside. I was grateful for being loved by both of them, though one's love feels like a warm hug on a winter morning and the others felt like they were trying to cage me inside to admire me. And if given a choice what would one choose? Thinking about her reminded me that she was ill. I told Haniya that i'd meet her later, it wasn't appropriate to stay longer as her parents would come back to check on things. Even though I would have liked to help her shift things , the other stuff was important too. I hadn't changed my clothes or showered since the last day. So I went back home, checked on Ezra, took a shower, ate the sandwiches she made for me and changed into a fresh trouser and shirt. So my sister was finally behaving like a grown up, huh? Ezra came from behind me and leaned on the doorframe. "So, is everything okay with you and Haniya?" She asked.

"You shouldn't have lied." I said.

"Look, I said sorry. I didn't know that you'd actually go to the airport. You knew that it wouldn't work right? This wasn't some bollywood movie where you'd end up preventing the plane from taking off and stopping Haniya."

"I knew, but I had to try before accepting the fact that she left me."

"Anyways, you know that there are others too who need your attention right?" She asked.

"Yeah I know, I am going there to meet her only." I said while fixing my curly hair in the mirror.

"You are going to meet mom?" She asked

"No, I am not. I am going to meet Alaia. As you told me earlier, she postponed the party because she was ill."

"And I was not talking about Alaia. You only care about her don't you? Mom called me this morning and was asking about you. Alaia had sent her the invitation too. So she was worried about what was going on in your life. Bhai, look at me." She said and I looked at her but in the mirror as she was right behind me. "She doesn't mean any harm to you, all she wants is to meet you. And then you can keep living your life as you wish. Dida has gone, it has been four years and you still haven't forgotten the things which didn't even include you. Whatever fights, arguments and misunderstanding there were, were between Dida and mom. Then why have you tied those with yourself? Can't you be a little bit understanding towards our mom?"

"Look, Ezra. I am not mad at her because of Dida. It's because she abandoned me when I chose Dida. I was immature to choose between them though she could have stayed, stayed for me. But both Mom and dad left the house and never came back. Did she try to talk to me? Did she call me even once? No. Why are you playing the middle-man here then? If she wished to talk to me, she'd call herself."

"I was trying to call you, my son. But guilt took over and I couldn't do anything. I am really sorry for leaving you. But sometimes leaving is the best choice, maybe it wasn't the best for me but it was best for your Dida. If we had stayed in that same household, we'd never live in peace. And she wasn't young, who would be able to stand it all. This is why we left, for *her* peace. She was happy with just *you* by her side, so we kept it that way." I looked for where the voice was coming from. For a moment I thought she was here, in my house but then Ezra showed me her mobile screen. Mom was on call with her all along, and now she spoke to me through the speaker. I didn't reply as I didn't know what to say to her. After all, I was listening to her speak after many years. It took me some moments before recognising that voice which was apologising to me instead of scolding. I almost teared up when she spoke again. "I am sorry my child, for dragging you between our adults quarrel. You weren't supposed to live alone, nor was it good for your growing mind. But I was glad that at least Alaia was there for you all along. Ezra told me about everything that happened between you two. But I think this was just your destiny, Haniya was your destiny. Indeed, the journey was cruel and yet it paid off at last. If you ever think of me or want to forgive me, come home, with Haniya. I desperately want to meet her, who came in your life as hope, as sunshine you lacked all your childhood." I gave up on holding back my tears when she stopped talking. Ezra came and side-hugged me. Mom was still on-call but silent. Ezra pushed the phone towards me and insisted that I talk to her. In between those tears and regret I said "I- I am sorry, I am sorry too, for holding things against you. You must know that I don't completely hate you, okay? It's just that… It'll take me some time to accept what you just said. And I am sure that you'll love Haniya when you meet her." I swear I heard a sniffle from the other side when I spoke. She must have missed me, I missed her too. I asked her about dad and she said that he still brings flowers for her every week. He still watches our old videos and laughs at the clip where I tripped or fell. And above everything else, he still has that one photo of Ezra and me in his wallet. Parents are so peculiar, they won't say upfront that they love you, but would carry your shoes in their hands because you were playing barefoot in the wet mud. I forgot what I was doing, or going to do as me and mom had a lot to catch up on. At least half an hour later I asked her to talk later as I was supposed to go to the University. She hung up saying that I should take care and teach some manners to Ezra while she was with me. I hurriedly took my laptop which wasn't charged properly but I thought I'd charge it in Uni only. I thought to stop by Alaia's on my way to the Uni and check how she was. But Ezra shoved a piece of paper towards me and said that it came for me this morning. She also said that it was from Alaia, and some cookies came along which she gobbled up alone. I opened the folded paper to find that it was another letter from her. I started reading the paper, this had to be important as we didn't need letters to communicate anymore but she chose to write me one and post it instead of calling some numbers.

Still with you.

THE LAST LETTER

Alaia

I was still in his embrace when I saw Shruti walking towards us. I immediately pushed him away. He didn't seem surprised, as he might have expected that. Shruti paused on her way as she sensed the awkward energy around but came forward when I shot a smile towards her. "Ma'am, are you okay? Why are you here? Weren't you ill? How are you? Should I bring something for you?" She seemed genuinely concerned. But before I could clarify anything Kabir spoke up. "Alaia lied. She isn't ill, at all. It's just that she is trying to do a good thing for the first time in her life." He gave me a small smirk. "Hey! She is your boss. You can't call her by just her name." Shruti reminded Kabir. "I can call her many things. Besides, I don't work here anymore." He said. And I remembered our first meeting where he had called me a mistress. My face flushed with just the thought of it. Mistress wasn't the word to be taken as a compliment, it was sexist and insulting but I had taken it as a compliment back then as I had known what he meant by it. He wasn't trying to insult me or something, but he had found me attractive and used the term 'mistress' to provoke me. His way of flirting was peculiar, but interesting. God! Was I even making any sense? I should have been mad at him that time. "What? Did you resign? When and why?" She interrogated me. "It doesn't matter. Now can you please let us talk, alone?" He said to Shruti who was surprised at his words. "Shruti, you are to leave whatever work you were involved in and start working as my assistant. And find me a new driver or just contact my old one and hire him back. As I can't go through another assistant hunting session. And don't let this word get out that I have come to the office today, for the world outside I am supposed to be ill for a few days. So I'd be working from home, I just came to take some of the necessary stuff. You are to report to me in another hour with your progress in learning about your work. Also, deliver this thing for me as soon as possible, please." I handed her the letter I had written to Aqeel this morning. I couldn't face him, after he made it clear that he didn't want to do anything with me. I was filled with guilt, guilt for causing him the problems he had to go through.

I realised I didn't deserve him at all. I wasn't even sure If I was in love with him, I had only started this whole thing because I wanted him. And I could have married him, despite not being in love with him but knowing that he accepted my proposal only because it concerned my honour. I couldn't do this. So I decided to write him a letter and then ask him to forget about me. Forget about my existence and start his life with Haniya.

I am sorry, Aqeel. I am sorry for coming back. I shouldn't have done that in the first place. Then it wouldn't have done this much damage to your life and reputation. I almost became the cause of your ruined career, and I swear that would be the last thing I'd ever want. All my life I had wanted you to become successful and happy. You did, you became all that you ever deserved to become. But I ruined it for you. I caused you sorrow and distress. Only because I wanted my old friend back. I lied to you, I didn't love you. I don't deserve to. I don't deserve love at all. I didn't know, But I have realised how selfish I could be sometimes. I thought, after losing everyone in life, I could have you. And yet, you weren't mine to have, you weren't mine to possess. You were yours. And still you chose me, upon everyone else and yourself. You were going to sacrifice yourself for me, you did. And I still didn't realise any of it. But when You told me that you loved me as a friend. I knew it was over for me. I didn't even deserve your friendship. You were going to sacrifice your love for Haniya, for a selfish friend like me. And god knows, if I had asked you to marry me, you would have done that for my sake. I couldn't see you slowly dying in front of my eyes, Aqeel. All I wanted was you, my childhood bestie, the one who loved me. Never did I think about you and what you wanted. So please for once, don't think about me. Think about yourself and Haniya. Forget about me. If I had made a mistake, I would have asked you for your forgiveness, but this isn't a mistake. It is a sin that I did. And I don't get to be forgiven. I get to suffer for my own doings. So let me be. Don't come for me. I have postponed the engagement saying that I was ill, I am not. And after some time, I'll cancel the party, and the blame would be on me. Please don't come for me, I am not going anywhere, but please don't come. I won't be able to look you in your eyes.

Shruti glared at Kabir and then left. Kabir held me by my arms and took me inside my cabin and shut the doors behind him. "What do you want?" I asked him, irritated at my own body who misbehaved with me. " Your time, patience and everything else." He said, still holding on to my arm. " Why? Why me?" I asked him. As I wasn't sure if I deserved anyone. I felt worthless, after what I did with my own friend. I wasn't capable of loving someone. I only knew how to dominate, but love was about submission. "Because, I like you." He uttered. And before I could object to him, before I could say that I was the wrong person. He pressed his index finger on my lips, and silenced me. "For once, can you let the other person talk? Please?" He asked me and I just blinked. "Alaia, I have been mesmerised by your beauty ever since I laid my eyes on you. But I never thought that I'd end up falling for you. I loathed you, for what you did to your friend. I tried many times to tell you that what you were doing was wrong. But you didn't let me, you did what you had to. And this time, I'll do what I am supposed to do. I won't force myself on you, but at least give me a chance. And I'll prove to you that it is me who you want, who you need. As I have noticed you, checking me out a few times, and your body reacts to me, to my touch. Even now I can hear your heart beating, and I for sure know it isn't fear or disgust. I know I am the last person you'd want to be with, but you are the first person I ever thought of. I love you. And you deserve the love. I deserve the love." And then he removed his finger from my lips, and left my arm. I moved back a few steps and remained silent. I didn't know what to say, I didn't have anything to say. How could he love me? After all that I did with Aqeel. He witnessed everything with his eyes and still loved me? How was it possible? He said he loathed me, I did too. But I didn't love me as he did. I couldn't, afterall I was worthless and undeserving. I left the office without looking at him again. And he didn't try to stop me. My head ached and my body shivered. I asked Shruti to come to my place on my way out. I drove like a mad woman, and reached my place in half the time. I spent the day working with Shruti. I was in a time crunch, and had to overwork so that I could present my designs on time. I used to be confident in my designs, and proudly showed them to my investors before finalising it. But this time I wasn't so sure about what I was doing. I keep zoning out throughout the day. How would Aqeel react to the letter? I hoped he would never talk to me again. I hoped he would abandon me. I was unworthy of the love I got from him or from anyone else. I was selfish and mean. Shruti was patient enough to work with me. She had learned her task from Kabir and me. Kabir, I had suspected about his likeness towards me, but I didn't think he would love me. He had seen me obsessing over Aqeel and trying to break his relationship with Haniya. He knew that I called the paparazzi and spread rumours purposely. So how could he still love me? Didn't he say he loathed me for doing that to my friend? If he was attracted to me, that would have been a different case, but he said he loved me. He shouldn't. Did he bring me my lunch, drove me wherever I asked him to even though he wasn't a driver, overworked himself, stood by me when Abbu died, trusted me, because he loved me?

I had thought him to be a workaholic, but turns out he was in love with me all along. Why? I am pretty, but that shouldn't be the only thing behind his feelings. What did I have, and didn't know, that he admired so much to fall in love with me? And if I was so easy to love, then why was it not Aqeel? There has to be something that he liked, which was unknown to me and others. What was it? If I wanted I could have asked him. But I didn't want to ruin another person's life. My mere existence destroys the balance in everyone's life. Though I'd have to exist, for me and my parents. I had wished to surprise them with their own Bungalow, though there was no one left to be surprised. And yet, I wanted to complete it. I talked to the builders who were working on it and asked them to resume the work with full force as I wanted it to be fully made by another month.

Shruti left somewhere around 10 pm and I kept working after that. It was around 2 am when I got up from my desk and went to sleep.

I was searching for a parking spot near the campsite, around the lake. The place looked abandoned and sketchy. No wonder why the students chose this place. I honked my car before turning right, as it was a narrow path and there was barely space for a car to pass by. When suddenly a guy with a buzz cut appeared in front of me. I panicked as there was very little distance between us and my vision got blurred. It was too late, and before I could hit the breaks, I had hit the guy. I covered my face in shock, leaving the steering wheel. It was a moment later, when I removed my palms to look outside, people were rushing towards us from across the lake. My hands shook and my whole body trembled, realising what I had done. A teardrop fell on my cheek, I was breathless. My car felt suffocative, and I immediately went out and sat on the mud outside drawing a deep breath. Then I crawled towards the guy I had hit with my car. He was bleeding, intensely. I noticed he was wearing headphones, which now lay beside him. Pop-music played through it in full volume. He was breathing, still. His head and neck were severely damaged and blood gushed out from the cuts he had to endure. All the blood made me feel nauseous, and it drained whatever energy I might have had while coming here. His breathing was getting slower and small by every passing second. His hazel eyes looked into mine with pain and agony. My hands trembled when I touched his wound and he winced in pain. People had gathered around us and they were all panicking at the sight. "Kabir!" they shouted as if the person lying down in pain would respond. I felt as if I was being dragged in the darkness myself. I could hear their rushed and panicked footsteps, when they all tried to lift him up. And I just sat there, with his blood on my hands. I had caused this accident. The person was dying because of me. And I was as helpless as him. I felt my own life being sucked from me. My stomach's content rising up to my throat, I closed my eyes to block my view of the blood and the injured body which was being helped inside my car. I tried to control it, but my head spinned a few times and I hurled it on the floor. When I opened my eyes, I was in my bedroom. There was no blood, no one injured, no accident. I had been sleeping. It was a nightmare. I wiped my face, and sat there on my bed. When someone rang the bell. I couldn't move, my body felt paralysed. I heard the bell but couldn't stand up let alone attend it. The doorbell rang, twice, thrice and then I lost count. My phone was ringing somewhere too. I couldn't find it. My hands were still trembling, and there was a sharp pain in my head. When I tried to stand up for the second time, my knees wobbled but I gained balance after a few seconds. I walked upto the door, and opened it. My head felt heavy and I couldn't lift it up to see who was there. I heard receding footsteps, but then it stopped and then I heard them coming nearer.

"Alaia! Oh my god! Are you okay?" He asked. I tried lifting my head a little, and it was Aqeel. "I thought you were dead. For god sake, Alaia. What happened?" He asked again. Why was he here? He shouldn't have come looking for me. I didn't deserve him. My knees faltered again, and I fell. But he grabbed me by my arms, and helped me up. Then I felt him, gently putting my arms around his shoulders and walking me to the couch. He sat me down and went to grab some water, mumbling on his way. I broke down in tears. Why? Why was this guy still helping me around? I held my head with both hands and sobbed. He came back with a glass of water and sat beside me. And then he gently pulled me into a hug, and stroked my head lightly soothing me. His warm embrace calmed me a little. And yet I kept crying, on his shoulders, fisting on his shirt. He held me like that for what felt like eternity. And I cried, until my tears gave up on me. "What happened to you, Alaia. Tell me. Are you okay? What's wrong? Please tell me, or else I'll die." He asked me, and I started crying harder. "Alaia, for god's sake. Please tell me what happened? Are you ill? Is it hurting? Should I take you to the doctor? Where is it hurting, tell me? I am here. Please tell me something, Alaia. Stop crying. I can't see you crying like this, my heart is ripping. Please." He was begging and yet I couldn't say anything. After a while, my sons got smaller and slower. "Please go away!" I cried. "Please, please, go away."

"I won't leave you until you tell me what happened. What is it that's hurting so much? Was it a nightmare? What makes you so shocked and upset that you can't control your tears.?" He broke the hug, and sat on the floor in front of me, cupping my cheeks. "My dear, What have you seen? Why are you not telling me? What happened to my strong buddy, that you are crying this much?" His eyes looked in mine with distress, and reminded me of those hazel eyes that were in pain. "Kabir." I whispered. " Kabir? What happened to kabir?" He asked. "I killed him." I said and fresh tears fell from my eyes. "WHAT?" He asked in confusion. "I killed him, in my dream." I said. I took a long breath before continuing. "It was an accident, Kabir. I didn't mean to kill him." I shook my head, and tears rolled down my cheeks. My lips trembled. "You said it was a dream right?" He asked, wiping my tears and snot. I nodded. He sat up again, beside me and pulled me in another hug. "It was a nightmare, Alaia. He'd be fine. He'd be fine." He repeated, and continued stroking my head. We stayed like that for another few minutes. I stopped crying.

And when I broke the hug and straightened myself a little. He looked at me and smiled. "Why are you here?" I asked him, sniffling. "I got your letter." He said, while fixing my hair for me. "I told you to not come, to not see me again, to abandon me. Then why did you come? Does my words not matter to you?" I asked him angrily. "It does. But I couldn't just leave you. After all, you didn't leave me in my worst. How could I ever think of leaving you?" He asked. "Still, you should have heard me. You should have respected my words." I said still sniffling. "Oh! Stop with that bullshit already." He seemed frustrated. My eyes widened in shock, after listening to him curse for the first time. "You should know Alaia, that you are my best friend. And I won't ever leave my best friend. It's impossible. I agree, I was a little hard on you because you weren't listening to me just as you are not listening to me right now. Have you ever heard of yourself? I don't deserve you...and blah blah." He mimicked me and I couldn't help but laugh. "My dear, you deserve the whole world. And I am not lying. You have to believe me, when I say that. You held me when I was in my lowest, and you think I'd leave you just like that? What do you think I am?" He questioned. "I know, things have been worse since we got back together. But that was because we were guilt-ridden, empty and unloved. I swear I felt bad pushing you away, but now that I know it wasn't love and you were just insecure. I am relieved. I am relieved that I wouldn't break your heart. And tell me one thing, why were you insecure. Why did you feel that I'd forget about you once I got into a relationship? What was the reason behind your insecurity?" He continued. "I wasn't insecure, Aqeel. I was stupid. I was stupid enough to think that you'd be the same, just like old times. But I forgot that you had moved on. That you could fall in love with someone else. I thought that I could have you, wholly to myself and I was wrong. I was wrong to think so. I am sorry Aqeel. It was my stupidity and not love. I called it love, so that I could attract you. I forgot that you were a human being, and not a dog. I tried to lure you with love and I failed. I failed miserably." I again started sobbing. "If you think that I'd leave you even for a heart beat. Then you are highly mistaken, my friend. You were my dearest friend, and you'd still be. No one can take your position. I say, no one. Not even me. I was with you from the start. And I'll continue to be. I promise you, I am here with you. Still with you. Our friendship will prosper, irrespective of the other people in our life. And that's a promise. Forget about what happened and live your life guilt free." He kissed my forehead, and hugged me. I hugged him back feeling relieved. His words weren't just comforting. They were heaven. No wonder, Haniya fell for his words and him.

"Also..Do you love Kabir?" He asked me. I was surprised at this sudden question, and so I broke the hug to look him in the eyes. "What?" I asked. "Do you love Kabir?" He repeated. "No.." I said. "Then why were you crying over a nightmare about him?" He asked with a smile. I released a breath. "I don't know."

"Then it's time to find out." He said and I got confused. He stood up and went inside my bedroom, then after a few minutes came back with my mobile. "Why have you saved his number as 'buzz-cut'?" He enquired. "Aqeel… what are you doing?" I asked. "Calling him." He casually said. And before I could stop him he was talking to Kabir. "Hey! Buddy. Looks like Alaia is missing you. Can you come to her place? She is crying like crazy…" "Aqeel!! Give me my phone back!!" I yelled and threw a cushion at him. He started laughing and kept talking to Kabir on the phone telling him about my nightmare. "Aqeel… for god's sake. Stop it! Give me my phone back!!" I yelled and ran towards him.

PROMISES

Aqeel

I didn't tell Kabir about Alaia's nightmare, I only pretended to do so, to tease her. I hung up the call as soon as he picked up. I hadn't expected him to pick up so soon, otherwise I wouldn't have called him. I didn't want to disclose Alaia's concerns towards Kabir, he deserved to hear it directly from her. I stayed with her for a while, as it was already late and going to University would be useless now that I had already missed my classes. She needed me at that time, I couldn't leave her. Afterall she was my friend, she was my first love, she was a treasure, a family member. And I couldn't see her begging me to leave. I wanted to tell her how important she was to me. But she didn't need hollow words, she needed to be taken care of. I realised that I must have ignored her at some point. Maybe I didn't look after her as much as I needed to, because I was busy after Haniya. They both meant alot to me, and I couldn't leave one for another. I was to learn how to love both of them, and how to care for both of them. And for my family too. Ezra needed me, Mummy and papa needed me. I realised how big of a mistake I had made. I only wanted my mother to reach out to me, I never wanted for her to apologise. Though I could have been the one to approach. I was their son, it was my duty to look after them. But I let myself think otherwise about them, I forgot them. I ignored them, and didn't try to understand their situation. Sometimes, people do need to make hard decisions, to avoid other problems. They left home, to avoid unnecessary quarrels and arguments. All they wanted was peace, for themselves and Dida. Maybe living apart gave them peace. I was just a lost piece of the puzzle. I made some decisions too, I got engaged to Alaia all the while I was in a relationship with Haniya, to avoid hurting Alaia. But I did hurt Haniya, though she didn't leave me. She stood by my side, and was even ready to sacrifice her own feelings for me. And what did I do? I kept no contact with my parents, lived alone as if they weren't alive anymore. I didn't try to reach out to my sister, who came and stood beside me. Help me. She was younger than me, and yet she was more thoughtful, kind and considerate.

Alaia was furious at me for telling Kabir about her nightmare. But I didn't tell her that I didn't do any such thing. Her anger towards me made her forget about the nightmare itself. She kept bickering at me, and I enjoyed that. I told her to wash herself as she stinked. Then she told me she had puked. "Alaia, you could have told me earlier. I hugged you?" I expressed disgust, even though I didn't mind it as there was no trace of filth on her. "I know, you wouldn't mind that. You hugged me when I was covered in sludge, all the way back in tenth standard." she reminded me. "Yeah. I did that to calm you. You were furious at those bullies who ripped my favourite book. I didn't mind as I had another copy, and besides I wouldn't wanna waste my time fighting with those rude bastards." I told her while mopping the puke on the floor. "Aqeel, you are cursing a lot these days. What happened to you?" She queried. "It's Ezra's influence. I mean I used to curse but not this much. Anyways I was supposed to fix her and not get influenced by her. And yet, look at me."I chuckled. "You know Alaia, I talked to my mother today." I said. "Really??" She gasped. "Yeah! Thanks to Ezra. She connected us." I smiled. "I am glad she is here. By your side. You need her." She returned the smile. "I need you all." I said. "Me too." She replied.

"Well, you should clean up now, till then I'll make some breakfast for you." I said. She came forward and hugged me, and I returned the hug. "You know what Aqeel? I did the right thing. I came back. I didn't realise how much your absence in my life tormented me. I am sorry. But I need you and others too. I'll fix myself. I'll fix my attitude, my ignorance towards y'all. I'll be good from now onwards. I promise." She whispered against my chest. I held her tighter and kissed her head. "Now you really should clean up, I came here all fresh and now I'd stink too as I hugged you several times." I teased her. "Oh please! I am not smothered in puke, for you to say that. Besides, I am more hygienic than you. You used to go weeks without showering and here you are complaining." We both laughed at that.

I made some frozen waffles for her, and hot chocolate to complement the weather. She was still in the shower when Kabir came. He was surprised to find me there, but I wasn't. My call to him earlier must have worried him. "Where's Alaia?" He asked. "She is in the shower. Would you like some waffles?" I asked. "Nah, I am okay. By the way, what are you doing here? She is okay right?" He interrogated rather worriedly. "Yeah, she is fine. She needed some reassurance from me and from you."

I said. "From me?" He asked. "Yeah, she is worried sick about hurting you. I am not telling you the whole story as she'd be furious at me. Though you need to tell her that you'd be fine." I said. "What do you mean by that? I am fine. What would happen to me?" He asked.

"Who's there Aqeel?" She yelled from inside. "Can you give me my clothes??" She asked. "I must have forgotten it, hand me whatever you can get your hands on." She continued yelling from inside. "Alright!" I yelled back. "Hey, can you do that for me? I have some waffles on the stove." I asked Kabir, who hesitantly nodded. Then he went inside and came back with the clothes and handed it to Alaia who was stretching her hands out from the bathroom door. Then he came back and sat with me on the dining table. "Aqeel…Where are my undergarments? You only gave me a tshirt and a pant. I can't come outside without my bra." She yelled. Kabir's face reddened with embarrassment and he looked at me with shock. I without waiting, went inside and grabbed her undergarments for her and gave it to her. "You two are *too* close." Kabir accused me and raised both his eyebrows in surprise. "I am sorry. It must seem weird, but it isn't like that. You are forgetting that we grew up together, like siblings. And don't you dare to think about me as a pervert. My feeling towards her were genuine. Besides, these things were normal between us. We used to discuss about her periods and everything in front of her mother. It was completely normal." I told him. "Its okay. You don't have to explain yourself. I understand." He said even though he didn't look comfortable. And I couldn't help but laugh. It was when Alaia came outside, all dressed. She was walking towards the dining table but halted when she noticed Kabir. She cringed. "Its okay." I mouthed. "Sorry you had to hear that." She said to Kabir. "Uh. Its okay, I guess. As long as you are comfortable." He said, biting on a waffle. "Kabir, there was no nightmare. Aqeel lied to you." I narrowed my eyes at her, she was the one lying. "Nightmare?" He jerked his head towards her. She looked at me in confusion and I bit my lower lip to suppress the smile. "Nothing! Why are you here?" She asked Kabir. "You called me. But didn't say anything and hung up the call. So I thought something was wrong. Hence, I came to check up on you." He told her and I smiled hearing that. She glared at me for doing that and moved on with the conversation. "You don't have to. I was completely fine." She said, "No you weren't. You were bawling your eyes out when I came." I interrupted. She threw a strawberry at me. And I dodged it. "You were?" Kabir questioned her. "She was, yes." I said. "Aqeel! Stop messing around, please." She yelled. "Okay, okay. You two carry on. I'll leave. My work is done here. You shall have your breakfast before it goes cold." I said and took my leave before she could object.

Since I didn't go to University. I called Haniya, and asked her what she was doing. She told me to come home and help her. So I went there, and found both her parents waiting for me. What did she mean to help her? Her parents looked disappointed and angry. I greeted them and went inside. Haniya was standing against her bedroom door, and her parents asked me to take a seat. The room was devoid of any furniture, so we sat on the floor. We sat in silence for some time, no one dared to say anything. I was finding it difficult to breathe as I was afraid of her parents. Then her father broke the silence. "Do you like my daughter?" he asked. I nodded. "Do you wish to marry her?" He asked. I nodded. "Then why are you sneaking into my house? If you wished to marry her. You should come right away and ask me for her hand, rather than sneaking around with her. You idiot! The guard told me, you were here late at night and stayed. What are you doing? Drowning your family's name and reputation?" He scolded. "I am sorry. We didn't do anything. I know my boundaries. I was going to ask you. It's just that, things weren't going the right way. I am sorry." I pleaded. "We know. Haniya told us everything. Besides, we know your father, we have known him for years. So you don't have to explain about yourself or your situation. It's just that, the act you both pulled isn't respectable at all. One should not indulge in shameless acts like these when they are in love. They should be brave and courageous to stand by their partners. I have respected your father for that. He married your mother and stood by her at all costs. And I am sure, you being his son, won't disappoint us. But you shouldn't have done that." He spoke coldly. "Son, I have known about you, even before Haniya said a word. I knew she spent some nights at your place. And I have scolded her for that. Though I trust both of you, and wouldn't accuse you of using my daughter. Although, I'd suggest you be more mindful of these things." Her mother spoke, rather warmly. I nodded. "I am sorry. I know we made some mistakes, and I'll make up for it. I do love your daughter, and I am willing to stand by her side, just like my father did. I'll talk to my mother and ask her to officially discuss it with both of you." I said. "That won't be necessary." Someone spoke from afar. I lifted my head to see my father emerging from Haniya's room. My mother followed him. I was stunned. How? My eyes softened seeing both of my parents standing beside Haniya with a smile on their face. They patted Haniya's head and came forward to sit with us. My mother's eyes were moist. How many years had passed since I last saw them? My mother looked beautiful as ever, a little old but elegant. My father looked strong and healthy. "Zubair Bhai, called us today and asked us about you. We were surprised to hear it from him. I have known Haniya since she was 16, and I have had a friendship with Zubair Bhai for 8 long years. Never in my wild imagination did I think, you'd fall in love with her. You are very lucky to have found her." Papa continued. And Indeed I was lucky to find her. I glanced towards her, and found her looking at me already. "We approve of you." Said Haniya's father. "And we approve of this arrangement." Said my father. Both our mothers nodded in agreement. I looked at Haniya again. She blushed and went back inside her room. My heart was in a serene state. I was both happy and grateful to Allah.

While our parents chatted, I slid myself inside Haniya's room. She was looking outside the window and had her back towards me. As I walked towards her, she turned and looked at me with a smile. "I didn't know, our parents were friends. When they asked me about you. I told them everything. They somehow connected your surname and called your father to confirm. Your mother told us that she had just talked to you about me. And that's how much you loved me. My parents did scold me, but approved of us. Isn't this magical?" She asked. "Yes, it is." I stood beside her. Watched her. "Haniya. I...I won't make hollow promises of stars and moons to you. But I'll promise you, that I will make your every morning as cheerful as ever, your afternoons filled with brightness, your evenings will be peaceful and serene, and your nights filled with dreams. And those dreams are mine to fulfil." I said. "I just wanted one thing. And I have been granted that. I can't be more grateful to Allah, than I already am. You were my wish, and it came true. Now I want to be the giver. I want to be the provider for you. I want to be the love you desperately seeked. I want to be able to fill your life with so much love and care that you won't have to look elsewhere." She said, while still looking outside. Then she looked at me with those beautiful brown eyes, ever so warm and welcoming. I took her hands in mine, and pressed my lips against it. "Congratulations, my future-wife." I said. "To you too, my future-husband." She said,

"Aqeel!" My mother called me. I went out to meet her. She immediately pulled me in a hug, and I snuggled in her embrace. I felt like a child hiding in his mother's arms ,as she congratulated me. My father came from behind and patted my shoulders while congratulating me. "Where is

Ezra?" My mother asked. "She is in my home. I'll take you both there." I said. Haniya's mother came towards us with sweets in her hand. She gave some to my father, fed my mother and was about to feed me when I interrupted her by saying I can't have it. "He is diabetic, mummy." Haniya told her mother. "What? At this age? Anyways it is not much. Have it, nothing will happen to you. You have our blessings." She said and I ate it from her hands. It didn't feel like I had just reunited with my mother, but it felt like I gained another one too. My mother embraced Haniya in a hug and fed her the sweets.

A NEW BEGINNING

Alaia

After Aqeel left me alone with Kabir. We were silent. I took the seat Aqeel had occupied a little while ago. He must have lied to me about telling Kabir everything related to my nightmare. Or Kabir was pretending to not know anything. He chewed on waffles and I sipped my hot chocolate slowly. "Why were you crying?" He broke the silence between us. I remained silent. "I asked you something." He said. "I wasn't." I said. "Your eyes tell otherwise." He met my eyes. "I was missing my Abbu, and Ammi too." I lied. "Oh. If there is anything else, please tell me."

"Thats it. There is nothing more." I said. "Are you sure?" He asked. "Yeah." I said. "Then…would you date me?" He asked. The sudden question left me speechless and stunned. "NO" I replied. My heart started beating faster, and my hands trembled. It was getting difficult to balance my mug, so I kept it down. "Why? Do you hate me?" He asked, looking down at his empty plate. "NO" I said. I didn't hate him. I was just afraid, I'd hurt him just like I hurt Aqeel. "Then why?" He asked. "Why don't you want to date me? Is it because I am younger than you? Or I am unattractive, unworthy of your attention?" He asked. "You aren't unworthy!" I blurted out. His eyes found mine again. His hazel eyes reminded me of him in pain, where I had dreamt of killing him. I couldn't see him. I couldn't maintain the eye contact. "Then?" He asked again. I remained silent. He stood up from his seat and walked towards me. Then he lowered himself and sat on his haunches, in front of me. " You don't think that I am unworthy of your attention and yet you wouldn't tell me why you were crying. You don't hate me or find me unattractive and still don't wanna date me. What do you want?" He asked me, I stayed still as I had no words. "I told you, how much I loved you." He said. His eyes, that looked into mine. Haunted me, reminded me of my dream. Reminded me, that I'd hurt him. My chest ached with the thought of hurting yet another person. Tears started welling in my eyes. He came closer and held my hands. "For god's sake Alaia. Talk to me. I can't bear your silence. If you hate me, ask me to go away. I'll go away from your life and I'd never come back. And If you like me, even a little bit then ask me to stay. Share it, Share whats haunting you so much. Why are you so upset?" He asked. "I don't want to hurt you or your feelings." I sniffled. "What?" He questioned. "I said, I don't want to hurt you." I repeated. "Why would you hurt me?" He asked. "Just like I hurt Aqeel. I'd end up hurting you. I don't want Kabir. I don't want to. I did see a nightmare. Where I had hit you with my car, the first time I met you. How do you think I can be with you after this?" I was crying miserably by that time. "Oh, Alaia! You got scared of a nightmare? About me? And you think you could hurt me? No, Alaia. You wouldn't. I know you. What happened is in the past. And I am sure it won't happen in our case. Alaia, trust me on this. I love you, and I'll make sure nothing bad happens in our case. I'll never hurt you, or let you hurt me. So please trust me. Besides, you didn't hurt Aqeel either." He said and came closer to wipe my tears. I felt butterflies inside my stomach. Why was it that these guys couldn't see me cry? Why did they all love me so much? "Can I ask you something?" I queried. "Yes, of course." He replied. "Why do you love me so much?" I asked. "Why is it that you love me, despite my flaws?" I continued. "Because, your flaws don't define you. You are much more than your flaws. You deserve the love, like everybody else. You are a human. And It's not like I can control my heart. If my heart found you lovable, if it found you worthy of my love and affection, I can't stop it. I have to accept it." He said. "This is why, I think I don't deserve you. I don't know if I am capable of giving back the love." I said. He tried to object to me but I continued. "But. If it means that I can have your love, I'll try. I'll try with all my being to love you, Kabir. I'll try to be nicer, kinder,and understanding. Will you help me do it?" I said, looking him in the eye. The nightmare, slowly fading in my memory. His eyes softened, and looked in mine, pupils dilating and minimising the hazel colour. His one hand held mine, and the other travelled up to hold my chin. "I'll help you with my entire being. I'll help you find love, and spread it. I'll help you become a better version of you. And I'll stand by you, before and after death." He said. I lowered my eyes, with the weightage of his love. I lifted my gaze again to look at him, and it was then that I noticed his outfit. He was wearing a simple white shirt, a few buttons were undone showing his bare chest. I couldn't help but stare, not thinking about how inappropriate it was to check him out after the confession we had. My heart beat raced, and not-so-innocent thoughts crossed my mind. He was still holding my chin with his hands, which he used to raise my head, So I could look him in the eyes. And before I could think anymore, he pressed his lips on mine. Slowly moving it against mine, brushing it. It was sudden, though I had been thinking about it too. So I parted my lips for him, letting him dominate, his soft lip grazing against mine, passionately sucking on it. My heart felt like it would burst out any moment. He stood on his knees to match my level, and let go of my hand to hold the back of my neck. I put both of my hands on his shoulders, to balance myself. And then he pulled away. I almost cursed him as I was hungry. Hungry for love and him. "I am sorry, I didn't wait for your consent." He whispered against my lips before pressing it again. I pulled out. "Kabir…just kiss me. Okay? Don't stop. You have my consent." I said before pressing my lips on his. And he smirked before invading my mouth with his tongue. "Oh my god! Alaia… you taste like Chocolate." He whispered. "Kabir… I'll kill you. Kiss me."I replied. "You are already killing me, Alaia. If I don't stop right now, I'll end up fucking you against this tiny dinning table of yours and I don't wish to do it outside wedlock." He kissed me more passionately than ever. My stomach flipped and I realised we both were having unholy thoughts about each other. I chuckled against his lips. He lifted his eyes from my lips towards my eyes. "You find it funny?" He asked. "No, I find it extremely sexy that I am going insane." I said. He grinned and licked his canines. We both kissed again, and he pecked me before pulling out this time. "I love you, my hot cocoa." He said. "I love you, too, my buzz-cut baby." I said. "Buzz-cut baby?" He chuckled and hugged me. I hugged him back.

EPILOGUE

A few months later.

Kabir

Alaia came to pick me up when I was still getting ready. She looked gorgeous in a pink suit. I wore a cream coloured kurta for Aqeel and Haniya's Nikah. Ammi was seated in the back with Alaia and I, their personal driver was driving the car. During our ride towards the venue, Alaia kept chatting with Ammi. And I kept stealing glances of her, as she was looking too pretty to ignore. Ammi knew about my feelings, long before I chose to acknowledge it myself. And she adored Alaia as her own daughter so when I broke it to her that we were dating. She was beyond happy and asked me to get engaged as soon as possible, although we wanted to take it a little slow. The engagement party of Alaia and Aqeel was soon called off, saying that they'd like to be nothing more than friends. And would continue to date others. People discussed them for a while before the matter died down a while earlier. Now I and Alaia were freely dating each other, and Aqeel decided to tie the knots with Haniya.

Once we reached the venue. We all entered together, Alaia and I both held my ammi's hands and walked in. We greeted Aqeel, Haniya and their parents. Then I went on to talk to Ezra, who I had become friends with.

Alaia

I was so overwhelmed after looking at Aqeel, dressed up in a simple Sherwani and Haniya who had a huge veil covering her face. They were yet to be bound to each other, so they maintained a good amount of distance. I looked at Kabir who trailed after Ezra. His hands on her revealing back. She was wearing a mint green lehenga with a matching blouse and dupatta. Aqeel was talking to me, while I was looking at them, far away from us. He must have followed my gaze and noticed them. "They make such good friends, right?" He asked. "Yeah, indeed." I gritted my teeth. "She is planning to work with him. They have been discussing their business ideas for quite a while." He said, but I completely ignored his words. "What are they talking about? And why does he have to be so close to her?" I expressed my concerns. "Alaia, they are just friends. Don't worry." He assured me. "What kind of friends touch each other like that?" I asked. "Well, he doesn't mind when I touch you. If he could trust you, you should trust him too. Besides, they are looking worried. Something must have happened." He said when both our phones rang. He picked it up and I did too. "Hey, Can you come to the ladies room? We might have a problem." Kabir asked me on the call. I looked at Aqeel. "They need us." He told me. "Let's go and find out." I said.

When we went to the ladies room, Kabir was standing outside. Then he informed us about Ezra's hook coming off loose and that he helped her prevent a wardrobe malfunction by holding her blouse straps together. "This is why I warned her to not wear such revealing clothes, but she won't listen to me. Ammi must have allowed her to wear this." Aqeel complained. I went inside the room and helped Ezra by fixing her loose hook. Then we both came outside and found the guys talking to each other. Aqeel was thanking Kabir who had helped her from getting embarrassed in front of the crowd. I felt bad for doubting Kabir and getting jealous of Ezra who was nothing but like a sister to him. Aqeel was about to scold Ezra, but I stopped him. As it wasn't her fault that her hook came off loose, it was a wardrobe malfunction that could have happened to anyone.

Out of guilt, I apologised to Kabir. But he shrugged it off and said. "I am pleased that my hot cocoa felt jealous and was being possessive of me. There is an ecstatic feeling in being owned by you."He said in my ear, and pressed a soft and quick peck behind my ears that sent shivers to my whole body.

Haniya

My heartbeats were so loud and fast that I was able to hear them, despite the noise coming from the crowd. I felt worry, anxiety, excitement and joy, all at the same time. My mother was seated beside me, and the Qazi was reading out the vows. On our request, our parents had arranged a joint Nikah. Though there was a veil covering my head, and a veil separating mine and Aqeel's side. I could make out him sitting in front of me. His family sat along with him. His face was covered too, and yet I was sure that he felt all the emotions I was feeling at that time. Looking back, my teenage self would have burst out laughing if I told her I was getting married to my crush. And here I was vowing to accept him as my husband. And he vowed and accepted me as his wife. Was this my destiny? Was he my fate? After all that happened last year, I was now his, and he was mine. This indeed was a miracle of Allah.

Aqeel

Despite the moderate weather,and the Ac working inside the venue. I was sweating profusely. Mummy kept wiping away my sweat, and gave me water from time to time. "You are worrying if you were the bride and not the groom." My mother teased me. I looked at Haniya, who was trembling when the Qazi spoke to her. And looking at her, I got more anxious. Papa patted my shoulders and whispered to me. "It's going to be alright, my son." And his words sent a wave of relief to me. There was nothing to be anxious about. If Allah has blessed us, he would surely look after us. And the path ahead of us was clear. We must remain loyal, faithful, and loving to each other.

PLAYLIST

Winner- Conan Gray

Dorothea-Taylor Swift

Perfect- Ed sheeran

Friends- Marshmallow and Anne-Marie

Wildest dreams-Taylor Swift

You belong with me-Taylor Swift

Enchanted-Taylor Swift

Still with you- Jeon Jungkook

Popular- The weeknd and Madonna

Closer-The chainsmokers ft Halsey

Until I found you- Stephen Sanchez and Em Beihold

I can see you-Taylor Swift

River like you- Maya Hawke

Till forever falls apart- Ashe and FINNEAS

Coverage- Maya Hawke

Heather- Conan Gray

Die for you- The Weeknd

You're On Your Own, Kid- Taylor Swift

Midnight Rain- Taylor Swift

Style- Taylor Swift

Love Story- Taylor Swift

Mr. Perfectly Fine- Taylor Swift

About the Author

Zaara Ali

Zaara Ali, a young girl with an old soul, was born and brought up in Kolkata, in a Middle Class Muslim family. From her childhood till date, she has proven to be a quiet but smart kid. She is always an introvert, but becomes an Ambivert at times. She completed her schooling from The Crescent School and is currently pursuing her bachelor's degree from City College, Kolkata. She has a soft corner for art and loves to spend her free time creating wonders. It was around her middle School that she started taking an interest in poems and stories. The world of fantasy and fiction fascinated the little girl's mind. And just like any other reader, Harry Potter served as a gateway for her into the fictional world. By the time she was in High School, she started posting her Poems and Poetry online for the world to know. Up till now she has been published a few times as a co-author and has completed her first novel. She is willing to be a full-time author and a part-time teacher.

www.ingramcontent.com/pod-product-compliance
Lightning Source LLC
LaVergne TN
LVHW041922070526
838199LV00051BA/2702